FUTURESPAN

GEORGIA DUFFY

Britain's Next
BESTSELLER

First published in 2016 by:

Britain's Next Bestseller
An imprint of Live It Publishing
27 Old Gloucester Road
London, United Kingdom.
WC1N 3AX

www.britainsnextbestseller.co.uk

Printed in Poland.

ISBN 978-1-910565-60-5 (pbk)

For all of the unfinished novels.

Futurespan Supporters

Maria Grundy, Sandra Maddison, Bruce McGurk, Karl Eckert, John Grundy, Penny Wales, Rebecca Pate, Claire Riley, Janet Duffy, Lee Keates, Frank Eckert, Miriam Pirt, Lisa Sharkey, Julie Peyton, Jonathan Kennair, Linda Roberts, Mark Lickley, Peter English, Kate Weightman, Stuart Wainwright, Katharine Lawley, Jylanka Mascari, Diana Clare, Laura Daly, Patricia Daly, Keith Blenkinsopp, Linda Blenkinsopp, Julia Monument, Pamela Burbidge, Lynn Burbidge, Elizabeth Brown, Rosemary Grundy, Nancy Maddison, Paul Hudson, Julie Whiting, Anthony Crammen, Joanne Pritchard, Jane Anderson, Susan Smith, Alice Priday, Rachel Bennett, Liz Collins, Jane Murray, Vanessa Turner, Matthew Luscombe, Rob Pailor, Gillian Foster, Andrea Woodhouse, Joan Wright, Janet McCoy, Catherine Jacques, Barbara Pritchard, Margaret Messer, Paula Long, Anita, Elizabeth Hutchinson, Adam Bates, Patty Miller, Margaret Macfadzean, Adelia Edwards, Marcia Werrett, Fiona Sharp, Siobhan Meadows, Maureen Davies, Avril Craig, Betty Smith and family, Becky Fleming, Mandy Gill, Rhea Ewen, Sylvia Grix, Hannah Whitaker, Diane Herman, Margaret Smith, Jean Wright, Kitty Shield, Audrey Upton, Mandy Cummins, Adil Iletmis, Natalie Day, Zoe Brookes, Emma Brown, Penny Wales, Clair Renfrew, Claire Ahmed, Christina Richardson, Aileen Ralph, Margaret Meynell, Pam Shannon, Fran Lestner, Kath Wilson, Joan Ellison, Jo-ann Midgley, Kelly Gaffney, Claire Robinson, Shirley Ashley, Marje McDonnell, Joan Turner, Megan Weall, Emma Burnup, Amy Lofthouse, Heather Peebles, Norma Wassell, Adam Welch, Eleanor Mockler, Debbie Brady, Alexina Thorkildsen McGurk, Katie Louise Tate, Margaret McFie, Evelyn Hutcheson, Myra Harrison, Janet Allison, Nancy Lane, Caroline Jamieson, Andrew Platt, Christine Platt, Brenda Armstrong, Audrey Hooker, Denise Leafe, Lole Faso, Lynne Hill, Chris Purdy, Moira Palmer, Angela McLean, Julie Dixon, Helen Mitchell, Dianne Gee, Mandy Bowen, Lillian Gray, Lynn Matheson, Gail Ferguson, Louise Terzza, Katherine

Tremaine, Mark Senior, Pamela Blades, Jessica Dalton, Janella Holland, Angie Hardie, Linda Smith, Kerry Daniels, Kim Jackson, Alison Kettle, Gilly Spence, Denise Battram, Helen Eastwood, Katie Kibbler, Adelle Kirby, Melinda Wallman, Claire Lancefield, Jackie McGurk, Ruby McGurk, Graham Millichap, Mark Pattison, Denise Stoker, Lynne Thistlethwaite, Tracy Teasdale, Louise Thistlethwaite.

Acknowledgements

Firstly, and most hugely I need to thank my amazing Mother. Without her this book would not have been published. She has raised me, and supported me throughout my whole life, and has been the driving force behind me reaching my 250 pre-order target and achieving a publishing deal. Through her very enthusiastic promotion she sold tonnes of books (and no Karl you can't have her as a saleswoman!). I can't ever say thank you enough, and I bet John is thankful the campaign is over now too! I still can't believe it is.

Very importantly I need to thank all of my wonderful, amazing, awesome pre-orderers – without you this book would not exist. Simple as that. You have all made my hugest dream come true, and I am forever grateful to each and every one of you. Thank you all enormously. Many were my Mum's loyal and lovely customers who have been so supportive of the campaign – you have all been amazing! And to Britain's Next Bestseller – my brilliant publisher, who has given me this amazing opportunity, this platform, that allowed the wonderful orderers to order… and this book to come into being.

To my wonderful Nan and Grandad who (along with my Mum) have made me who I am today. I get my reading from my Grandad – the only person in our family to read more books than me (enough to fill more than one bookcase I might add!). You have both always been there for me – and I am forever grateful for everything you have done for me, and everything I am because of you. You are the very best people. And I see the goodness in the world because of you.

Karl, for being a bigger dreamer than me and always believing in my dream of wanting to be an author – here it is! Thank you so much for always being there for me, despite the Buffalo in the house. And for letting me fly your laptop 1200 miles to Portugal where 10% of Futurespan was written in our beautiful villa. And who has bought enough books to fill a bookcase! Let's hope this is the start of both of our dreams becoming realities.

Special thanks also go to Suzy who was the first person I told about the characters and story of Futurespan, very late one night, somewhere in Harrogate. You listening meant so much and gave me the courage to keep writing. To Claire whose interest in the story, also told late one night, made me realise that people would want to hear this story, and made me brave enough to show it to the world. And to Katharine who was the first reader of Futurespan. Her glittering review both verbal and then written were overwhelming, and made me glow inside - thank you so much! Thank you to Siobhan for all of your support both covert and public, much appreciated! And for being able to talk to you about my characters as though they are real! Thank you also to Jylanka for your much needed reassurance, to Sara for always having faith in me and to Bunmi for believing in my dreams. I am blessed to call all of you guys my friends.

Thank you so much to Diana who purchased many books! And to Joshua, Jemima and particularly Danielle who has followed the campaign online, and is the happiest! To Frank, thank you hugely for all of your encouragement. I am so blessed by all of your support and the family's faith in me, and making me so welcome in your lives – thank you all.

Thanks also to Lee for using your salesman powers to 'gently encourage' an unsuspecting business partner to purchase several copies! And for ordering your own.

To all of my other friends, colleagues, family, fellow writers, unicorns, acquaintances and complete strangers who have been excited, supportive and encouraging – seriously guys it means the world.

Finally thank you to Futurespan – for not melting away, or turning into anything else, and allowing me to get the words down on the page to make you real – it has taken 10 years for this to happen with a story! And I'm so glad it did with this one.

And thank you to you, for reading it…

Prologue

Amelia stood in the bedroom of her prison sure that she had finally found a way out: a way to end it. Having been trapped for what felt like a very long time – and indeed it had been most of her short life – she couldn't quite believe that she was actually clutching salvation in her small hands. It was heavy, the gun, but she grasped it tightly. The metal was cold against her palm as she held it steady, shaking only a little she kept it pointed firmly at his sleeping chest. She watched the slow rise and fall, contrasting with her own quick, shallow breaths as she surveyed the gross sleeping form of the man on the bed. Him with his slack, fat face, and his great beer-belly protruding out from his grubby vest: he repulsed her. But she fought the urge to bolt, even though this time he couldn't have stopped her, and she stood summoning the last little bit of courage she needed to actually do it.

She took a deep breath, praying that he wouldn't wake up, squeezed her eyes tight shut and then pulled the trigger, three times in quick succession, just to be sure.

The force of the gun took her by surprise and her hands were shaking terribly as she lowered it. On opening her eyes she saw that there wasn't as much blood as she had expected. What was there was a dark, barely red-black ooze pouring slickly from the wounds in his chest and being sucked into the mattress. He hadn't even woken up, but sick gargling noises had escaped his chest as the bullets had ripped through his lungs, allowing blood to pool in them and still his breath for good. He had convulsed briefly and then stilled. Amelia stared at him. Dead. She could barely believe it. The scene she had imagined so many times was finally before her eyes.

'Bye, Dad,' she whispered as she dropped the gun on the floor. It landed with a final clunk, and she did not look back.

In the hallway outside she slouched against the wall, feeling as if she was finally able to breathe again. A strange feeling filled her chest: somewhere between elation and panic. She waited expectantly. But she waited long enough for her breathing to completely return to normal: for what, deep down, she knew was much too long, and nothing had happened.

Grim realisation settled in her stomach and she slid to the floor as great, shaking sobs shook her. Wrapping her arms around herself she rocked, devastated: it had taken everything she had to pull the trigger. She sobbed and sobbed. *Maybe it hasn't worked,* she thought with a small glimmer of hope. She pulled herself up with renewed purpose, wiping hot tears from her cheeks as she went.

From the doorway he did look dead. He was laid there splayed and still, but reluctantly she went over to check, picking up the gun and using it to prod his face. This elicited no response, and no breathing was evident. He was dead – had to be – but then why was she still here? So she put the gun to his head and fired it, taking no chances this time, the bullet launching out of the gun straight through his frontal bone. Black-red goo erupted from inside and she was splattered with it. She looked at her now undeniably dead father and screamed in horror and frustration. 'I did it!' she screamed to no one. 'I did it! He's dead!' She wiped her hands on his chest, covering them with blood and goo. 'Look!' she screamed, holding up her hands. 'He's dead. Look!' Her voice broke and the sobs came again, unwelcomed. She sank onto the floor, her back against the bed. 'He's dead and I'm still here,' she cried desperately.

Wherever here was.

The Stairs

Feeling as if she were falling, as in that odd time between wake and sleep, Tabitha jolted, suddenly awake and completely unsure of where she was.

Shaking herself internally she pushed herself up and found that she was, in fact, on a small landing: a tiny, non-descript ten foot square of concrete. Marking the edges were two sets of concrete steps: up and down. There was nothing else. The light was strange, so dim, that things looked blurry. Tabitha rubbed her eyes, but it didn't change a thing; everything was dulled. Instinctively she felt in her trouser pockets for her phone but she found she had nothing but the clothes she stood up in.

'Hello?' she called, her voice echoing in the concrete stairwell for what sounded like a very long way. Looking down she tried to work out how high up she was but all she could see was the descending flight of stairs, giving her no idea of the scale of this strange place.

'Hello?' she called again.

There was no answer.

Preferring not to wait on this featureless landing in the semi-darkness she weighed up the two options. Down definitely seemed – and felt – darker somehow, as if it was deeper. Deciding to go up felt easier in her heart. Perhaps it was some primordial instinct to get above ground, she wasn't sure, but she instantly felt a little better once she began her ascent. And at least it meant she was doing something, and would hopefully find something. There was a sense of strangeness in the air; she felt as if she was breathing it in. There was something about the whole place that was like nothing she had ever experienced before, and she couldn't even begin to articulate exactly what it was, even to herself.

It took twenty steps before she reached another landing, which was equally as trim and dreary. She wondered again where she was, and still saw no doors, no signs, not even any potted plants. It was quite unlike any other stairwell she had come across. But she persevered: she wouldn't get any answers by standing still.

On crossing the sixtieth dull step and the third dreary landing she still saw no end to all the greyness. In fact, her eyes were starting to become accustomed to it. It was just a shame there was only concrete to see. Sighing, she pushed on up the next flight. There had to be something. Didn't there?

With the perturbing thought that this staircase might actually be never-ending, Tabitha paused on the next landing and strained her ears, listening for any sign of – well, anything. Anything that would break the strange, silent emptiness of this place. But there was nothing.

Somewhere around the seventh landing she paused again, willing herself to hear something. The silence was as oppressive as the greyness, if not more so. Panic was rising in her chest, as she felt trapped in this place, and scared she would never find anything. She was terrified she had died and ended up in some sort of limbo, the emptiness more of a torturous thing than any kind of hell she had imagined before. But she turned away from this thought as soon as it came; it was too awful to contemplate. Instead, with a new determination, she stormed up the steps. She would find something. She had to.

Pausing a few more landings up she listened again. At first there was nothing but after a few seconds the faintest sound of a voice echoed from not far above her and she wondered if she had imagined it. But she continued, hopeful that the voice was real and that she would soon have some company in this desolate place. Maybe company who could shed some light on things, both literally and figuratively, she thought as she surveyed the unshifting gloom. She hoped whoever it was would be friendly, though she had no reason to think she would encounter someone hostile. No reason except for the oddness of the place, the eerie not-quite-rightness. She shook off the thought. The only way to find out was to keep going, and she was getting a little sick of her lonely climb. Any company was better than none, surely?

A few steps on she heard the quiet murmur again, and this time she was sure it wasn't just in her head. As she rounded the next landing she rejoiced that she could hear the voice more clearly now. Her heart felt a little lighter knowing there was another living person here, and that she wasn't doomed to wander the concrete steps alone. Pausing, she listened to it; in fact it sounded a little angry. *Annoyed,* Tabitha corrected herself, *definitely annoyed*. She approached the next landing quietly, sure she would find the source of the voice there, and hoping her worry had been unfounded.

The horizon line of the eleventh landing came into view, and instead of grey emptiness it was decorated with a woman crouching on the floor. The woman was about Tabitha's age, maybe a few years older – or she seemed it, anyway, perhaps because of the harsh set of her jaw, and the long, lined forehead. She was fiddling with her perfectly straightened black hair, and luckily she looked fairly normal, except that she was whispering angrily at what Tabitha first thought was the floor.

Tabitha approached with caution; the fact the woman was talking to herself made her look a little mad, and despite the pull of another human soul Tabitha wanted to pass on keeping the company of a madwoman. Or maybe she was hostile, and maybe solitude was preferable to that. Tabitha waited, hoping the woman wasn't as mad as she seemed. Then another voice joined the conversation. It was male, and its source was blocked from Tabitha's view; it came either from the other end of the landing or maybe the next set of stairs. Tabitha couldn't hear what they were saying but, slightly more satisfied that the woman wasn't mad (at least she wasn't talking to herself), she ascended the last few steps and stood carefully on the landing. The boy looked younger than the woman, maybe twenty, but Tabitha couldn't see him clearly. He was curled into himself, nestled tightly into the corner with his eyes fixed on the next flight of stairs, like an animal caught in a trap, with the stairs as the hunter.

'Dig, you really need to get a grip. We're not going to spend the next god-knows how long here just because you think the bogey monster is hiding up the stairs!' said the woman.

'It's not safe,' the boy whispered sheepishly.

'You're mad. This is ridiculous, Diggory, even for you,' said the woman resolutely, crossing her arms. Yet she didn't make a move for the stairs either.

They were too preoccupied with each other, and the stairs, to notice Tabitha, despite her being only a couple of feet from the woman. Tabitha coughed tentatively, not wanting to stay there unannounced. The woman looked at her and did a double take before scrambling up and putting a few more feet between them.

'Aarghh!' screamed the boy, looking at Tabitha and then putting his hands over his face. 'It's not safe. It's not saafe!' he screamed, his last words descending into sobs.

The woman stood to the side of the boy, her back firmly against the wall, staring wide-eyed and wary at Tabitha. 'Be quiet, Diggory,' she said, absentmindedly tapping his head. 'Who are you and what are you doing here?'

'I'm Tabitha, and I'm, erm, well, I'm not really sure.'

'Oh.'

'Not safe. Not safe. Not safe. Not safe,' said the boy quietly, in time with his rocking.

'What's wrong with him?' asked Tabitha.

'Just try and ignore him. That's my usual tack.' The woman seemed to relax a little.

'Who are you two? You're the first people I've seen in this *place*.'

The woman just stared at Tabitha, and for an awful moment Tabitha thought she wasn't going to say anything.

'I'm Rin,' she said with the small hint of a smile. 'And this, unfortunately, is Diggory, but call him what you like for all I care. Digging lunatic at the moment,' she said tutting.

'Right. Well, hello.' Tabitha smiled weakly. 'Do you know where we are?'

Rin stepped into the middle of the landing and spread out her arms, letting out a small laugh. 'No idea. None at all. You?'

'Aside from some sort of staircase I'm none the wiser either.'

'Well, here we are,' said Rin, sitting down again.

Tabitha sat down too, opposite the still-rocking Diggory. 'How long have you and Diggory been here?'

'Well, here as in this landing I don't know, an hour, maybe. Brave Diggory here won't budge. And here as in this grey, never-ending staircase of nothing: what feels like forever. Probably about half a day.' She looked up, thinking. 'I want to say all morning, but who knows if it actually is.'

'So you've been up there?' Tabitha pointed to the next flight of stairs.

'Oh no, we came from further down.'

'Same as me. How far down were you?'

'Not sure, but we walked a long way up. I lost count at the twelfth flight. I reckon that one there would've been at least our fifteenth, if Mr Scaredy-Cat here hadn't flipped out on me.'

'You came from further down than me,' Tabitha said. 'This is the eleventh landing I've seen.'

Rin continued fiddling with her hair, whilst Diggory rocked and murmured quietly to himself.

'Why does he think it's not safe?' said Tabitha.

'God knows. On some sort of come down, I think.'

'Oh right.' Tabitha surveyed the boy again, but didn't glean anything, except that he was wearing fairly normal, wide-legged jeans with frayed edges. Poking out from the bottom were scuffed Converse trainers, and she could see a silver chain hanging from the jeans' waistband on one side. That was some sort of teenage fashion, Tabitha recalled; those that liked heavy rock used to wear chains like that. From what she could see he didn't look like your typical user, but then again appearances could be deceptive. 'Drugs?' asked Tabitha cautiously.

'Not like you mean, no,' said Rin.

They sat there for a few minutes of awkward silence, listening to Diggory's chanting, before Tabitha asked, 'Are you together?'

'Ha!' Rin laughed. 'No. That would be wrong.'

'Oh, I didn't mean it in that way, sorry. I just meant do you know each other, you know, normally?'

'Always. Unfortunately.'

'And you being together would be wrong because he's turned into some sort of, what did you say, digging lunatic?'

'No, it would be wrong because I don't practise incest,' said Rin.

'Ah, I see.' Tabitha looked over at Diggory whose head was still buried in his hands. 'I couldn't really see to notice the family resemblance.'

'It's weak anyway. And you can't see a bloody thing in this light,' said Rin.

'I know, it's like being in an old movie, all black and white.'

'Tell me about it! It's depressing, I feel like I've travelled back in time.'

'You don't think we have, do you?' said Tabitha. 'I don't see how but…'

'That'd be some sick joke, wouldn't it? Surprise! You've travelled back to the 1930s, and just to prove it you're stuck in a black-and-white movie – excellent. And with a demented brother to boot.'

'I don't think they had so much concrete in the 1930s,' said Tabitha, unconvinced.

'Well, I don't think we've really travelled back in time to some weird 1930s movie either, have we.'

'No, I know.' Tabitha paused. 'But still the light's weird, well, it's not the light is it, it's like everything's changed colour. I'm sure these trousers used to be navy, but look at them – they're dark grey.'

'Yeh, it is weird,' said Rin, looking down at herself. 'I'm sure this top was red.'

'And look at our skin, it has a greyish tinge, like we're half-dead.' Tabitha shuddered a little.

'Not a reassuring thought,' said Rin, looking purposefully at Diggory.

'You don't think we are dead, do you?' asked Tabitha.

'No I don't.'

'Not safe, not safe, not safe,' came Diggory's voice.

Rin ignored him. 'Do I look dead to you?' she said to Tabitha. 'I'm breathing, I can feel my heart beating. I feel alive. Don't you?'

'Kind of.'

'Kind of? So you feel dead then?'

'No,' said Tabitha, pausing. 'I just don't feel, quite, I don't know, right. Don't you feel like that?'

'Well, I think a little unease is acceptable given the circumstances, stuck on a never-ending staircase in some black-and-white version of Neverland, for Christ's sake. We're bound to feel a little out of kilter, but it doesn't mean we're dead,' said Rin. She continued in slightly hushed tones, gesturing over to Diggory who was still rocking. 'And the last thing Diggory needs to hear is that we're in some messed up version of hell. *That* will be anything but helpful.'

'Sorry,' said Tabitha.

They sat there for some time again, rather awkwardly, listening to Diggory quietly chanting and rocking. Rin had started playing with her hair again, and was now sucking on a strand of it, staring off into the distance. Tabitha felt her adrenaline rising as she looked up the staircase. Despite it being just the same as all the many stairs she had already encountered, she couldn't help feeling that maybe Diggory had a point: there was a sense of foreboding about it. It was a niggling, nagging feeling in her gut, telling her that there was something not quite right. Something dangerous, maybe. She tried to push the thought away, preferring to think that it was just Diggory's fear that had morphed into a monster in his head.

She told herself not to be stupid; at least she wasn't alone. It was just her mind playing tricks. *It's a happy place,* she thought to herself. *Everything is okay.* Even though she was fairly sure it wasn't.

'So were you just planning to wait here until he calmed down or something?' she asked, breaking the long silence.

'Something like that,' said Rin. 'Maybe it's been long enough.' She went over to Diggory's crumpled form and stroked his arm. 'Dig, come on now, have you calmed down?'

'But it's not safe, Rin,' he whispered meekly. He did seem calmer, though, and at least the rocking and chanting had abated. Tabitha thought he seemed rather depleted, spent from the exhausting effort of maintaining his fear.

'I'm sure it's fine. Come on now, why don't you have a stand up for me?'

He peeled his hands away from his face and his eyes darted towards the staircase, and then towards Tabitha. Tabitha looked into his pupils which were ringed with a colour more greyscale than the normal human eye, but by the light tone of it she guessed his eyes were ordinarily blue or possibly green. Whatever the colour, they were haunted, deep, scared-looking eyes, and they were staring right at her. The bags under them aged him far past his years, and he was much paler than her or Rin. He looked ill. She wondered again if he was an addict: the eyes fit the bill if nothing else.

'Who's that?' he asked, looking back towards Rin and clinging to her arm like a scared babe.

'That's Tabitha, Dig, she's lost here just like us.'

'Hello,' said Tabitha.

'Tabitha,' he said, his lips forming the word slowly.

'That's it. And I'm Rin, remember?' Rin smiled sarcastically. 'Now how about we stand up?'

Slowly, with Rin helping him, Diggory rose to his feet. He was looking quickly in all directions, as if he could see things on the bare floor, and indeed maybe he could. He did seem more than a little crazy, Tabitha reflected; he could probably see ghosts, or indeed monsters. She looked again at the next set of stairs and shook her head. *Happy place,* she thought.

'Right now, let's get a move on, see if we can find anything in this goddam place,' said Rin. 'Come on Dig, one foot in front of the other. Follow Tabitha.' She looked expectantly at Tabitha, smiling a plastic smile.

Tabitha took a look at the stairs, her gut tugging at her to go back the other way, but she already knew what lay down there, for at least fifteen floors if Rin was right. At least up presented a new possibility, so she started, shaking the thought of monsters firmly from her mind. Monsters didn't exist. They were just in your head.

'It's not hers, though,' said Diggory, momentarily more aware, as he and Rin started to follow Tabitha.

'That's it, Diggory, follow Tabitha, huh? Up the stairs we go.

There are no monsters I'm sure, now come on, you're too big to be dragged up.'

Onwards and upwards in the happy place, sighed Tabitha mirthlessly.

As they were about to start the third flight, even though Diggory had been whimpering all the way, being coaxed a little less than gently by Rin, Tabitha did think it felt a bit lighter. Lighter or warmer? She wasn't sure. Just more alive, somehow; things didn't seem quite the same dull-dead grey as the lower levels. It almost felt electric here. The uneasy feeling still nagged at her but now there was something more like a kind of magnetism that was drawing her in.

Looking up, she could see something on the wall of the landing ahead: a solid, dark grey line protruding just above the horizon line of the last step. It was still grey, but at least it was something and as Tabitha approached she could see it was a sign. Finally, there might be some clue about where they were. Bolting up the last few steps she saw it was a typical directional sign that would have been at home in any hotel stairwell. It was small and dark grey, with white numbers and an arrow pointing upwards. It wasn't a particularly interesting sign, but it was the most exciting thing they had seen here – the only thing, in fact. It read:

7039320

She stared at it. She had no idea what it meant, but she was thankful that there was some clue at last.

The Numbers

There was nothing else: just that one very long number, or seven little numbers, depending on your perspective. No tidy little logos, no lettering, and no clue as to what the number actually pertained to. Only the number and the arrow pointing up.

Diggory staggered onto the landing, clinging to Rin.

'I found something,' Tabitha said, pointing at the sign. 'Don't really know what seven million, thirty-nine thousand, three-hundred and twenty has to do with anything though.'

'Me neither,' said Rin, stroking the whimpering Diggory. 'It's okay, Dig, look! A really unhelpful sign. It couldn't get any better.'

'Well, I suppose we'll find out what it means. The arrow points up,' Tabitha said.

'Yeh, come on Dig.' Rin tugged at his arm. 'Time for some sort of answer, I hope.'

Diggory tore his flitting eyes away from the uneventful floor, and looked up at the sign. His eyes widened, his pupils dilated and he stood transfixed. Rin tugged at his arm again.

'Come on, Dig, we don't know how much further we have to go before we see something more than godforsaken concrete steps. Oh, and the one solitary sign that explains precisely nothing. We waited long enough at the last landing.'

But he didn't budge; he just stood there.

'Diggory, come on, move it. There aren't any monsters here, and I don't think seven million and whatever is going to turn out to be a monster's den, do you? '

Tabitha looked on curiously, wondering if the number meant something to Diggory.

'It's mine,' said Diggory resolutely, as if in answer. Then he started up the stairs, taking them several at a time, reminding Tabitha of a child suddenly happy after a long sulk.

'Okay then,' said Rin, exchanging a glance with Tabitha. 'Well, at least it's an improvement, I suppose.'

'Yeh.' Tabitha fell into step with Rin, and they both followed Diggory like owners walking a new puppy. 'Has he always been like this?'

'Not exactly. He's normally on medication; it's pretty heavy stuff. I think all this must be because he hasn't had it.'

'I see. What's it for?'

'All sorts really. Anxiety, mainly, and other psychological things, you know. He has some issues. Very up and down, as you can see.'

'It doesn't run in the family then?' said Tabitha as they cornered another landing.

'What do you think?'

'No, I guess not.' Tabitha smiled. 'Poor Diggory though, it must be awful.'

'Yeh. He's much better on the meds though. He's a sweetie really but I haven't seen him this bad for a long time – not since the beginning, anyway.'

'The beginning?'

'Yeh. When it all started. But it doesn't matter, just some bad stuff. Just need to work out where the hell we are and get him to a hospital or something.'

'Hopefully this seven million carry-on will help when we get to it. Let's hope it's not another ten or twenty floors. Or seven million. Surely there can't be that many.'

'No,' said Rin uncertainly. 'I hope it isn't far. I need to get Diggory out of here.'

'Come to think of it, I can't remember how I got he –'

A high-pitched, excited squeak came from the floor above. Rin ran up the steps, with Tabitha following behind. They reached the next landing, and nothing. They ran up the flight after that; he had sounded closer than he was. As they approached what she assumed was the next landing Tabitha could see the sign: 7039320, with no arrow this time. And no small square landing either; instead it opened up into a long corridor.

'Never thought I'd be so happy to see a corridor,' said Rin.

'Me neither.'

There was no sign of Diggory, but it looked as if there were doors further down. Doors, plural: after so much of nothing they could barely believe it. It briefly crossed Tabitha's mind that maybe they were like mirages, like water in a desert; on a never-ending concrete staircase doors were what you wished for. And she did really hope they were real. She kept her eyes fixed on them, scared that they might disappear. As ridiculous as it was they didn't seem to be getting any closer; in fact they seemed to be getting further away. It was just a really long corridor, that was all. Had to be.

'Diggory!' Rin called, to no response.

They hurried on and finally reached the end of the corridor where they saw there were indeed three doors: one directly in front of them and one on each side. Tabitha longed to touch them to prove that they were real, but something stopped her from actually lifting her hand. They all had numbers on them. Long, long numbers:

70393040798

70393190514

70393060620

'What the hell is with the numbers?' asked Rin.

'God knows,' said Tabitha.

The door on the right, with the numbers ending in 040798, was very slightly ajar.

'Look,' said Tabitha, indicating the door. 'He's probably through that one.'

'Come on then.' Rin headed tentatively towards it. 'Dig,' she called out. 'You in there?'

Slowly she pulled the door far enough open to peer through. All she could see was some kind of white smoke, like an indoor fog, which reminded her of smoke machines in nightclubs. 'Diggory?' she called through the fog, holding her breath as she listened but no response came. She leaned back out and breathed.

'What is it?' asked Tabitha, looking over Rin's shoulder.

'No idea, I can't see anything, just this white stuff. Diggory, I don't want to have to come in there after you! Can you just come back please? I can't see a thing.' She paused, waiting again: nothing. Exasperated, she leaned back in and shouted again, 'Diggory, come out of there!'

'Maybe he isn't in there,' said Tabitha. 'Maybe he just took a look and thought, I'm not going in there.'

'You mean like I'm thinking now?' Rin leaned back to look at the other doors, all sat squarely in their frames. 'I don't know, funny that it's the only one ajar.'

'I guess.'

'And I feel kind of drawn to it,' said Rin. 'Weird right?'

'No weirder than anything else,' said Tabitha.

'No. Well, it doesn't look like he's coming out, whatever he's doing. Plus it can't be any more boring than the million-step staircase and the grey corridor, can it?'

'No, I very much doubt it.'

'You never know, maybe it's the way out,' said Rin with only a hint of sarcasm.

'Maybe.'

'Only one way to find out.' Rin took a deep breath and walked into the white fog.

The Other Side

Tabitha followed Rin, literally a second behind her, but she couldn't see or hear her. There was nothing but, well, nothingness. Whiteness and blankness lay all around her. Her breathing quickened and her palms were clammy; she almost went to turn back. There was nothing except the fog pressing on her, slightly cold and tingling next to her skin, almost as if it wanted to get in. She shook her head and opened her mouth to call Rin when she felt and heard a whooshing, as if somehow she'd been moved, and now all of a sudden felt as if she were somewhere else. Then the fog began to clear just a little and she heard Rin right in front of her.

'Oh my good god,' Rin said in an empty voice.

'What is it?' said Tabitha as the fog finally cleared enough for her to see what Rin was seeing. 'Oh, wow, I'd started to forget there were colours in the world.'

They were standing in the corridor of what looked very much like a small family home. There was a staircase to her left, with a worn but deep red carpet. On the end of the railing was slung a bulky array of coats: blues, greens, beiges. There was a side table to the right, with a phone, a notepad with scribbles on it and different sized shoes on the floor. Straight ahead was the living room with green and gold cushions; the colours were as bright as harsh sunlight to their grey-accustomed eyes. Tabitha could see through the narrow door and the far window that there was a garden beyond. A garden! *I must be dreaming,* she thought. They were too high up for there to be a street, or maybe they had been underground; she didn't know. She didn't feel she knew very much anymore. The impossible, it seemed, was here.

The kitchen was to the right, a little way ahead. Rin hadn't moved. Tabitha could hear the TV, something on the news about

Prince Edward's marriage, and the new currency, the Euro. Tabitha was puzzled; the Euro had been around a long time. Rin looked very pale.

'Where are we?' asked Tabitha. 'Are you okay?'

'No,' said Rin.

'What's the matter? Do you know where we are?'

'It's our old house. But it isn't possible.' Rin's voice sounded choked. 'But it is. And what the hell it's doing on the apparent seventh million floor of hell knows where I do not know.'

'This just got a whole lot weirder. That's a street outside,' said Tabitha, peering through the kitchen window. 'A street with grass verges and trees and a bright blue car.'

'You're telling me,' Rin said.

'And I'm guessing you didn't have some kind of bizarre concrete house extension?'

Rin looked at Tabitha, but seemed to look straight through her.

'It's like an episode of Dr Who,' ventured Tabitha.

'Yeh, and we're the idiots who are going to be eaten by the monster. Maybe Diggory was right.'

'Hopefully not,' said Tabitha.

Rin hadn't moved, except for her head which was slowly scanning the scene she obviously knew so well. 'It looks exactly the same. It isn't possible.'

'Maybe we should just fetch Diggory and go back. I thought anything would be better than the monotonous concrete, but this? I'm not so sure.'

'Me neither. Not much to go back to but anything is better than staying in this place.'

'Perhaps one of the other doors will be better – maybe even the way out.'

'I doubt that. Let's find him first.'

Rin stepped forward slowly, making her way towards the living room, poking her head inside the kitchen on the way past, and looking down as if he might be hiding behind the island. Tabitha followed a little way behind, cautiously looking up the stairs and seeing no sign of anybody.

'Diggory, are you here? Stop messing about if you are. You know I can't be here,' said Rin.

They reached the living room and it was like walking back in time. It was redolent of some of the living rooms from Tabitha's childhood: the living rooms of family friends of the 'lesser class' as her father had put it, or sometimes the living rooms of 'the workers'. Rin scanned the living room and walked towards the patio doors to look out onto the garden. It was a small typical terrace garden: narrow and long, it stretched out, mostly grass with the odd forlorn-looking shrub, to a shed at the back which was wonky; Tabitha thought that it probably consisted of rotting wood. There was nothing else of note in the garden. No Diggory. Rin turned and let out an exasperated breath.

'This is not possible. It is just not possible. This has to be some kind of dream.'

'It feels too real. Not like any kind of dream I've ever had.'

'You're right, it's a nightmare,' Rin said. With that she stormed back into the hallway with heavy, determined strides. Tabitha followed her as she clomped up the stairs.

'Diggory, this is not funny anymore. Come out here!'

They emerged at the top of the stairs onto a miniscule landing with four flimsy white wooden doors leading off it. Rin paused momentarily and took the door that was directly in front of her. Tabitha followed her, pleased to see there were no silver numbers in sight. She smiled to herself and then stumbled as she ran into a stationary Rin.

'Oh. Sorry,' Tabitha muttered but Rin didn't budge. She stood there, mesmerised by something inside the room. Something that Tabitha couldn't see. 'Rin,' she said. 'Is everything okay?'

A choked sound escaped from somewhere deep in Rin's throat. It was somewhere between a sob and a scream. Tabitha felt as if it had cooled the air. 'Rin?' Tabitha shook her shoulder gently and craned her neck to see what she was looking at. 'Rin, can you hear me?'

Then Tabitha heard another voice from inside the room. It was a small voice, high-pitched. 'Rin-Rin!' said the voice. 'Come and play.'

'Oh my god,' said Rin, clasping her hands over her face before turning, almost knocking Tabitha out of the way as she made for the landing. She leaned over the banister and drew long heavy breaths into her lungs. She looked as if she was about to be sick.

Tabitha stood in the doorway but didn't look inside. Whatever, or more to the point whoever, was in the room could wait. She went to Rin and tentatively put a hand on her shoulder.

'Just breathe slowly, nice long breaths. In and out,' Tabitha said calmly.

'Oh my god, oh my god,' Rin repeated over and over, as her breathing became faster. She was stealing glances over her shoulder as if scared something was coming to get her. But whatever it was Tabitha wasn't worried. The voice had sounded like a child.

'Rin, just try and slow your breathing down, a bit slower.'

Rin took a few deeper breaths and then said, 'This. Cannot. Be. Happening.'

'It's okay, Rin, that's it, nice and slow.'

'It. Is. Not. Okay. Tabitha. It is not okay. This can't be happening. The house was one thing, one awful, awful thing – but this. It isn't possible, Tabitha, it isn't. *He* isn't possible.' Rin pointed towards the door. She was taking large gulps of air now, swallowing it as she rocked back and forth beside the banister. Now Tabitha could see a family resemblance.

She heard light footsteps and turned to see a small boy, about six years old, dressed in grubby but colourful Superman pyjamas. He was holding a paper aeroplane and smiling broadly.

'Rin-Rin, come play,' he said, tugging on Rin's leg. Rin continued hyperventilating, rocking back and forth, trying to ignore the child. 'Come on, Rin-Rin,' he persisted. 'Please! I've got lots more airplanes, come look,' he said, bounding back into the room.

'Rin, was that?' said Tabitha, her half-finished question hanging thick in the air.

'Impossible,' whispered Rin to herself. She had her eyes

squeezed shut and was wildly shaking her head. 'Impossible. Totally impossible. Maybe you were right about Doctor Who. That back there is a big bloody concrete time machine.'

Tabitha went back to the door to get a better look at the offending child. He was clutching several paper planes in his left hand and holding one high up in the air with his right, turning it this way and that.

'Zoooom, zoooom, zoom,' he said in time with the movements. He bounced happily around the room, largely ignoring Tabitha except for zooming around her a couple of times. He did have a look of Diggory about him, in his manner and his movements. Tabitha thought that his eyes were familiar, except they had lost their fear. This little Diggory seemed like a totally different person, content flying his paper plane.

'Come and look, Rin-Rin, zoom, zoom, zoom!'

Tabitha went back out to the landing, thankful to see that Rin seemed a little better. She wasn't rocking as much now and her breathing had slowed, but her eyes were still tight shut.

'Rin. Are you alright?'

'I don't understand this,' Rin whispered. She looked right into Tabitha's eyes then and grasped her hand. 'I'm really scared.'

'I know, I'm a bit scared too. It's beyond weird. What should we do?'

Rin paused for a long time, taking several deep breaths. 'I'm not sure, but I can't stay here.'

'Zooooom zoooooooom.'

'I don't think we should leave the little Diggory here. It isn't safe. I need to get him out of here.' Rin let go of Tabitha's hand and marched into the room. 'Come on, Diggory, move it. It's time to go now.'

'No, Rin-Rin! I want to play,' he whined as she plucked him off the ground, where he had been zooming aeroplanes along the blue carpet. On unsteady feet he stumbled as Rin took his arm firmly and proceeded back down the stairs, following Tabitha. The paper aeroplane he had been clutching fell to the floor.

'Rin! No!' he whined at the bottom of the stairs, and grasped the banister, hugging it with both arms, and wrapping his legs around it too.

'Diggory, stop being a little brat; we need to leave. Let go now, come on,' said Rin, sternly tugging at his arms.

'No!' said Diggory, before screaming at the top of his lungs.

Tabitha winced. She was only a couple of feet from the door now – what she imagined would have ordinarily been a typical front door, probably UPVC with a fake stained-glass effect or frosted flowers. Instead there a dark grey doorframe, with no visible door, and only white fog to be seen inside it. Who knew if behind the white fog the concrete would still be there? She wouldn't be surprised if there was something else. She stood there wondering, torn between wanting to find out and wanting to stay here, basking in the colour, safer perhaps from any more surprises for now.

It took Rin a good couple of minutes to prise Diggory's hands apart and pull him away from the banister. She bundled him into her arms, as he kicked and scratched at her to be free, screaming madly the whole time.

'No, Diggory, stop fighting me, you're not staying here. It's not happening again. Not on my watch. Come on, Tabitha, move it!' Rin said.

'What about the grown-up Diggory?'

'It doesn't matter. At least this one isn't crazy. Maybe he never will be if I can get him out of this goddamned house. I can't stay here a minute longer; are you just going to stand there all day?'

'N-no, sorry,' said Tabitha as she scrambled to the door and into the fog, with Rin and the little Diggory following right behind her.

The Not-Blue Door

Amelia woke on the landing, a safe ten floors below *the* landing: her landing, or more to the point *his* landing. She half expected him to emerge from up the stairs. Shuddering at the thought she turned to check and saw gratefully that they were empty. It felt safe here but she carried his shadow around with her wherever she went.

Having arrived in this strange place only a landing away from *his* landing, she had walked unsuspectingly up the twenty steps and had frozen in fear at the number four that hung awkwardly on the door. Her *home,* she scoffed in her head. Some home. It was her supposed 'family' home: a two-bedroomed, cramped flat in a dismal Leeds tower block. Lindsey Mount, Lindsey Road, Harehills: not the kind of neighbourhood most people would venture into. But Amelia thought the streets were much safer than the horror behind that blue door. At least if she was knifed by some thug the hospital was across the road, and if she didn't make it there then the end would come quickly, and she might finally have some peace. Amelia was never scared of the rough people in her neighbourhood, just the monster living at the same address.

On discovering it she had stood outside the door, briefly confused, thinking that she must have been coming home. She had vaguely noticed that the stairs leading up to the landing were different, but it hadn't really registered yet how different they were: on seeing the door she thought everything that had preceded it had been a daydream. There was nothing different; she was outside her familiar front door, the same as always. The only thing that niggled at her was the strange colour of everything – as if she had been transported, somehow, and shoved in an old-fashioned TV show. Someone was playing a cruel joke if that was the case, like some sicker version of The Truman Show. The blue door didn't really look altogether blue either: there was only the tiniest hint of a grey-blue present. Even her skin had a grey tinge. That was when she became convinced that it was not altogether real – not in the usual sense, anyway. But it felt more real than anything. She had felt more scared than ever looking at that not-blue door.

But she had gone in anyway, as usual; where else was there to go? Plus he would be expecting her, and if she was late it only made things worse. So she crept in quietly. There was nothing new about her not wanting to be there, but it was all that she knew, and she didn't have a choice. There was nothing different, greyness aside, just Amelia dreaming, as usual, of an escape. Perhaps the greyness signalled new heights of her imagination: either that or the start of madness. The greyness perhaps echoing her dull, grey boredom with her life.

Music blared out from the TV in the living room ahead, the open door allowing the sound to permeate the small space. She walked past the bedroom door first, and shuddered a little, involuntarily, as she knew before she passed that it was empty. He would be in the living room slouched there as usual, beer can in one hand with his eyes glued to the screen. And indeed as Amelia advanced he was sitting there on the far side of the sofa, in his spot that she imagined would one day mould to his exact shape. That was something she had seen on the Simpsons before and it had made her chuckle. Marty Ramsdon and Homer Simpson were not all that dissimilar after all, except for the yellow colouring. Marty was more of a pasty white: sickly looking. In fact Amelia learned that sometimes real people can actually turn yellow. She had thought the teacher was joking but he showed pictures; it had a posh scientific name that sounded a little like 'Janice', and it happened when there was something wrong with your liver. The amount of beer Marty drank she wouldn't be surprised if there was something wrong with his liver, and she very much hoped that there was. Maybe it was just a matter of time before he turned yellow, and then the transformation to Homer would be complete. She smiled a little to herself at the thought, thinking also that if he really did turn into Homer perhaps she would be able to rub him out or Tipp-Ex him or something. And then at least it wouldn't be murder. You couldn't go to prison for killing a cartoon character. But it was not to be today and probably not ever. He was sitting there, very much real, very much illegal to murder, and too strong and scary to try it anyway. Nothing new.

'Hi, Dad,' she said meekly.

'I'm watching the footy,' he said without looking up. 'Dishes need doing.'

Amelia padded through into the small adjoining kitchen and surveyed the mess, unable to remember when she had last cleaned it. She ran a dish full of hot soapy water and went to work. This was her normal daily reality, and in a way it was her comfort. He left her alone to do the 'women's work', happy that she was 'in her place'. And Amelia was happy, relatively at least, to be out of the way and to have some sort of control over a part of her life. So she scrubbed, and rinsed the dishes plate by plate and glass by glass before leaving them to dry whilst she set about clearing the worktops. The numerous beer cans were carefully tidied into the plastic bin that was shoved underneath the sink.

It had been this way for so long now Amelia could barely remember the before. All she had now was herself busy playing the role of wife, with nobody else here to care. She cooked, she cleaned and she ironed, keeping the scruffy flat as best she could. Not out of pride, or out of anyone else to show, but because it was something to do, something to immerse herself in, something that was at least hers in this place. Something that meant, for a while at least, he left her alone.

That had never been enough for her mother. Amelia didn't blame her: often she thought she would have left too. Except she was sure she would have taken her daughter with her. But he would never have let them both go, not without a fight, and her mother hadn't had any fight left in her. Like an injured animal it was all she could do to skulk away and lick her wounds. Amelia still thought she would've fought him; for a daughter she would have. Maybe she did blame her mother a little for that. It was three years since she had left her alone here, and Amelia was teetering just on the edge of sanity. How her mother had managed ten years she would never know. But she blamed him for that. Only him.

Amelia was looking forward to being sixteen. It was only three years away, and she liked the symmetry of that as often she thought she was halfway through. You could get a job at sixteen, and if she had a job she would have real concrete hope. She could get together some money and find a way to leave. A part of her knew it would never be quite that simple, knew she would probably be too scared of him to do it and she would be left waiting for him to turn yellow. But she clung to her little hopes, using them to keep her on the knife-edge of sanity, to keep her from falling off into the depths where she was sure she would either kill him or herself. He would push her to the edge eventually, she knew that. For a mother to leave her daughter, that was somewhere *way* past the edge. It was just a matter of time and Amelia hoped that she had enough of it left to get out with her sanity at least somewhat intact.

It had been a long three years for poor Amelia. The night before her mother had left she had suffered one of the most violent attacks, breaking the all-time record for their hopeless partnership. Her father had beaten her mother so badly she hadn't even been able to get out of bed the next day to send her ten-year-old off to school. Amelia had been rudely awakened by his fist on the door – the same fist that had turned her mother's eyes black. Her mother had always been up on a morning. Always. Even though she had stopped braving the school gates with sunglasses on some years ago at least she got up to pack Amelia's lunch and send her off with a kiss on the forehead. But not that day. Amelia thought he had probably kicked her ribs so hard she could barely stand the pain to get out of bed, and thought that was also why she had barely taken a thing with her. What hurt most was the abandoned box of baby photos.

Amelia had got herself up that morning, got herself ready, and plucked up the courage to ask for some lunch money after checking and seeing the fridge unusually devoid of sandwiches. The only response she got from him was that he couldn't be wasting his money on her fattening herself up, even though Amelia was teetering on the small end of the normal scale for her age. If she had been at a good school they would have suspected anorexia, but at a school with serious behavioural problems ranging from violence to drug dealing, neglect was not a primary concern. So Amelia left that morning, passing by the bedroom on her way out, getting one last glance at the beat-up wreck of her mother, sleeping restlessly in the monster's bed.

When Amelia had got home from school that afternoon she had returned to a scrawled note from her mother, saying she was sorry and that she had to leave. Even at such a young age Amelia understood. Never having had the loving mother-daughter relationship most children enjoyed – her mother was too busy worrying about him – Amelia didn't feel the loss as acutely as most children would. The sense of abandonment had been somewhat longstanding. She grieved for her mother, but she was glad to no longer feel so powerless, waiting in her room listening to her mother's screams, hoping that when she fell silent it wouldn't be forever.

Initially Amelia ceased to fully grasp the repercussions and the permanence of her mother's departure, but she was happy she wouldn't have to see him hurting her mother anymore. The thought that she would fill her mother's shoes didn't even cross her mind until much later. That was when she started to really wish her mother had stayed.

When the monster came home from his usual Tuesday night outing to the pub he screamed at her to tell him where her mother was and reluctantly she showed him the note. He smacked her across the face so hard that she fell to the floor, but he didn't touch her again for over a year. In that time, and afterwards, she increasingly slipped into her mother's shoes, starting with the washing and cleaning, and progressing to much more sinister things. She shuddered to think of it all, of how much things had changed. It was strange that the year after her mother had left had been one of the most peaceful. At least she had things to occupy her time with, and she only had herself to worry about. Naively she thought as long as she was good, as long as she cleaned the house and did what he said, that he would leave her alone. Unfortunately she had been very wrong.

It had started slowly. The odd angry word and him grabbing things from her progressed to occasional bouts of violence that ended in broken crockery or holes through the flimsy wooden doors. It progressed so slowly that it became normality for Amelia, and indeed violence had been an ever-present feature in her life. It took an awfully long time for her to see how very wrong things were, and to realise how she really didn't want to live her life being scared and violated all the time. She wished he would leave her alone. Her purest wish was that she could leave, but she didn't know any different, and didn't think anyone could help, so she just made the best of it, waiting until she was sixteen, until money might offer a shining way out of hell. At least that was her meagre plan, the best she could do. Except for murder, but she wasn't sure whether she had the guts. If only he were yellow.

And here she was, stuck in the same hell as always, clutching her one solitary dream that her life would amount to more than this. That was all. Amelia didn't have any grand ambitions. She was far from stupid but not being at the best school, and having little support at home didn't work in her favour. At best she was an average student, and knew she wouldn't be going to college or university. If nothing else she couldn't wait that long to get away. The plan was to work lots when she reached sixteen: not just a little part-time job that some of the college kids did; she needed more than that. But sixteen was still a long way off.

Thinking all this through as she cleaned the dishes she started to get the sense that something more than her imagination was at work. The greyness of everything was odd. Surely she couldn't imagine things were grey? However dull her life was surely that wasn't possible. You couldn't just imagine things had changed colour. Testing the theory, she squinted hard at the plates, trying to make the previously blue stripes blue again. As hard as she tried they remained grey. How could it be possible?

Once Amelia had finished putting the grey plates away in the grey cupboards she wandered into the living room in a daze, staring at the not-brown sofa and the not-red curtains, and the way her dad's skin was no longer the sickly off-white of alcoholism, but the grey of the undead. Her eyes followed his to the TV: Marty's first love reduced to black-and-white. Not the usual sparkling colour of the hundred-pound knock-off her mum had sacrificed a week's wages for. She wished her mother were here; at least she could have asked her what to do about her sight. She could have asked her if everything was black-and-white for her too.

So Amelia stood stupidly in the middle of the living room staring at the black-and-white figures running around the grey pitch.

'What do you want?' he said, turning briefly. 'I'm watching the footy.'

'It's black-and-white,' said Amelia, still in a daze.

'Are you stupid? It's an away match, they play in blue. They only play in white at home. Everyone knows that.'

'No. The picture's black-and-white.'

'What you talking about?'

'It looks black-and-white. Not colour.'

'It's a colour TV, LCD backlit. Top of the range. Does it look bloody black-and-white to you?' He paused, taking a loud slurp from his can of Special Brew. 'Don't they teach you nothing at this school? Can't even teach you to see properly.'

'No, Dad. Sorry,' she murmured.

'Now I'm watching the footy. If you've got any more stupid questions ask the bastard teacher, not me. You hear?'

'Yes, Dad,' said Amelia, making her retreat. As fascinating as the black-and-white footballers were, they were not fascinating enough to risk her father's heavy hand. She didn't want to see if her bruises would be black-and-white too.

She looked back to the living room and watched her supposed father happily watching the match and consuming his beer, not giving her a second thought. He was slurping from a second can now, the first lying crumpled and forgotten on the floor. He had more consideration for that can than he did for her. She looked away. There was a bigger mystery to solve here. Perhaps something had happened to her vision. Maybe she should take herself to the hospital, since nobody else would. Either way, she needed answers.

She opened the door carefully and peered out onto the landing, which was of course grey – no surprises there. Glancing over her shoulder again, and seeing her father unmoved, she left the flat, closing the door without a sound. She padded down the stairs in the dim, strange light but she didn't find the usual ground floor three floors down, nor the usual exits off to other flats on each floor. There were no exits or doorways. Five floors further on – what Amelia imagined was like going below ground – there was still nothing. It dawned on her then that it wasn't her eyesight: she wasn't in the tower block at all. She was somewhere else altogether.

And initially she could hardly believe her luck, and felt no desire to find a way out of this place; she felt an overwhelming sense of peace and freedom. For the first time she had somewhere that was hers. Her father hadn't seemed to notice anything wrong with the colours, and she thought it would all be the same for him when he opened the still-blue door. So she had settled a few more floors down, ten floors below *his* landing. Happy, for now, to have some peace.

Grown Again

As they entered into the nothingness again Tabitha felt the cold creep of the fog and the whooshing, just like before. She kept walking forwards and as the fog cleared, she saw with mixed feelings that it was all the same as it had been: the corridor unchanged, everything with the same grey-glow, and with the same humming feeling of energy that she had sensed earlier.

Facing the door she waited for Rin and the little Diggory, wondering what it meant for Diggory's future. She watched as Rin had to drag him through the door by his wrist, only just managing to tug him over the threshold before falling on the floor. Tabitha gasped and she and Rin looked on, awestruck, at the little Diggory. As he was just over the threshold he started to transform, mutating right in front of them. His arms and legs and then his whole body lengthened back into their fully grown-up form. Even his clothes transformed, and he was back exactly the way he'd been before going through the door, as if nothing had happened at all.

The newly grown Diggory stood on the precipice of the doorway, a little stunned. His eyes were bleary and he awkwardly half-stumbled a step or two away from the door. Rin, still breathless from their struggle, reached out and firmly closed the door. Tabitha thought if there had been a lock available she would have used it and incinerated the key. Rin sank to the floor, breathing heavily.

Tabitha stood staring at Diggory as he rubbed his eyes and glanced around him, like a child waking from a nap, unsure of exactly where he was.

'Are you alright?' asked Tabitha.

Rin shook her head between ragged breaths. Diggory didn't look much better. 'What happened?' he said, rubbing his eyes.

'I don't know, Diggory, you tell me,' snarled Rin.

'I don't know, Rin,' he said, looking around. 'I don't know. I'm scared now; maybe I should just go back in there.' He looked at the door. 'It felt better.'

'What the hell, Diggory? Why did you even go in there? Why didn't you get out the minute you realised you were in that place, instead of trotting upstairs and playing aeroplanes like a goddammed good boy? What's wrong with you?'

'I felt safe, and I was a little boy.'

'Safe? Safe! In that place, in that awful place. I couldn't bear it, Diggory, what were you thinking? I don't even know how our house is even here. I mean, how the hell is our old house behind that door? How is that possible?' Rin's voice was shaking.

'I don't know,' he said, sitting down and putting his head in his hands. 'I felt like I did back then: back then, before. It was like I wasn't really me, not this me, and it was safe and I was safe. I was happy.'

'You don't go back in there, do you hear? Because I won't be coming to get you,' Rin said between choked sobs. 'And that little boy you somehow turned back into didn't want to come out. And what would have happened if I hadn't been there, Dig? Would you have just been stuck in there forever?'

'I don't know, Rin. It's all fuzzy, but it felt better in there. I don't like it here,' he said, whispering the last sentence.

'I know, and I'm not exactly jumping over the moon here either, Diggory, but you can't go back in there. It's not safe and you damn well know it.'

'It was once,' said Diggory glumly. 'It felt just like it did when it was.'

'Yeh, well, that didn't last very long did it.' Rin wiped her eyes and turned to face him. 'Look, Diggory, look at me. It was just some kind of cruel illusion, some sort of, I don't know, projection of the past and it isn't real. It's gone, and it was never really real anyway, was it. Not the safe part. That was just an illusion too. So you can't go back in there, you mustn't. It's a trick, okay?'

'Okay,' he said reluctantly.

'I mean it.'

'Okay.'

'It was a trick, Diggory. What was it?'

'A trick.'

'Yes,' said Rin, drawing in a deep breath. 'Now let's get away from this place.'

'What about the other doors?' said Diggory.

'Never mind them. That one was a trick, who knows what's behind the others and I don't want to find out. I'm not following you through another one. We need to get out of here.' Rin got up from the floor. 'Come on, let's go now.'

Rin walked past Tabitha and back down the corridor towards the landing again. Tabitha hung back, watching Diggory as he sat on the floor like a lost little boy. She could almost see him as the six-year-old he'd just been, sitting there alone without anyone to look after him. Except this version wasn't happy. He looked about him, his gaze fixing on the door before he caught Tabitha looking at him. He looked sheepish.

'You okay?' Tabitha asked.

He sighed. 'I don't know. I don't feel so good.'

'It'll be okay,' said Tabitha, as Diggory became distracted by the door again. 'I don't think that's a good idea though. Think Rin might kill you, anything else aside.'

'Yeh.' Diggory laughed. 'You're probably right.'

'Come on,' said Tabitha, holding out her hand.

'Thanks.'

'No problem,' she said as they began walking down the corridor. Diggory took a look back at the doors, and severed the connection between their hands. There was deep regret in his eyes.

'It's for the best,' said Tabitha.

'Yeh, maybe,' he said.

'At least you're not rocking on the floor now. Do you feel better than you did at first?'

'A little,' he said with a small smile. 'This isn't a good place though. I still feel that.'

'Hmm, it's a strange place, that's for sure.'

'It isn't safe, you know.'

'You said that a lot before,' said Tabitha. 'Why isn't it? It doesn't seem dangerous to me, just strange.'

'I can't really say why, it just doesn't feel safe. Probably sounds stupid, but the only time I've felt safe since we got here was behind that door. And a big part of me wants to go back through, even though I know Rin's right.'

'Well, hopefully we can find a way out soon.'

'Yeh, I really hope so.'

'You better be behind me, Diggory,' came Rin's voice from down the corridor.

'I am,' he shouted back.

'Sisters, huh?' smiled Tabitha.

'Always been the same, wouldn't change it, I guess,' he said distractedly as he looked back at the doors.

'Have you always been close?'

'Yeh, I guess, had to be. But I don't really want to talk about it.'

'Sorry.'

'It's okay, just forget it.'

'Maybe you'll feel better once we get moving again,' said Tabitha.

'I feel better here,' he said sadly. 'It feels safer here, anyway: not good, but safe. Mine. You know? I don't like the rest of here at all.'

'Maybe we can find a way out, Diggory; try and keep it together. Keep strong.'

'Easier said than done.'

'Think happy thoughts, think about what you want to do when we get out of here.'

'Don't know if that'll be all that motivating, life's kind of a mess,' Diggory said.

'At least you won't be stuck on an endless concrete staircase.'

'That's a point,' he said with a small chuckle.

'What are you two doing?' snapped Rin. 'I want to get out of this place, we haven't got all day. If it even is day. We need to get out of here.'

'I kind of want to stay here, sis,' said Diggory. 'Can't we stay here tonight? There's more room here.'

'Don't even think about it. It's a trick, I told you. It's not a good idea staying near those doors, Diggory; I want to get away from them… There must be a way out, now move it. Up the stairs and away from here,' Rin said sternly.

Tabitha gave Diggory a gentle push towards the stairs, along with a reassuring smile. Reluctantly he moved towards the first step, looking back over his shoulder again. He hesitated, his foot hovering just above the step, his eyes focused on the doors. For a second Tabitha thought he was going to bolt towards them, and she braced herself to get out of his way, knowing she wouldn't stand a chance of stopping him. Rin stood with a hand on her hip, staring intently at Diggory, with a pain in her eyes visible just below her hard exterior. She let out her breath as he put his foot on the step. Finally he turned his attention upwards and slowly started his ascent. Rin followed him with a small nod of her head and a sliver of a smile, and Tabitha relaxed and prepared to climb again. She had lost count of the number of steps.

More Numbers

They had moved over ten floors away from Diggory's doors after what felt like half a day's climbing. Just as they were preparing to sit down for a rest at the next landing, all of them exhausted, Tabitha spotted a new sign on the horizon. It proclaimed:

14019114

They all reached the landing and considered it. It had an arrow pointing upwards, just like its predecessor. Again, Diggory was assessing it with the wide eyes of understanding. He looked straight at Tabitha and plainly said, 'Yours.' He then promptly plonked himself down on the floor, and curled into himself. 'It's yours,' he whispered.

Rin sat down slowly next to him. Tabitha looked at her, her head tipped to one side. 'You heard him,' said Rin, shrugging her shoulders. 'It's yours, and I want nothing to do with any more bloody numbers. I'm with Dig. And I'm exhausted.'

'Me too. I'll go tomorrow,' Tabitha said.

'Doesn't feel right calling it tomorrow does it? It doesn't really feel like any time at all,' said Rin.

'No, I guess not, but it's the closest description, I guess.'

'Yeh. Anyway, I'm not coming with you.'

'Okay.'

'Not after last time.'

'I understand,' murmured Tabitha as she settled down on the other side of the landing.

The light was always the same here, but she was exhausted and knew she needed to rest. She looked anxiously at the next staircase: her staircase, she supposed. She didn't want to think about what was up there waiting for her so she tried not to think about anything at all. It was a difficult thing to do as she couldn't ignore the strong waves of energy she could feel pulsing down the stairs. She felt them washing over her, and it was oddly comforting, like the beating heart of a loved one. She listened to the slow, contented breathing of Diggory who was now curled up and sound asleep. As she focused on his breathing she forced her own to match it, breathing slowly and steadily. In. Out. In. Out. Eventually sleep came: uneasy, fitful sleep, filled with the past. Filled with her mistakes and regrets, with all the bad feelings she had ever felt.

She woke with a jump what felt like hours later, and she felt more than a little sick. Rin and Diggory were still asleep but Tabitha knew there would be no more rest for her. So she got up and stepped slowly towards the staircase. There was no point in delaying the inevitable. The sense of foreboding she had felt since arriving in this place was about to be realised. She climbed the stairs one by one, the feeling of the heat and warmth of other people slowly slipping from her with every step until she felt utterly alone by the time she reached the landing. What Diggory had known somehow by the numbers, and what she knew in her heart: it was hers.

The sign proudly proclaimed '14019114' on a small grey plaque.

Just as she thought it would, it opened up to a long corridor, just like Diggory's except this time the three doors were hers. She walked down to them and stood amongst them. Surveying them she felt drawn towards the right door, the one with 140191020914 written on it. Diggory would probably have known what to make of it, but all Tabitha knew was that it was hers, and it was tugging at her, as if it wanted her to open it. Energy seemed to pulse out of it, coming from inside it and rushing outwards. If she squinted Tabitha could almost see it pulsing in and out; it looked a little like it was breathing.

She took a deep breath. This was her door. She was glad Rin had stayed with Diggory because she could empathise with how easily Diggory had strolled through his door and into the past. It was as if it was inviting her in, and it took a lot not to grasp the handle and go straight in. She made herself think, two thoughts conflicting: what if she got trapped as Diggory could have done? But what was the point of the doors if not to be opened? They were hers. She was meant to go through this one. Of that she was utterly certain.

Without another thought she grasped the handle. As she pulled open the door the familiar white fog seeped out into the corridor; she could feel it surrounding her, wrapping its wispy, invisible tendrils around her limbs, ready to pull her in. She felt if she stayed there long enough she would have been hauled through. Not wanting to wait for that to happen she took small, cautious steps towards the precipice, all the while the tendrils curling around and coaxing her in. It was all an inevitability. Tabitha stepped over the threshold and the door creaked and closed softly behind her. She was sucked into the fog fully now; it surrounded her, permeating her skin. She stood clothed in it, shaking, taking uneasy breaths of moist air, her head filled with the noise of her rapidly beating heart. She felt the rushing whoosh, a sensation not unlike falling, and then the fog began to clear.

She looked down at herself, and saw that her clothes had changed: now she was wearing a plain blue T-shirt-type top, the style that she knew would have a coloured band at the back to indicate the size, and she knew that the band would be yellow: small. Standard NHS issue. Her trousers were matching, a very slightly different shade of blue with the same over-washed feel to them and a string waist-band tie that was also yellow. Her shoes were comfortable, New Balance trainers, and she felt an unfamiliar weight around her neck. She moved her fingertips up to investigate and felt the cold, smooth finish she knew she would. The cold metal was shaped into a round disc at the end: a stethoscope. Her stethoscope, engraved with the initials T.E.H., the kind her mother had been going on about buying her as a graduation present. She ran her fingers over the indents on the engraving, feeling the sharpness against the smooth of the metal.

The fog cleared and she saw that she was standing in the doorway of what was clearly a hospital room. There were four bays, each with a trolley, separated by thin blue curtains and surrounded by a miracle of equipment. There was an x-ray tube in the corner suspended from its ceiling tracks that spanned the room. It looked very much like a resus room. Tabitha's heart sank. Of all the doctoring she didn't want to do this was at the very top of her list. If she had to pick it would be something a world away from the stress and bustle of emergency medicine. She would have picked a nice, calm, controlled specialty – maybe dermatology. No fast decisions required. But now she found herself here.

Looking at the clock she saw it was one a.m. The night shift. *Another perk of the job,* thought Tabitha. In the end bay there was a patient surrounded by a team of doctors, with an anaesthetist busy passing a tube into his throat because he could no longer breathe for himself. Just being in that atmosphere filled Tabitha with blind panic. She wouldn't want to be the one responsible for that patient, yet here she was with an engraved stethoscope around her neck, expected to know what to do.

Thankfully the other bays were empty.

Turning around she saw that where the door to the rest of the Accident and Emergency Department should have been there was only the dark grey door frame containing the white fog, masking the ever-grey corridor beyond. She looked back at the anaesthetist, now struggling with the patient, unable to pass the tube through the delicate passageway, and she tried to turn for the fog, for an out. But she found that her body didn't move; she was still, watching the scene she didn't want to see. She had merged with this future version of herself. She felt her body walking forwards, outside of her present control. The future Tabitha walked towards one of the empty beds, while the Tabitha of the concrete wasteland watched on.

A nurse appeared, seemingly from the fog. 'Doctor Hamilton?' she said with a small smile. 'ETA is five minutes. They could only spare me, I'm afraid; I work on acute medical usually but it's chaos out there.'

'How bad is it?'

'We're bursting at the seams. Lots of very injured people, and smoke inhalations, walking wounded filling all of minors and the waiting room. We need the room in resus for the majors that are coming; it's taken them a while to stabilise them on the scene.'

'What are we getting?'

'Motorcyclist first. Part of the pile up. It doesn't sound good: burns, head injury, unresponsive.'

'Are the seniors coming in?'

'They're managing the chaos. Dr Smith is in CT with a child who was a passenger. We're waiting for Dr Lawson to come in. Dr Mitchell is with the lorry driver over there. They're going to ITU. He'll be back with us shortly, I'm sure. We can manage until he gets back.' The nurse sounded as if she was trying to convince herself.

Tabitha waited nervously, her mind completely blank as to what she was supposed to do with a motorcyclist with a head injury. She felt as if she needed treating herself for an acute case of panic. But before she had time to think anymore the paramedics rushed past her with the motorcyclist. They were babbling about his BP, GCS, heart rate, vital signs and injuries. They might as well have been speaking a foreign language. A foreign language that she was expected to understand.

The future version of herself looked down at this broken man and listened with her stethoscope as the boom of his irregular heartbeats echoed loudly. The paramedics departed, and her future, inexperienced self uncertainly started her work.

Both Tabithas were thankful he was still breathing. He needed a CT but would have to wait his turn after the child. His leg was a mess; Tabitha set about examining it as the nurse cut off the cloth. It was a nasty compound fracture, the tibia protruding awfully from the skin.

'We'll need orthopaedic consult for this,' said Tabitha.

'I'll bleep them,' said the nurse.

Whilst the nurse was busy on the phone Tabitha carried on assessing the man, feeling his abdomen for signs of internal bleeding. He wasn't fully conscious but her examination elicited terrible groans from deep in his throat. Tabitha stopped prodding, and the nurse came back.

'We'll need a CT abdomen as well,' said Tabitha. She turned to the monitor and assessed the ECG. Worryingly she saw the telltale saw-tooth pattern of the waves, indicating an unstable heart rhythm. 'He's in VF! Get the crash trolley ready.'

The nurse rushed to get it from the corner. The future Tabitha listened again to the man's heart, and watched the worrying irregular lines wiggle their way across the monitor. Both Tabithas were panicking. They watched as the line on the monitor went flat, and his chest fell silent.

'I need the crash trolley now! He's arresting,' said the future Tabitha.

The nurse was tangled in the corner, prevented from coming across the room momentarily by Dr Mitchell and his team as they raced past with their newly intubated patient. The future Tabitha reached for the drugs cabinet and grabbed the adrenaline, drawing up the vials with shaky hands. The nurse was there then, already applying the defibrillation pads and charging up the machine.

'200 J biphasic, Doctor?'

Tabitha nodded.

The nurse applied the paddles. 'Charging. Clear!'

Both Tabithas watched as electricity flowed through the damaged man, and caused him to jump with the force of it. The monitor was unchanged. The future Tabitha plunged the full adrenaline syringe into the cannula and depressed the plunger all the way. There was still no change.

'360,' said Tabitha.

'Charging,' said the nurse. 'Clear!'

Again the man's body jumped violently, but his heart rhythm did not return. Tabitha started CPR, pushing down repeatedly on his chest, pushing the oxygenated blood sluggishly around his damaged tissues. It was to no avail. After two minutes she stopped.

'360 again,' said Tabitha.

The nurse nodded. 'Clear!' she shouted.

His body shook again, Tabitha saw that his tibia wobbled grotesquely as his body rocked. The line was still flat. The nurse started CPR this time as Tabitha watched in vain. She didn't know what else to do. They shocked him again, and there was no change. Thankfully that was when Dr Mitchell rushed through the door.

Tabitha updated him as the nurse continued CPR. He looked sombre.

'How much adrenaline has he had?'

'Erm,' said Tabitha as she grasped around for the vials. '10mg.'

'10mg! How long have you been resuscitating?'

'I'm not sure, that was the fourth shock.'

'You should have given 1mg after the third shock. 1mg, not 10! And then continued with 1mg a time. Did you give it as a bolus?' he said, furious now.

'Yes,' said Tabitha, her voice shaking.

'When?' he demanded.

'After the first shock,' she said.

'You've ruined any chance this man had,' he said, all the anger gone as he went to the patient.

Tabitha stood there, feeling impotent as the consultant battled to do anything he could for the dying man. Tears flowed down her face as the fog clouded her vision and transported her back.

She flew out of the door, slamming it behind her and almost running into the wall opposite. She fell to the floor and collapsed in a heap, gasping for breath. Shaking, she crouched down, leaning against the wall, feeling as if someone were crushing her heavy chest. Unable to catch her breath at all she was panicking, breathing faster and faster. Hot tears were pouring down her face.

'Tabitha?' came Diggory's voice.

She barely heard him; her head was buried in her knees, the tears dampening her trousers. Diggory sat down next to her, close enough that his body was almost touching hers.

'Tabitha?' he asked again. Loud sobs were escaping her now as she held herself tight. Diggory put his hand tentatively on her arm. 'Are you alright?'

'It was terrible, Diggory,' she said between sobs. 'Oh god, I'm a failure. It's such a mess. I'm such a mess.'

'I'm sure you're not,' he said. 'Can't be as much of a mess as me.'

'Oh god, I am. If I ever even become a doctor I'm going to kill someone. I'll be a murderer, instead of a life-saver. I didn't even want to be a life-saver. I never wanted it.'

'You're a doctor?' Diggory said.

'No,' said Tabitha, her sobbing quieter now. 'I'm meant to be – soon, I suppose. I'm in my final year; I just have a couple of months left.'

'Wow, definitely not as much of a mess as my life.'

'At least your life is your life,' said Tabitha glumly. Diggory looked at her confused. 'My life hasn't really been mine,' she went on. 'Not properly, anyway. I suppose a lot of that's my fault. In fact pretty much all of it is. Oh god, and I'm going to make even more of a mess of it now.' She started sobbing again.

Diggory stretched his arm around her shoulder, and Tabitha leaned into him, letting him cradle her in his arms as she sobbed heavily. Diggory rubbed his hand up and down her arm, unsure of what else to do with this sobbing girl he barely knew. He didn't feel so great himself; the sickness he had felt in his gut, and the fear clawing at his head, trying to crack open his skull and intrude with sharp, pointed nails to squash his brain, were growing. He had gradually calmed as he got over the initial shock of the place, but he wanted to get out and was worried the fear would drive him mad. Maybe so mad he'd open his skull and welcome in the claws, welcome the dull silence that would follow. He shook the thought from his mind. Looking at Tabitha, with tears running down her cheeks, he realised he didn't feel so scared with her next to him. He felt better.

'It's okay,' he said, pulling her closer. 'There's no one to kill here. Well, except me and Rin, I guess, but you don't strike me as the murdering type.'

'Not the cold-blooded sort, no,' she said flatly. 'From the looks of it I will be a murderer – feels like I already am. I mean, is that real?' She gestured towards the door. 'It can't be, surely? Because I'm back here but it definitely feels real. I feel like a murderer, Diggory. Maybe I am, maybe I will be. Is that the future? Set in stone?'

'I don't know, Tabitha. Mine was the past,' he said, rubbing her shoulder and trying a small smile.

'And it was exactly like the past? Every detail?'

'Yeh, but it has to be, doesn't it. It's the past.' He shrugged. 'And I guess there wasn't you and Rin in the past so that was different, but the house and everything was the same.'

'Oh, I don't know. I don't want to go back in there.'

'You don't have to,' he said, pulling her closer. 'You can stay right here.'

'I can't bear it. I really hope it won't happen, Diggory. It can't, surely, because I've seen it now, so I know. I know to just not go to the hospital that day. Not go into a hospital at all, because I'd only make another horrible mistake. I don't think I want to be a doctor anyway. It's always scared me, and that…' She jabbed towards the door. 'That proves it. I'm not cut out for it. I never even wanted it, not really.'

She sobbed a little more, quietly to herself, as Diggory rocked her gently. He was content there, with Tabitha's heat seeping onto the surface of his body. He could feel her heart beating a little too quickly, and was comforted by it. He felt complete, less alone and less afraid. For the moment at least he was happy, for the first time in a very long time. He smiled to himself. Not everything about this place was bad after all.

'It's okay, Tabitha. You can decide now.'

'Yes, I guess you're right,' she said, a little calmer now. 'Thank you. I'm sorry I'm such a mess. It terrified me and it hasn't even happened, I don't think. Hopefully it will never happen now. God, it was awful.'

'It's okay now. And I'm here.'

And he held her until she drifted to sleep. The trauma of seeing one's life falling apart had a rather soporific effect.

Onwards and Upwards

Tabitha woke up from what was a very deep sleep with her back to the wall and Diggory's arm around her. She'd almost forgotten what had happened until her gaze fell on the door, with the numbers still glinting in the bizarre twilight. Then the sinking realisation came and she felt sick. Turning her head away she turned her attention to Diggory instead, who was also slumped against the wall in a kind of half-doze, just starting to wake up. He looked at her, surprised.

'Morning,' he said groggily.

'Morning, Diggory,' she said, pausing a little awkwardly. 'Sorry I was such a mess, it just wasn't what I was expecting in there.'

'It's okay, you were upset. How you doing now?'

'Yeh, better.' She detangled herself from his arms. 'Sorry,' she said, wincing. 'Your arm must be dead.'

'I'll live,' he said, smiling. Their eyes met briefly and his arm lingered around her waist.

'Hello! Diggory! Tabitha! Hello?' came Rin's voice, echoing from the lower level. It was quiet up here. Tabitha couldn't help thinking they shouldn't be able to hear Rin so clearly, but here it was. Diggory's face was only a few inches from hers, but he smiled and pulled away.

'Up here, Rin!' he shouted down the stairs.

They walked back towards the landing and soon Rin appeared around the corner, looking up at them. Tabitha felt reluctant, despite her experiences of the *night* before, to leave her floor. There was still something comforting about being there: something familiar. Her feelings mirrored Diggory's: it was something very like coming home.

'Where have you been? I thought you'd both disappeared into thin air or something. Wouldn't surprise me in this place.' Rin was slowly walking up the stairs. 'There're more doors up here, aren't there?'

'We knew that,' said Tabitha.

'I guess. How many this time?' said Rin.

'Three.'

'Again?' She shrugged, peering towards the hallway. 'Not like this place is big on variety anyway. Anything else up here?'

'Not that I can see. Same layout.'

'You went in, didn't you?' said Rin.

'Unfortunately.'

'What about the other doors – did you try them?'

'They're all hers,' chirped Diggory. 'They're not the way out.'

'Well, was worth an ask. Suppose I knew the answer anyway, just want to get out of this place now. What happened, anyway? Did you go in as well?'

'No, I came to see if she was alright,' said Diggory.

'It was awful,' said Tabitha, looking straight at Rin.

'Yours too, huh? Hope I don't have any. The only door I want to see is the exit.'

Nobody said anything. After a moment's pause Tabitha spoke up. 'Well we'll only know if we carry on, I suppose.' She looked at the ascending the stairs. 'I don't really want to leave this floor, though. Does that seem silly? One door was awful and I'm too frightened to go through the others but I still want to stay here – crazy, right?'

'This whole place is,' said Rin.

'I understand,' said Diggory, looking forlornly at the descending staircase.

'But there's no point just waiting here I guess. We might as well see what else there is. Hopefully a way out.' Tabitha started ascending the stairs, looking back briefly at the three doors – her doors. The number 140189020914 boldly glinting there. Taunting her. She could almost imagine the grim reaper behind the door, standing over the bed of the poor, dead motorcyclist. All because of her. At least now she knew for certain her being a doctor was a bad idea.

So they began their slow ascent again.

'So what happened?' asked Rin as they rounded the next landing, far enough away, she thought strangely, for it to be safe to talk about it – where the doors wouldn't be able to hear.

'I killed someone,' said Tabitha, struggling to get the words out, but needing to face up to the reality of what had happened behind the door – what, perhaps, would really happen.

'You what?' said Rin, taking a small step back.

'It's not like it sounds,' said Diggory. 'She isn't a murderer or anything Rin, it's okay.'

'Well, that isn't what it's called, but it's what it is,' replied Tabitha.

'It's different,' said Diggory.

'Far as I can see there's murder and murder, not really anything else. So does someone want to tell me what you're talking about? Did you kill someone or not?' said Rin, her posture closing up as she looked suspiciously from Tabitha to Diggory and back again.

'She's a doctor,' said Diggory.

Rin's eyes widened. 'A doctor? Oh well, that makes it alright then.'

'Well, technically I'm not; not yet anyway,' said Tabitha, more to herself.

'So this is to do with what happened behind the door?'

'Yeh. It was horrible, Rin. I was the doctor, the only doctor, and I didn't know what to do. I killed him.'

'So you didn't mean to kill him?'

'No, I wanted to help him but I didn't know what to do. I gave him too much adrenaline. I never wanted to be a doctor. I shouldn't be. I'm clearly not very good at it.'

'Being a bad doctor doesn't make you a murderer,' said Diggory.

'It still means I'll kill people.'

'Wait a second,' said Rin. 'It wasn't a flashback? It wasn't the past?'

'No. It hasn't happened yet.'

'Yet?'

'Yes, it was in the future. In about four months' time when I'm due to be a junior doctor, but it couldn't have felt more real. It felt as if I'd just missed out the in-between and landed there as that doctor, not knowing what on earth I was doing.'

'Maybe that's because you're not there yet. You haven't learnt everything,' said Rin.

'Well I pretty much have, and no, it wasn't like I'd just been dropped there unprepared, it didn't feel like that. It felt like I was inside that person's head, like I was watching the future me, and I still didn't know what to do.'

'It was a bit like that for me, like I had no recollection of my future. I was pretty much that little boy, in body and in mind.'

'It's weird, I can remember it all like a memory, even though it hasn't happened yet.'

'Stop saying "yet",' said Rin. 'We don't know that it will happen at all, we don't know what any of it means.'

'It felt pretty real, Rin. I'm going to be a murderer – an incompetent doctor who will probably be struck off.'

'Well, now you know what happened behind the door you can find a way to avoid it, can't you – like a warning.'

'Even if I stayed away from that patient, it would just happen with someone else. I'm not ready to be a doctor. I didn't ever really want to be one.'

'Maybe now you don't have to be. Now you know you wouldn't be any good at it,' said Rin, standing with one hand on her hip.

Tabitha gulped. 'Try and tell that to my mother.'

'Sorry?' said Rin.

'Never mind. It's difficult to do very much else with a medical degree. That, and not to mention I've wasted five years of my life.'

'It'll be okay,' said Diggory.

'I don't know about that. But at least I know I'd make a terrible doctor. So you're right Rin, I guess it is like a warning.'

'I usually am.'

'Always,' said Diggory mockingly. And they laughed.

They carried on trudging up the seemingly endless steps. Tabitha couldn't shake the image of the motorcyclist from her mind, and she thought the horrified, disappointed look of the consultant would stay with her forever, real future or not. Having spent her entire life trying to avoid becoming a disappointment, that was the one thing she didn't want to be. And this was so much worse; she wasn't just a disappointment, it wasn't just her mother's pride and her community reputation at stake – it was peoples' lives. She wanted to get out of this place more than ever; it was like a torture chamber for the mind. Doors with people's futures and pasts secreted within. Maybe doors to the future? Her own floor, her own door. Hers. Who knew what the others held?

'Diggory?' she asked. 'How did you know it was my door, and yours was yours?'

'The numbers,' he said simply. Tabitha and Rin looked at him, puzzled. A small smile tugged at the corners of his lips. 'The first doors were obviously mine, 70393. My birthday, the 7th of March 1993. And the rest of it was the date. Simple really.'

'You always were a clever thing, Dig, I'll give you that,' said Rin with a rare grin.

'Yeh, I didn't even realise with mine, 140191, the 14th of January 1991. But how did you know that was mine?'

'That's a point,' said Rin. 'How did you?'

'Well, it wasn't mine or Rin's,' said Diggory.

'Hm, that didn't mean it was mine, though,' said Tabitha.

'Who else is here?' Diggory shrugged.

'Who knows, I only found you two. This place seems to go on forever, there might be others,' said Tabitha.

'I guess,' said Diggory. 'But we haven't seen anyone else, have we.'

'Do you think we will?' Rin asked Tabitha.

'Maybe. But you knew, didn't you?' she said, closing in on Diggory. 'You knew they were my doors?'

'I don't know what you mean,' said Diggory.

'Yes you do. I don't know how but you knew.'

'That would be silly,' said Diggory. 'How could I know?'

'Hm, silly or not, it's true, and we both know it.'

'You can keep thinking that, Tabitha,' said Diggory. 'But really it was obvious. The numbers just make sense. At least they do to me.'

Tabitha let it drop; maybe that was all it was, but Diggory did at least seem to have more insight into this strange place than she or Rin. And he was the one who had said it wasn't safe; she was beginning to think he might be right.

They continued on their lengthy climb. Tabitha was feeling a little torn, simultaneously happy to leave her dreadful future behind her, and more than a little sad to leave the comfort of something that was undeniably hers. What had she been thinking? She hadn't wanted to be a doctor. Had known deep down that she wouldn't make a good doctor, and there she was in the future actually being a terrible doctor. Causing someone to die. She felt a sickness in the pit of her stomach, like a long-repressed illness that had always been there; now it reared its ugly head, commanding her full attention. It was time she took control of her life. She had seen what happened when she didn't.

Be Careful What You Wish For

Amelia stood outside staring at the familiar door. It should be blue. It had always been blue: a dirty, petrol blue with chips that showed the cheap chipboard beneath. And the number four, although wonky, was gold. Yellow gold. Now it was all grey. It didn't make any sense. *How's it possible?* she thought. *How can it be? How can the whole of the flat be too?* Maybe she should go to the hospital – perhaps something was wrong with her sight. But she couldn't get to the hospital, because instead of exiting out onto a dark Leeds street there were more stairs. Flights and flights of them. And where had the other flats gone? Where was she? How could the flat be *here?* Wherever *here* was.

Maybe this was a dream. *That's it,* she thought. *I'm dreaming.* Except with a sinking feeling she knew it couldn't be. She had slept floors below, and if she had been dreaming all this surely when she awoke she would have been back to her grim but very real reality. Somehow she had ended up here. Maybe the answer was behind the now-grey door. Maybe if she went back in she would gain some insight; there was after all nowhere else to go.

Reluctantly she approached it, not really wanting to go back through. The strange, grey concrete was a sanctuary. But it was lonely, desolate and confusing. Where was it anyway? And why? For all she wanted some peace, after much sleep and hiding on the floors below she decided she wanted something more. She wanted answers. Answers about where she was, and how to get back to her sorry life. At least it made sense. She had always dreamed about escaping, but she had never wanted to escape to a concrete wasteland. She wanted to escape to something more than that. This certainly wasn't the escape she had in mind and as bad as her life was she couldn't change anything from here; she needed to get back. Perhaps it was all waiting behind that door, all as awful as before, and back in colour, as if nothing had happened. She grasped the door handle: time to find out.

The moment she opened the door she heard it: screaming.

There had been plenty of shouting and screaming over the years, but this was in a category all of its own: high-pitched, skin-tingling, screaming-for-your-life screaming. And she knew it was her mother. Interspersed between the screaming, and the gasps for air, were loud empty-metal banging noises. Amelia felt sick.

All of a sudden the screaming stopped, but somehow that was worse.

Slowly Amelia walked into the hallway, and turned to see her father in the bedroom, holding a golf club. A thick, grey liquid that should have been red dripped from the end of it. He dropped it with a clunk and his dark eyes fell on Amelia; he glared at her, and then, grunting like an animal, he charged headlong into her. He pushed her to the floor and paused like a predator sizing up a kill, his huge, hunched shoulders heaving up and down with each grunting breath. A look of disgust crossed his face and he turned abruptly into the living room. She wasn't worth it.

Looking into the bedroom she saw her mother's feet protruding from behind the bed. They weren't moving. Amelia clambered up and went to her. She was lying semi-prone on the floor, curled up in a vain attempt to protect herself, but Amelia saw sadly that it hadn't worked as her arms were covered in patches of dark grey, the worst in a long line of bruises. Her hair was stuck to her head with what Amelia knew was blood. It lay there in a thick, sickly warm puddle around her head. There was too much of it.

Amelia brushed her mother's hair to one side to see her face – the right side was grotesquely swollen. 'Mum,' she said, shaking her gently. 'Are you okay?' She tried to hold back the tears. Her mum didn't even murmur. Amelia leaned in close and couldn't hear any breathing. 'Mum,' she said desperately.

She watched, holding her mother's limp and battered arm, as she saw him walk past without a second look and then she felt the vibration of the door she didn't see slam.

Suddenly hot anger erupted inside her and she rushed after

him. As she got up she tripped over the golf club covered in the grey slime that she knew was the last of her mother's blood. She picked it up in one quick sweep and went to the door. But there she dropped it; she wasn't a monster. She followed through the door, thinking he must be in the concrete wasteland now too. Surely he would realise there was something off now. He'd have to realise something was wrong now, wouldn't he, when he couldn't get out. *Wake up Amelia*, she scolded herself, *there is something very wrong in here. She's lying dead in there on the bedroom floor.*

Dead. This is what would have happened if she had stayed.

Amelia ran down the stairs, sure she would stumble across him but he was nowhere to be seen. She ran back up the stairs, her anger giving way to floods of tears. She ran as fast as her legs could carry her; wanting desperately to be with her mum. Wanting to hold her and hope she would come round, even though she knew it was a sorry hope. Even though her mother had left, at least she had been alive. She hadn't been there for Amelia but she had had a mother in the world. Someone she could go to one day, maybe. Someone whom her father hadn't killed.

She ran straight into the flat and through to the bedroom and stopped suddenly. The space where her mother had been lying was empty. *He must have moved – no, it couldn't be.* There wasn't any blood. She knelt to touch the floor; it wasn't damp or even stained. It wasn't possible. She hadn't been gone that long. Even if he'd moved her, and wiped up the blood, which he wouldn't have done anyway, there hadn't been enough time for it to dry. And if she had moved herself then she would have left a trail.

She left the bedroom in a daze wondering if she had somehow imagined it all and from the hallway she watched as her father was returning to his chair holding a cold can of lager.

'What are you staring at?' he said.

'What've you done with Mum?'

'Well, where do you want me to start, love? It was my seed that conceived you so we've obviously gone all the way. Thought you were old enough to understand these things.'

'Don't talk about that,' she said, her voice breaking. 'What have you done with her body? It was in there.'

'What's the matter with you? I haven't seen your mum in years stupid.'

'She was here a minute ago, and then you stormed out. I don't understand. I went after you but you must have come back, and she's gone. How can she be gone?'

'She was gone three years ago, Amelia. She hasn't been here. She left you remember. And I've been sat here watching the match, and it's half time. It'll be back on in a minute. Go and do the washing or something, will you.'

He left her standing there and went to sit back down, not giving her another moment's attention. Amelia went back to the bedroom. There still wasn't any blood. It couldn't have just happened. It wasn't possible. And her father hadn't had any blood on him either. Maybe it hadn't happened at all.

Amelia went back to the door; she didn't want to stay here. She had seen him murder her mother and somehow it had been real.

Rin's Torment

A few more flights on and a strange feeling began to descend on Rin. Unable to put her finger on it at first, she tried to ignore it, hoping that it would simply go away. As far as she could tell Tabitha and Diggory were fine, and she tried her best to shake off the feeling, thinking she was perhaps just imagining it.

'Why didn't you tell us you're a doctor?' asked Diggory.

'Probably because I've been trying to ignore that very fact. Silly, I suppose. I've spent most of the last five years learning a million things that doctors need to know. I guess I was just going along with it. I never seriously thought much about actually being a doctor.'

'Seems a lot of work to just go along with it,' Rin said.

'I know. It seems like such a waste looking at it now. Looking at it after seeing how useless I would be.' Tabitha sighed. 'I guess I just kept thinking that it would grow on me. That nobody feels ready, and everyone's scared. I was always getting good feedback on assignments and endless encouragement from my mother. I thought this is what I'm supposed to do. I just ignored the fact I didn't really agree.'

'At least you've realised now. A doctor that kills people is no good.'

'No,' said Tabitha uncertainly.

'And you haven't hurt anyone,' said Diggory. 'Not really, because it hasn't happened.'

'It feels like it has in my head though. I don't think I'll ever be able to forget it.'

'Just be thankful it wasn't something that has actually happened. You can change whether that happens or not. Some people would give anything to have had a warning like that. You're lucky,' said Rin.

'I guess,' said Tabitha.

Rin increased her pace, putting some space between her and the others. This place was messing with her head. As she walked, listening to Diggory reassuring Tabitha, the strangeness she had been feeling did nothing to abate, and as they continued to ascend it turned into a palpable feeling of dread. A few floors further on it had developed into full-blown dread and anxiety that made her feel as though her insides might slip away. Rin felt like a caged animal, completely unable to get out. She didn't say anything to the others but she slowed, not wanting the feeling to intensify. A big part of her wanted to turn around but she knew the exit wasn't that way, and she didn't want to take Diggory anywhere near another one of his doors. He was already broken enough.

So they carried on walking, Tabitha and Diggory making some sort of small talk, as Rin shrank back into herself, worrying about the feeling and what it meant. *Not safe, not safe, not safe,* echoed in her mind, unsettling her; she wondered if this was how Diggory had felt when they were approaching his floor. The feeling in her gut made her think it was, and she knew what that meant. She was trapped; neither direction would give her what she really wanted – which was for all of this to go away.

As they approached another landing the feeling inside her had risen to a pitch. The panic was starting to consume her, and it was all she could do not to scream. Just when she thought she might herself be reduced to rocking in the corner, Tabitha announced that she was feeling tired and maybe they should stop there on the landing and rest for a while. They had all given up saying 'for the night', as honestly, who knew? Rin was beyond thankful Tabitha had suggested it as she didn't want to face any questions; she just wanted to bury her head in the sand. And get some respite, for now, from the intensifying dread.

Tabitha and Diggory lay close together, still murmuring, and if Rin hadn't been so distracted by trying to breathe she would have taken more interest in their interest in each other. Instead she lay there trying to block out thoughts of the last time she had felt like this. She lay there as Tabitha and Diggory fell into sleep, still feeling as though something were crushing her chest. The panic had settled a little, but she felt more that she had become more used to this new state than that it had actually improved at all. She felt as if she had fallen into an abyss and her eyes were starting to get used to the dark.

Long after Tabitha's and Diggory's murmuring had ceased, and the calm, regular sounds of their breathing had replaced it, Rin realised that sleep was not going to come for her. As she lay there in the dimness she came to the sad conclusion that not knowing was worse. This feeling of anticipation was like torture, and unable to take it anymore she rose, wanting to see for herself and do something about this feeling before the others realised how badly she was affected. She was always the strong one; she needed to be for Diggory lest he end up rocking on the floor again. Especially, she did not want him to see her rocking on the floor: that might break him entirely. There was only one thing for it. She had to find out if her fears were true. So as Tabitha and Diggory slept Rin ascended the steps alone.

Just as she'd expected, two floors up there was a sign. Her sign. It read 18098446. Just as Diggory had worked out. The 18th of September 1984: it was hers alright. Diggory's little system worked. Rin disregarded the last two numbers: they must have something to do with the doors.

A floor above and she would find her doors, but she didn't need to see them to know what was coming. So, with a feeling of dread so thick she felt as if she was walking through it, Rin approached her landing. Looking down she could see there were three doors here, too. With a grim, reluctant determination she approached, knowing she couldn't turn back now, however badly she wanted to. Sure, she was going to be plunged into that terrible past if she opened it. But she carried on because she had to see. See if this place was as sick and *not safe* as Diggory had first thought.

It was the door on the right, she knew it without looking. It felt wrong. When she did look at it she saw confirmation in the numbers: 180984300402, shining there innocuously. The feeling of sick fear made her stomach turn over. The 30th of April 2002: nausea and panic swept through her. She wanted to run but she found herself unable to, and instead she just stood there, looking at the numbers, unable to believe what would lay behind that door. It wasn't possible. But she knew that it was – if this place could shrink Diggory to a six-year-old then it could make her relive the worst day of her life. She knew that, but standing outside the door she still couldn't comprehend it.

Rin was so overwhelmed by disbelief she found the courage to reach for the handle, her brain unable to fully believe that it was all really behind the door. How was it possible? As she neared the handle this confidence slipped away and she shrank back, unable to even touch it. The memories came flooding back and she didn't need to relive them; she already had and she wanted to avoid them forever, to never think of them again. What she had been trying to do for the last twelve years was to bury the memories deep, so deep they would never resurface again. She hadn't quite succeeded but she had been doing her best to ignore them.

She couldn't do it. She couldn't relive it again. Why was this door here? Why that night? This place truly was a concrete version of hell. Her life had been enough of a hell since that night, and now she was expected to go through it again. *No. Not again.* She screamed in her head. *No!*

Still unmoving, she stood staring at the door, expecting something. Hoping it would disappear. Of course that wasn't what happened.

As she stared she heard a strange liquid seeping sound, and looked down in horror to see blood seeping out of the door towards her feet. It was the thick heavy, bright red stuff that would have been more than at home on the set of a Tarantino film. Rin screamed. The blood almost touching her grey trainers before she backed away into the door opposite. Pressed against it, barely able to catch her breath, she watched as the blood followed her – so much of it. Her horror broke and she bolted, running from the door, the blood and the landing; she didn't stop until she was a floor below her sign where, pausing mid-flight, she collapsed onto a step.

She sobbed until there were no tears left. Until the sadness turned to burning hot anger pouring from her. She had done all her crying: had done enough to last forever. It wasn't the kind of thing a person could ever get over, or get past, but she'd got around it and got on with her life. It had hardened her and isolated her beyond all measure, and that one stupid door had brought it all back in an instant. That one door had destroyed her well-built defences easily, and replaced them with all the sad, sorry helplessness and the panic. The dizzy, sickening feeling of your whole word turning on a knife-edge, of it having been irrevocably changed forever. Rin didn't want to feel like this again. It had nearly destroyed her the first time.

Why was this place doing this? She didn't know. She was exhausted beyond all measure, but wearily she made her way back to the landing, away from her doors.

As she came back down she saw Diggory and Tabitha sleeping, backs to each other, just a little too close. She wanted Diggory to be happy. Not that she'd ever imagined happiness might come in a remotely Tabitha-shaped package, but, if nothing else, she was pleased he was no longer rocking on the floor – for now, anyway. He had been walking on a thin knife-edge of some semblance of sanity, between madness and the darkest depression on each side. He had fallen off many times, and both Rin and the struggling mental health services had done their best to catch him. It was no wonder though: not really, Rin thought. She sometimes wondered about how much of a knife-edge she herself walked on, but she had never really strayed far enough to find out. She had walked the straight line of her life a little too severely since she had had to grow up far too fast and become everything to Diggory. There was never a choice about it, and she had never stopped to think long enough about what she wanted life to be like. She just kept walking in her painstakingly straight line, head held high, each foot placed precisely in front of the other.

Rin took up her place on the floor again next to Diggory. She looked at his calm, sleeping face and smiled; he looked as peaceful as he had being that little boy, the one from years ago, and the one from a few floors down. She closed her eyes and willed herself to sleep, wishing she could sleep as peacefully as Diggory, but images of her door and the blood invaded her mind. She tried to push them away: she didn't want to think about the door or about what must lie behind it. What was it doing here? Was she meant to go through it? Because she couldn't. She could not do it. Wouldn't even if she could.

Rin pushed away the image of the blood seeping from the door; she felt as if it was seeping into her mind. Willing it to go away she squeezed her eyes tighter but all she could see behind her lids was red, and all she could feel in her gut was sickness. What lay behind that door was so awful she didn't just not want to think about it ever again, she wished that she could cross it out of the timeline of her life somehow and never have to feel that pain again. But the repercussions were so far-reaching it could never be that simple. It never had been but Rin had kept herself busy walking her straight line and looking after Diggory, and never looking back. But now the past was standing right in front of her – or two floors above. It felt as if it was pushing down on top of her: that and what Rin guessed to be the hundreds of floors above it. She felt as if they were all pressing down on her chest. It was hours before she drifted into an anxious sleep.

Wishes and Dreams

Amelia couldn't believe what had happened. She ran back down the many stairs, until she felt as if she was underground, burrowed away safely. He couldn't get out of the flat at least. Of that she was now sure. This was a safe place, even if she was stuck here. It was safe from him.

Her thoughts were stuck on that pool of grey blood around her mother's head, and the silent sound of her still chest. The bruises covering her haunted Amelia; they were somehow worse in black-and-white. They made her feel sick, and sad, and angry. Somehow it had happened, and then somehow her mother had been gone.

The door was showing her what would have happened if her mother had stayed. Amelia thought after the last violent attack that had driven her mother away, perhaps she had known the next time might be her last. There was only so much somebody could take. She had seen him kill her mother, and now she wished more than ever that she could kill him. With thoughts of murder filling her young, spoiled mind she drifted into uneasy sleep.

Rin's Resolution

Tabitha and Diggory woke long before Rin. 'Do you think we will find a way out?' asked Tabitha.

'I don't know,' said Diggory. 'I have a feeling the way out, for me at least, is down there.'

'Your door? But you were a child?'

'Not that door.'

They sat there for a few moments, two strangers contemplating their fate in this strange place. Tabitha was wondering if he was right, and her thoughts turned to concern about what new horrors might lie behind her other doors. If they were anything like the first, then getting out of here wouldn't be so easy.

'Why have three doors?' said Diggory. 'We must be supposed to go through them. If there was a big door saying "way out" up there somewhere, then why would we each have three doors?'

'Hmm,' said Tabitha. 'Makes sense in a way but I kind of hope you're not right. One was awful enough. And what about Rin? We haven't found any doors that are hers.'

'I think we will.'

'It would follow. Suppose it wouldn't be fair if she didn't have any, would it.'

'No,' said Diggory.

'You really think they're the way out?' said Tabitha.

'Yeh. It's the only thing that would make any kind of sense. Otherwise there would be no point us each having doors if there was an easy way out.'

'Well, I hope the other doors aren't as bad as the first one, otherwise I might never get out.'

'Maybe if Rin ever lets me go through mine I'll see what they're like. If I'm a kid again I don't think I'll stand much chance of getting out either.'

'No.' Tabitha laughed. 'We'll see what happens.'

'We will.'

Soon after that Rin woke up from the longest sleep she had had here. Tabitha and Diggory were thankful she was awake, as they were sick of checking on the rise and fall of her chest.

'You okay, sis?' asked Diggory.

'Hmm,' said Rin, still groggy.

'You slept for a long time,' Diggory said.

'We were worried,' said Tabitha.

'I'm okay. Just tired. Sick of walking up these steps.'

'I'm with you on that,' said Diggory.

Tabitha and Diggory looked at Rin, both picking up that there was something that wasn't quite right with her.

'What's the matter, Rin?'

'Nothing, Diggory. I'm just tired. Maybe we could just stay here and rest for a bit.' She shuffled back towards the wall, resting her back against it and rubbing her eyes.

'You don't want to press on and find the way out?' asked Diggory.

'It's not very likely, is it.'

'Well, there must be some way out,' said Tabitha.

'Hm, I don't think it's going to be as simple as stumbling across the exit though, do you?'

'Maybe not,' said Diggory. 'But we need to try. We can't just wait here forever, can we, like you said to me.'

'No,' said Rin. 'But we don't have to go now. I'm tired now.'

'You've just been asleep!' Diggory said raising his voice. 'What's the real reason Rin? Why don't you want to go up there?'

'I don't know what you mean. I'm tired.'

'You can't be. There's something you're not telling us.'

Tabitha and Diggory looked at Rin; she was hiding her head in her knees.

Rin sighed. 'I went up there last night. And I don't want to go up there again.'

'Why? What do you want to do then – stay here?' said Diggory.

'What was up there?' said Tabitha.

'Look, I don't want to talk about it, and I don't want to go up there. I just want to sit here for now, and not think, okay?'

'You found a door, didn't you?' said Diggory.

'Did you go through it?' said Tabitha.

'Look just leave it, I don't want to talk about it.'

'You did find a door. I know you did,' said Diggory.

'I don't want to talk about it,' she glared at him, and turned away.

They left Rin alone with her own thoughts for a while, both of them backing away to the other side of the landing. Rin couldn't get the image of the blood seeping from the door from her mind. She'd thought the doors were safe unless opened, and realised now that wasn't the case – at least not with her door. Why did it have to be that night? Of all the things that could be behind that door, it was the most horrific thing imaginable. The worst thing that ever happened to her. Something that she could never change. It wasn't fair. She just wanted to get Diggory out, and to get out herself.

That was what they had been trying to do, Rin reasoned. She had saved Diggory from his door, and kept him away from the others. And they had been trying to find an exit. Somehow she didn't think it was further down than they had been. So it must be further up. They would have to go up. Having protected Diggory once from the blood she didn't want him to go up there and see it oozing from the door.

She would have to face it.

That or risk Diggory seeing it. Or stay stuck in the monotonous limbo of this place forever. She would have to go through and see what horrors would lie behind it.

The others have been through their doors, she thought. *I just need to go through mine*. With a new kind of horror she thought of

Diggory's door and of how they had followed him through it. She didn't want Diggory to follow her through hers. The thought of it turned her insides to ice. That couldn't happen. She wouldn't let it happen. She had to do it now, and quickly, before he got any crazy ideas.

She pushed herself up. 'I need you to go back down.'

Tabitha and Diggory looked at her, wide-eyed.

'What do you mean?' said Diggory.

'I need you to go down,' said Rin.

'We already know what's down there,' said Tabitha.

'Yes, and it isn't the way out,' said Diggory. 'And you said for me to not go near my doors again, Rin.'

'I know. But I need to go up. And I need to go up alone.'

'We can come with you,' said Diggory. 'There's nothing down there except what we've already seen.'

'No. I need to do this alone. Please will you just go down and promise to stay there, just to the next landing. Not to yours.'

'Okay,' said Diggory. 'If that's what you want. But we'll still be here for you.'

'Okay,' said Rin. 'Whatever happens though you wait for me, you don't come up to my floor. I don't want you to.'

'Okay,' said Diggory and Tabitha.

'We'll see you soon then,' said Tabitha.

'Be safe, sis,' said Diggory. 'We'll be here.'

They descended the stairs, leaving Rin to face her fate alone.

Salvation

Bleary-eyed and drowsy, Amelia pulled herself up. She was glad to be out of her uneasy sleep but felt worse than she had before she closed her eyes. She yawned, half-debating curling up and going back to sleep, but the atmosphere felt electric and the buzz of it melted away the bleariness. Looking around her she was unhappy to see her surroundings hadn't altered: same old concrete landing, same awful steps up to *that* place – his place.

Except there was one difference.

It was sat boldly on the fifth step, twinkling in the twilight. Amelia couldn't believe it: her dream had literally come true, sparkling before her eyes. Tears blurred her vision, but she could still see the object on the step: it was undoubtedly a gun. As she neared she saw that it was an old-fashioned ladies' revolver, with ornate carvings on the handle. It was the type she imagined strong ladies in America would have carried at some point in history, partly for fashion and partly for protection. She wished she was as strong as those women, but she couldn't have cared what kind it was. She was just glad that it looked small enough for her to manage.

She ran to it. Looking down on it from above she admired the shining surface. It was too good to be true. Had to be. She barely dared to reach for it, afraid her fingers might slip through it and it would disappear into a puff of smoke. She longed for it to be real, for her to be able to reach out and touch the cold metal, to pick it up and run it through her fingers, to hold it in her hand and to realise her only dream. To enable her to end the nightmare of her life for good. Elation welled up inside her at the thought. The feeling came flooding upwards, spilling out of her, down her arm giving her the power to reach for the gun. She stretched down and grabbed it before the feeling dissipated, and the elation peaked in her chest as she felt that it was real. The metal was as cold and smooth as she imagined, and she was very relieved it hadn't slipped through her fingers. Turning it over in her hand she felt its weight: heavier than she'd thought, but manageable.

Amelia had never held a gun before, but she had spent long nights dreaming about it in her cramped box room. Dreaming about how she could get her hands on one. She'd heard the people in the apartment down the hall were dealers and she'd heard that dealers had guns. She knew they did. But she was too scared to even look at the O'Connell brothers, let alone speak to them and ask them about guns. Besides she didn't think their firearms were for sale and even if they had been she barely had money for pick and mix, let alone an illegal gun. In truth a part of her was scared that even if somehow she managed to get her hands on a gun, she wouldn't be able to pluck up the courage to actually use it. Despite the torture of all the things he had done, all the torment he had put her through, she just didn't know if she had it in her. Didn't really want to have it in her. As badly as she wanted him gone.

But now she found herself stuck in this place. Either forced to relive her past over and over, or see new and more terrifying versions of her future. That or descend the never-ending staircase in eternal limbo, loneliness and misery. And she couldn't carry on this way, didn't want to, and now here was a way out, weighing heavy in her hands. She looked down at it, shining, standing out from the dullness of everything here like a beacon of hope in the dimness. Amelia smiled. Finally she had a solution. A way out. She held salvation in her palms.

Behind the Darkness

Rin stood outside the door close enough to feel the darkness pulsing out, imagining it as a dome pushing outward from the door and threatening to engulf her in its protruding centre the second she stepped just a little closer. Even this close was more than she'd thought she could manage; she'd never thought she would be able to stand here even for a few seconds. She was glad there wasn't any blood this time – at least not out here. So she stood, struggling to believe that she could tolerate this reminder of the hideous past. It brought back every awful emotion. And yet she stood there, basking in it uncomfortably.

Rin had stepped into this old darkness, and she didn't run or bolt this time: she stood still. Stood there defying it. Defying its power to control her, to take everything from her and strip her bare leaving her with nothing except that awful poisonous dread seeping through her skin and filling every crevice of her body. *No,* she thought as she stood up straight, fists clenched, whole body leaning forward slightly pushing against the force of the dome. Letting it pulse, letting it get in. Unwilling to let it defeat her. Unwilling to be as scared as the rocking Diggory. She was stronger than that. It wouldn't defeat her. She let it in but not all the way. She didn't let it have all of her. *No more.*

No more – and with that she strode into the dome, the darkness engulfing her with a coldness she couldn't name seeping into her body. She reached out, knowing there was only one way to make it stop. To release the hold that day had had on every facet of her life: on every feeling, every decision, every distrustful relationship. It ended today. *No more,* she thought, growling the words in her head, letting them fill her up, their power racing down her shoulder, through her arm, giving her the strength to clasp the freezing handle. With a last deep, cold breath she flung the door open and walked into the fog.

The adrenaline was pulsing in her veins, and she was shaking with the cold, impatient to get it over with. Impatient to get back to Diggory and exist in that strange place without this terrible fear. To find some way out of the concrete hell. To protect Diggory from these horrors for a second time.

As the fog started to slowly clear fear rose in her, swelling in her throat as she tried to push it back down, threatening to overwhelm and control her. The fog swirled and she started to feel different; the adrenaline was draining from her and the fear was subsiding, as if it was all slipping away, out through her feet, pooling on the floor. She imagined it there as a black sticky liquid. As she patted herself down she noticed that her grey clothes had melted away, and had been replaced by the clothes she would never forget. Jeans that were actually blue coated her legs and where they ended her white plimsolls were clinging to her feet. She was wearing her favourite floaty top, the black one with the lace back. The fear may have slipped mostly to the floor, but being back in these clothes made it all far too real. She couldn't do it, so she tried to turn back, knew she'd been wrong to think she ever could have. *No!* she cried, as her body refused to obey her and she realised it was too late. She was that girl again: the frightened little Rin of twelve years ago. She was seventeen and she was standing in her hallway, the older Rin nought but a spectator in her young head, reliving the whole thing.

The old house looked just the same as it had that day, almost identical to the house she had dragged little Diggory from, except this one was a couple of years on. The décor was slightly different, and it was dark, but it was the same house.

She walked through the hallway, shrugging off her denim jacket and hanging it on the stairs, listening to the quiet of the sleeping house. She walked silently up the stairs and crept into Diggory's room, where she saw he was quietly sleeping underneath his Pokémon duvet. She bent down and kissed him gently on the forehead. 'Sweet dreams,' she whispered. He was perfect like that, when he was still and peaceful. She envied him such calm sleep.

Rin padded towards the bathroom and was about to go in when

she noticed her parent's bedroom door was open. She poked her head round the door, and saw that strangely they weren't there. It was late, well past midnight, and she hadn't heard them downstairs. Uneasiness settled in her stomach. She bypassed the bathroom and went directly downstairs. They wouldn't leave Diggory. She knew that but her stomach knew that something wasn't right. In the hallway she whispered their names to no response. She looked briefly into the kitchen as she passed and went to the living room and still they were nowhere to be seen. *They can't have gone out and left Diggory,* she thought, *they can't have, whatever the emergency they wouldn't have just left him* – but the uneasiness was at a pitch and was now more real fear. Something was not right.

She went back to the hallway to pick up the phone, when she saw over the kitchen island that the door to the garage was open. As she rested the phone back on the stand she walked slowly towards the open door. With each step she felt more scared. 'Mum,' she whispered. 'Mum, you in there?' *What would they be doing in the garage after midnight?*

Rin wasn't far from the door now and she could feel the cold draught coming through it. She gulped as she got closer, never having been so scared in all her life. She passed the kitchen island and the entrance to the garage came into view. She gasped and stumbled back against the island. Heavy, hot breath caught in her throat as she stared at the floor in front of the garage door, and the thick red liquid that lay there.

'Mum? Dad?' she whispered, as she grasped the island top behind her. The liquid was slowly seeping towards her feet. 'Mum? You in there?' she said as loudly as she could, which was little more than a whisper, as her throat felt closed tight. It was as if her fear had morphed into a ghostly hand squeezing her throat.

She walked forward, knowing she had to see. Knowing something terrible had happened and knowing that it was a lot of blood. The older Rin at the edge of her mind was powerless to stop any of it, powerless to even close her eyes. She was inside the past-Rin's head, screaming. Screaming at her to turn around. But the past-Rin walked on, unaware there was an audience. There was no way to walk around the blood; it was pooled around the doorway. She leant forward, trying to peer inside; she didn't bother even trying to speak now, but it was no good, as she couldn't see anything. The blood was a good foot or two from the door. She took a deep breath, tentatively put one plimsolled foot into the blood and put her weight through it. Feeling wetness through the sole of her foot she fought the urge to throw up.

As she walked forward slowly, not looking down, she heard the splashing of her feet in the blood, and hoped it wouldn't be deep enough to creep over the plastic and seep into the fabric. Slowly she edged through the mire, rounding the corner, finally able to see into the garage. The blood extended towards the car, and seemed to be originating from somewhere near the front of it. Rin couldn't see the source of it yet. As she opened her mouth once more to try to speak she found her throat felt swollen and choked. She closed her mouth and took a deep breath.

She saw her mother first. The blood surrounded her chest in a bright red pool. Rin opened her mouth to scream but couldn't. She tried to gulp for air but found she couldn't do that either. Her mother was pale, and as she went to her, she felt the wetness against her foot and had to turn to vomit. Rin was shaking as she grasped her mother's arm, but it was cold. There were small cuts there, but Rin turned to her face, seeing sadly that her eyes were stuck wide open. Rin squatted to vomit again, but only retched: she was utterly empty. Finding her voice she managed to whisper 'Mum? Can you hear me?' There was of course only silence in return. Rin reached out to her, cradling her head in her arms, huge sobs shaking her. 'Mum,' she wailed. 'Mum, what happened? What happened?' She looked down seeing that there was a large patch of blood in the centre of her white top. She felt at it and her fingers went inside a little; she shuddered. There was a large wound there. Rin had no idea how it happened but that was where all the blood had come from.

Rin looked around her, lost. Wishing she could scoop some of the blood back into her. Wishing there was anything she could do to help her. As she turned her head she saw her father. He was further over, a few feet away, sprawled on his back with his own pool of blood around him. Rin's eyes fell on the knife that lay discarded next to his hand, and she saw the self-inflicted wound on his neck. Then a noise that did not even feel like it was hers erupted from her chest. She clutched her mother's lifeless body and pulled her protectively away from the monster lying on the floor.

Rin sat like that cradling her mother for a long time, unable to believe it, expecting her to wake up any moment. She wanted to take her mother away from him, and away from the awful, freezing tomb. Her mother didn't deserve to die like that. Alone and bleeding in the cold garage. Rin felt sick. She didn't understand how her father had done such an incomprehensible thing. She tried to shuffle herself and the dead weight of her mother further towards the wall of the garage. It was a lot of effort. She shuffled her own body that way first, her arms stretched out in front, still clinging onto her mother, her wrists scraping against the floor, weighed down by her mother's body. She pulled hard, leaning backwards, using her body weight to try and haul her mother towards her. She tugged as hard as she could and fell backwards with the effort, her mother's body tumbling to the floor. Rin cried out, screaming sobs shaking her.

'Rin.' She heard a small voice echo from the hallway. She scrambled up, kissed her mother's head for the last time, and left her there; she couldn't let Diggory see this.

'Rin?' came his voice again, sounding a little closer. She raced out of the garage, slipping on the blood, one leg ending up coated in it. She pushed herself up and ran into the kitchen to see Diggory in the hallway. 'Don't come in, Diggory,' she gasped. 'Just stay there.'

'Rin? What's the matter?' His voice was croaky from sleep.

'Just stay there, good boy,' she said as she shut the garage door, trapping the ghosts in there, hoping to shield her young brother from them.

He was standing forlornly in the hallway, his teddy dangling from one hand. It was the saddest thing Rin had ever seen. She shut the kitchen door firmly too and ran to Diggory, gathering him up in her arms and holding him tight, amazed at how warm his little body was. 'Your shoes are all red, Rin-Rin,' he said, perplexed. She was thankful that was the only red he had seen.

'I know, Dig. I know.' She tried to hold back the sobs rising in her, threatening to erupt from her.

'But they're all red, Rin-Rin, and your leg,' he said in his whiny childhood listen-to-me voice.

'I know, it doesn't matter,' said Rin distractedly, even though it did matter. It mattered a great deal. The sobs threatened still; she felt as if they were at the very top of her throat. She choked them down as best she could, not wanting to frighten him any further. 'Come on, Dig, it's late, go back to bed.'

'Can't sleep,' he said sulkily.

'Just go and try again for me, Dig. I'll be up in a minute, okay?'

'Had a bad dream,' he said, clutching his teddy.

She didn't want to press the issue and knew she needed to get some help – not that there was much anyone could do now. At least she wouldn't be alone with this terrible secret, teetering just on the edge of holding it together. She needed some help now.

'I need you to sit here a minute then,' she said, plonking him down on the first step. 'Okay? Don't move.'

'Okay,' he said sleepily, his brow furrowing in worry.

Rin picked up the phone and went down the hallway, hoping Diggory wouldn't hear. Tapping the nine button three times she gulped in air, trying to control herself, hoping she would be able to speak. She could still feel the coldness of her mother's body lingering on her palms. She shook her head, trying to concentrate. The automated voice asked which service she required, and she was about to say ambulance, a part of her unbelieving that it was too late. Sadly she caught herself, knowing her mother was too cold for that, and said in a low voice, 'Police.'

'What's your emergency?'

'Erm…' said Rin, struggling with what to say. 'S-something's happened. I need someone to come. I don't know what to do.'

'What's the address?'

'It's 23 Elmwood Avenue.'

'Can you tell me what's happened?'

Rin glanced over, seeing Diggory sitting there rubbing his eyes, and she turned away from him further to face the living room. 'Two people are dead,' she whispered. 'Please come now, I have to look after my brother.' She took the phone away from her ear, could hear the rumble of the voice, indiscernible, on the other end, but she put it down firmly on the receiver. She couldn't talk about it anymore, and she didn't want Diggory to hear. It was all too much to bear. Both Rins were sobbing now. The past-Rin hugged Diggory to her as the phone rang, shushing his demands that she should answer it. 'It doesn't matter, Diggory. They'll ring back.' *They'll be here soon,* she thought.

'But you don't know who it is,' protested Diggory.

'It's okay, Diggory. It'll be okay. I'm here.'

'Is it sauce?' said Diggory, leaning down and prodding the sticky substance on her leg. He held his finger up curiously. Rin grasped it and rubbed it vigorously on her shirt. She didn't answer his question. She couldn't. She just gathered up his little hands in her own and hugged him to her, and they waited in silence like that, Rin grasping little Diggory so tight she was probably hurting him. He knew something was wrong, and he knew not to ask anything else. Rin remembered that they had waited, waited until there were flashing blue lights shining in through the frosted glass of the front door, and there were knocks at the door and the announcement of 'police', which was followed by Diggory asking if it was a policeman at the door. Rin told him it was. Except this time the front door wasn't frosted, there was just the doorframe suspended with fog swirling in the middle, leading the way back to the concrete, and an escape from reliving this hell. She got up from the stairs, mirroring the way she had all those years ago to answer the door to the police that were too late to save her mother, except this time she walked through into the fog. Turning, she took one look back, seeing Diggory's sad young face as he sat there all alone on the step, before the fog blurred and removed him from her vision.

Rin stumbled back through the door, glad to be free from that horror, only wishing that the door could have taken her back sooner. She wished above everything else that she could have saved her mother. The thought that if she'd have come home sooner instead of getting tipsy and flirting down at the pub whilst her mother lay bleeding to death had haunted her for years. It wasn't until the police informed her that her mother had been dead for over four hours when Rin had found her that the guilt had abated a little; there was no way she would have come home that early. And there was no way she could have known. Still she had wished that she had stayed in, had gotten sick and needed to come home, had been there to stop him. Yet the logical part of her knew he wouldn't have done it if she'd been there; at least she didn't think so. It would have just been on a different night. And there was never any clue. Nobody expected Nigel Caplin to murder his wife.

She slammed the door shut and backed away from it. Once was bad enough, and she had been reliving it over and over in her head for years, every day. That was terrible enough but to relive it in every awful little detail was painful beyond belief. Rin was shaking; with tears streaming down her face she ran away from the door.

Waiting

Diggory woke up. He sat bolt upright, feeling as if he had been electrocuted.

'Diggory, you okay?' said Tabitha.

Diggory rubbed his temples. 'She must have opened the door.'

'Oh,' said Tabitha, rubbing her eyes. 'Do you want to go and see if she's okay?'

'No.'

'Shouldn't we?' Tabitha paused. 'What if she can't get out without help, like your door?'

'She wanted to do it alone,' said Diggory. 'And it isn't like my door.'

'How do you know?'

'I think I know what's behind it. It's the only thing that would make Rin act like that. Rin won't want to stay there, no way. And she wouldn't want me to see it. Imagining it is bad enough.'

'Is this what changed everything?'

He nodded. 'Everything.'

'You going to be alright?' asked Tabitha. Diggory didn't look like he was doing so well; Tabitha imagined that he might start rocking again. His cries of *not safe* echoed in her mind.

'Yeh, I'll just wait for her to come back.'

They both shuffled with their backs against the wall, waiting as Rin had asked them to. 'Not like I've got anywhere else to be,' said Tabitha, and Diggory smiled at that. After a pause she said, 'I'm sure Rin will be okay.'

'As long as it doesn't break her,' Diggory said sadly. 'It very nearly did last time.'

'She's a tough one. Not like me. She's strong.'

'She is. You're different to her but in a good way; Rin's too tough sometimes. I guess she's had to be to look after the mental case here, but I'm glad we found you.'

'Me too... I thought for a while when I first got here that I was completely alone. I was worried I'd never find anyone.'

'Good job you did,' smiled Diggory. 'You've been kinder to me here than Rin. You're more like that; she's always been cold since everything that happened. She cares in her own way though.'

'Thanks, and you're not a mental case, Diggory. I'm glad I met you too. I'm more myself than I've ever been.'

'That's good,' said Diggory. 'Are you sure you don't think I'm a mental case? I was rocking on the floor when you found me.'

'I don't think you're mad,' said Tabitha, looking straight at him. 'You were scared, that's all. I think maybe you feel this place more than the rest of us. You knew about the numbers.'

'Really?'

'Really what?'

'You don't think I'm mad?'

'No, I really don't think you're mad,' she said as she smiled at him.

'Most girls think I'm mad,' said Diggory.

Tabitha leaned closer, pausing with her lips a few centimetres from Diggory's, gauging his reaction. His breathing was fast and shaky now; he was unsure of himself. Tabitha moved quickly before she changed her mind, and she pressed her lips full against his.

'I don't,' said Tabitha, pulling away.

'Good. I'm glad,' said Diggory, smiling nervously.

Tabitha leaned against him, and with their hands intertwined they fell back to sleep, content together. All worries for Rin forgotten for the moment.

After the Darkness

'Wake up,' shouted Rin. 'Wake up now, we have to go back down, we have to go back down and find a way out. Get up!'

Diggory and Tabitha stirred slowly. 'What's the matter?' said Diggory to the back of Rin's head as it disappeared down the stairs. 'Rin, wait! What's wrong?' He got up to chase after her.

Tabitha was right behind him. 'Did you go through the door?' she called to Rin who was still racing ahead of them.

'Rin, wait!' shouted Diggory as he ran.

Tabitha caught up with them on the next landing. Rin was trying to descend the next set of stairs while Diggory was holding onto her arm. She tugged against him. 'Let me go, I need to get away from it, I need to go and get out of here. I've had enough now. Let me go.'

'No, we've been down there, we've probably been even further down than we have up and there was nothing, don't you remember?'

She shook her head, still trying to tug away from him, her right foot almost at the edge of the step. Tabitha hoped she wouldn't pull too hard and go tumbling down the stairs. She didn't know what would happen if Rin fell in this place: would she break every bone in her body or would she somehow just bounce? Diggory must have read her mind as he put his other arm around Rin, drawing her safely away from the step.

'Come on now, Rin, come and sit down or something, think about it for a minute. There isn't a way out down there, we tried it.'

She was shaking her head still, trying to tug against him with tears rolling quietly down her face. 'I played along when you were terrified, Diggory. Now it's my turn.'

Her dark hair hung down, obscuring one eye. Diggory held her tight. 'I know but there isn't a way out down there. I know you want one, I do too, but we tried down there, we did and there wasn't one, was there?' She stared at him, her nose a few inches from his face. 'Was there?' he repeated, shaking her a little.

She shook her head slowly.

'And to be honest, Rin, I don't think it's a good idea to go back to my doors, because a part of me wants to find out what's behind the others, and that probably isn't the best idea, after what happened last time. And you didn't want me to either, remember?'

'No. Don't go near the doors, Dig, please,' she said, her voice breaking. 'I never want to see another door again unless it's the way out of this goddamned place. I feel like I'm being tortured all over again.' She collapsed into his arms and started to sob on his shoulder.

'I hate it here too,' whispered Diggory.

Tabitha leant against the wall and waited, feeling thoroughly unsettled. This strange place was bad enough, and now all these torturous doors. It was all too much for her. Even the way she felt about Diggory was too much, and guilt nagged at her, tugging at her intestines like an incessant rat. He deserved better. But the thought drifted from her mind, as thoughts seemed to do here. She could face it another time.

It took a little while for Rin to calm down, but despite Diggory's pleas she wouldn't sit down. Once she'd stopped crying, she spoke firmly. 'I know what you're saying, Diggory, but I just need to get away from that place, at least for a little bit. I need to get further away. I can still *feel* it. It's making me sick, and terrified, and I feel like it's coming to get me. I've never been so scared and it isn't any better, please, please don't stop me; I need to get away from it.'

'Okay,' said Diggory. 'Okay, we can do that, just for a little bit, until you feel better, okay?'

'I just need to get away,' she said, as she broke away from him and started down the stairs, a little unsteady but determined.

Tabitha and Diggory followed.

'Is she okay?' Tabitha asked.

'I've never seen her upset before. Not like this. I've barely seen her cry.'

'It must have been pretty awful whatever it was.'

'It was,' said Diggory. 'I mean, if it was what I think it was. It was awful. And I don't know anything else that could have upset her like that.'

'What was it?'

'It was what happened with our parents. A few years after what was behind my door. I was too young to understand really, but it nearly broke Rin in two. She's always been so strong, but once I was older I understood how tough it must have been for her. Well, I understand as much as it's possible to anyway. It was really bad.'

'You don't have to talk about it.'

'I haven't talked about it much. Doesn't seem much point, people only end up being awkward or feeling sorry for you. But we've got plenty of time in here. Maybe I could explain. I think you're the kind of person who might understand. But I want to make sure Rin's okay first.'

'I'm not going anywhere.'

They quickened their pace, as they'd lost sight of Rin and couldn't even hear her footsteps now.

'Rin, wait up will you?' Diggory shouted, his voice echoing. She didn't reply, but he knew she needed some space and she would be okay in time. Well, as okay as Rin could ever be now.

A few landings on Diggory rounded the corner and found her. He was sad to see his strong sister curled up there on the landing, her back against the cold concrete.

'I just need some space, Dig,' she said quietly.

'You know where I am,' he said. She nodded slowly, sucking a strand of her hair. 'We'll just be up here. Don't keep going down though, we might lose you.'

'I won't,' Rin said in a small voice.

So Diggory went back up, leaving Rin to deal with things on her own, as had always been her way. At least since Diggory had been paying attention. 'Always been the same,' he said. 'Best left alone for tonight. Well, for however long we usually stop for – you know what I mean.'

'Yeh,' said Tabitha. 'And don't feel like you have to tell me anything. I understand. It's personal and it's okay if you want to keep it that way.'

'I know,' said Diggory. 'But if I don't you might never understand Rin. You'll probably never understand Rin actually, but most people completely misunderstand her and a lot of them dislike her – even hate her. But they have no idea what she's been through, or how strong she is, or what she did for me. I feel bad for her. People don't know why she's like she is.'

'She can be a little hostile sometimes; I bet a lot of people think she doesn't like them.'

'Yeh, I can see how people get that impression,' said Diggory, chuckling a little. 'But she has a warm heart really. It's just encased in some pretty heavy-duty stuff.'

'You mean because of what happened?'

'Yeh. Look, I'm not telling you for sympathy or anything, for me or Rin, just so you understand.'

'Okay,' said Tabitha. 'I understand.'

'Our parents died when I was eight. If anyone asks me now I just say they were in an accident or something equally as ordinary, but that isn't true.' Diggory took a deep breath. 'The truth is my mum was murdered, and Rin found her.'

'Oh my god, that's so terrible. What happened?'

'My dad killed her, and then killed himself. Rin found them in the garage. She was only seventeen. I remember coming downstairs and knowing something was wrong. We sat on the stairs and waited for the police. She had come out of the kitchen in a hurry, and closed the door, which was odd because we always left it open. I thought there was a fire or something had gone wrong with the cooker since Mum had told me not to play with the dials and that it was dangerous so many times I was scared of it. All I remember is sitting on the step, waiting for something, and staring at Rin's shoes which were covered in red. I thought it was sauce, from the cooker.'

'I'm so sorry, Diggory.'

'Yeh, everyone is. Sorry. But you do get sick of it. I know you mean well and there's not anything else to say but it doesn't change anything.'

'I know,' said Tabitha. 'Why did he do it?'

'That's the question. He always had problems, depression and stuff, but none of us realised it was anything like that.'

'Was he violent?' asked Tabitha gently.

'No,' said Diggory. 'That's just it. Maybe we would have expected something then. Maybe Mum would have realised he was a monster and left. I can't say this in front on Rin anymore but he was a good dad. I know that sounds so wrong because of what he did but before he did that he was a good dad. He was fun and strict in the right amounts, and he looked after us, he really cared for us. It's been so hard for me because for a long time I couldn't see past that. Didn't even really understand what he'd done. I was just sad that my wonderful ice-cream-buying, story-reading parents had disappeared.'

'And you couldn't talk about how you felt with Rin?'

'No. She hated him. Really hated him. She still does, she's so angry all the time. I can't blame her really, but it's like she's forgotten all that happened before, like it has all disappeared into nothing, and it makes me so sad because I can understand how she feels about Dad, and her wanting to forget him because of what he did. Even if I don't feel like that myself, even if I should, I know why she does. I understand. But Mum didn't do anything wrong. She was wonderful – she was kind, and caring, and the most loving mother. And Rin never talks about her, never remembers her. I worry the only way Rin even thinks of her now is in a pool of blood.'

'I'm sorry,' said Tabitha, reaching out for his hand. He didn't move it as she rubbed the back of it. 'It must have been so difficult for Rin.'

'It was. I know it was. I just wish she hadn't let him taint all the good memories. It was bad enough what he did, without letting him do more.'

'Poor Rin,' said Tabitha.

'At least now you understand. She isn't like it on purpose.'

Tabitha nodded and rubbed Diggory's arm. This put how she felt about her parents into perspective; her mother was overbearing and she irritated her, but she wasn't a murderer. And her father had died sadly of a heart-attack, and she missed him, but nobody had killed him. And as much as her mother annoyed her, Tabitha was very glad she wasn't dead. She felt a sadness for Diggory in her heart, and she felt it even more strongly for Rin, who had been his rock, and had ended up turning to stone.

The Gun

Amelia walked up the stairs finding the familiar door easily despite the dark, the black and the grey of everything here. She hovered her hand over the handle, pushing the grim sickness in her gut away. Empowered by the feeling of the cold metal dangling from her left hand, she took a deep breath and walked over the threshold, quickly grasping the gun in both hands and holding it up in front of her.

She stood in the bedroom of her prison sure that she had finally found a way out. A way to end it. Having been trapped for what felt like a very long time – and indeed it had been most of her short life – she couldn't quite believe that she was actually clutching salvation in her small hands. It was heavy, the gun, but she grasped it tightly. The metal was cold against her palm as she held it steady, shaking only a little she kept it pointed firmly at his sleeping chest. She watched the slow rise and fall, contrasting with her own quick, shallow breaths as she surveyed the gross sleeping form of the man on the bed. Him with his slack, fat face, and his great beer-belly protruding out from his grubby vest: he repulsed her. But she fought the urge to bolt, even though this time he couldn't have stopped her and she stood summoning the last little bit of courage she needed to actually do it.

She took a deep breath, praying that he wouldn't wake up, squeezed her eyes tight shut and then pulled the trigger, three times in quick succession, just to be sure.

The force of the gun took her by surprise and her hands were shaking terribly as she lowered it. On opening her eyes she saw that there wasn't as much blood as she had expected. What was there was a dark, barely red-black ooze pouring slickly from the wounds in his chest and being sucked into the mattress. He hadn't even woken up, but sick gargling noises had escaped his chest as the bullets had ripped through his lungs, allowing blood to pool in them and still his breath for good. He had convulsed briefly and then stilled. Amelia stared at him. Dead. She could barely believe it. The scene she had imagined so many times was finally before her eyes.

'Bye, Dad,' she whispered as she dropped the gun on the floor. It landed with a final clunk, and she did not look back.

In the hallway outside she slouched against the wall, feeling as if she was finally able to breathe again. A strange feeling filled her chest: somewhere between elation and panic. She waited expectantly. But she waited long enough for her breathing to completely return to normal: for what, deep down, she knew was much too long, and nothing had happened.

Grim realisation settled in her stomach and she slid to the floor as great, shaking sobs shook her. Wrapping her arms around herself she rocked, devastated: it had taken everything she had to pull the trigger. She sobbed and sobbed. *Maybe it hasn't worked,* she thought with a small glimmer of hope. She pulled herself up with renewed purpose, wiping hot tears from her cheeks as she went.

From the doorway he did look dead. He was laid there splayed and still, but reluctantly she went over to check, picking up the gun and using it to prod his face. This elicited no response, and no breathing was evident. He was dead – had to be – but then why was she still here? So she put the gun to his head and fired it, taking no chances this time, the bullet launching out of the gun straight through his frontal bone. Black-red goo erupted from inside and she was splattered with it. She looked at her now undeniably dead father and screamed in horror and frustration. 'I did it!' she screamed to no one. 'I did it! He's dead!' She wiped her hands on his chest, covering them with blood and goo. 'Look!' she screamed, holding up her hands. 'He's dead. Look!' Her voice broke and the sobs came again, unwelcomed. She sank onto the floor, her back against the bed. 'He's dead and I'm still here,' she cried desperately.

With every beat of her fragile heart she felt as if a hole was being torn through its vital tissue, getting larger with every squeeze. She had nothing else left. She was stuck here alone.

The Descent

Tabitha rolled over, half-asleep, her arm landing on Diggory. He groaned at the impact, and Tabitha half-opened her eyes.

'Sorry,' she murmured, as she removed her arm. 'Morning.'

'Morning,' he replied, and smiled at her. 'If that's what you can call it, eh?'

'Yeh. I think I've forgotten what sunshine looks like,' she laughed.

'Me too,' said Rin, standing over them. 'I wasn't even one for sunrises, but I think I finally understand the fascination. People are not meant to live underground like moles.'

'No,' agreed Tabitha, as she pushed herself up, conscious of how close she was to Diggory, and of Rin's watchful eyes on them.

'And you want to go further down,' said Diggory. 'If we are in some underground somewhere then surely going down is a bad idea.'

His statement hung heavy in the air. Tabitha stood up and busied herself, rubbing her eyes, smoothing her hair, and keeping out of it. Rin looked at her feet and then up towards the stairs and the door that had diminished her to tears. She was still frightened of it. 'I can't do it again,' she said quietly.

'You don't have to do it again,' said Diggory. 'Maybe we can just walk past it and keep walking like we did with mine and Tabitha's?'

'I don't want to go near it.'

'I know you don't want to but it makes more sense to keep going up,' said Diggory.

'Maybe it does, but I can't face it right now. It was too much the first time.'

'Okay, well, let's go down a bit more; it might make you feel better. But I think we'll have to turn around at some point.'

'We'll see.'

So they descended, with Rin clearly in her own little world, her face still puffed and blotchy. Tabitha and Diggory didn't feel much like talking; it felt a lot like they were going backwards, but neither was too bothered about that. Each of them was also preoccupied, thinking that they were heading in the right direction to get to their floors again, and their doors. They both mused, individually, that they should have been filled with much more a feeling of dread; instead this was more like excitement.

They trudged down the many stairs, none of them keeping count, Rin walking a little ahead of Tabitha and Diggory. She was at least two staircases ahead of them. Tabitha spoke quietly. 'Do you think she's okay?'

'I'm sure she will be,' said Diggory, his worried look at odds with his words. 'Let's catch up with her.'

They rounded the corner onto a landing a few more staircases down and came across Rin slouched against the wall near the far staircase, looking as if she was well on the way to sleep. Diggory shrugged and sat down too, a little way from her. Tabitha followed suit and it wasn't long before they were all sleeping.

The Man with the Chair

Tabitha awoke bleary-eyed and blinking. Diggory was sleeping so close to her that she could feel the heat radiating from his body. Rin was across the landing, curled up into the wall, murmuring something in her sleep. There was an odd shuffling, scraping sound and the occasional bump of what sounded like wood against concrete, and Tabitha realised this was what had woken her up. She was startled by the outline of a large figure carrying something awkwardly down the stairs. Diggory and Rin didn't even stir, but Tabitha had always been a light sleeper. She squinted at the staircase, wondering if she was still dreaming, but saw with certainty that there was indeed a figure: a huge chunk of a man coming down the stairs, huffing and puffing with the effort of carrying what Tabitha could only describe as what appeared to be the largest chair she had ever seen.

'Diggory,' she said, shaking him awake. 'Diggory, there's someone coming down the stairs.' She spoke with a quiet urgency so as not to draw the huge man's attention to them. Diggory groaned. 'There's someone coming down the stairs, carrying a huge chair. Wake up.'

'You what?' said Diggory sleepily.

'There's a massive man coming down the stairs. Wake up!'

He turned over and looked towards the staircase, and there he was. Five steps from being on their landing. The man looked like a giant; Diggory wagered he would top his own nearly six foot height by at least half a foot. And he was built, as his grandmother would have said, like a brick shithouse. Diggory was glad he was carrying a chair, and not a gun or something, but then again he didn't fancy his chances against a chair that size, nor the man carrying it. Thankfully the man didn't look particularly hostile, despite his imposing size.

Before Diggory or Tabitha thought to wake Rin, the huge feet of the man were planted on their landing, followed by the feet of the chair. He huffed with the effort, and was out of breath. He looked at them both as if he knew them, and made no move to introduce himself; he just stood there grinning. Tabitha and Diggory exchanged a glance before looking back at the man.

'I'm sorry but who on earth are you?'

'I'm Jetson,' he said, his merry voice booming in the small space, causing Rin to stir.

Rin opened her eyes and saw the huge bulk of Jetson above her. She did a double take and moved quickly away from him, clinging onto Tabitha's arm. 'Who is that? Why didn't you wake me up?'

'Sorry,' said Tabitha. 'He just appeared.'

'I was just saying I'm Jetson, and I'm pleased to meet you folks. No need to be frightened, lassie, I mean you no harm,' he said, as he sat on the chair. 'Newcomers, I take it?'

'Newcomers?' said Rin. 'We've been here for what feels like forever.'

'But probably not actually that long,' said Tabitha. Rin glared at her.

'I thought not,' said Jetson.

'What's with the chair?' said Diggory.

'Ah, this is Cheryl, my trusty companion, my noble steed. Although it's more a case of me carrying her, as you can see,' he chortled.

'You take *this* everywhere?' said Rin, looking sceptically at the huge chair. It really did look more like a wooden throne.

'Once you've been here a while you get sick of sitting on the floor, and this is the only chair I've found – only one in this whole place, maybe. The Futurespan Throne, some call it.' He chuckled. 'Hopefully you kids won't come to understand.'

'Futurespan?' said Diggory.

'That's what I call this place,' said Jetson. 'I think it's quite fitting myself. Don't ask me why it's called it though.'

'At least it has a name.'

'How long have you been here exactly?' said Rin.

'Long enough,' said Jetson smiling. 'How about you lot, how many floors have you climbed? Looking for the way out, I take it?'

'Yes,' said Rin hesitantly.

'Well, it ain't up there,' said Jetson.

'It isn't down either,' said Diggory. 'Not for a long way if it is.'

'We've climbed over probably thirty floors at least. I lost count of the steps,' said Tabitha.

'It's not for an even longer way up, I can tell you,' said Jetson.

Rin sighed. 'Wonderful news. So we're stuck.'

'He didn't say that, Rin,' said Diggory.

'Well, there's no way out downwards, unless we go all the way back down the god knows how many floors we've already passed, and then however many more after, and still maybe nothing. Probably nothing. And according to Jetson here there's no way out up there either, so it was pointless us going up there. So we are stuck, Diggory.'

'You've been up too?' said Jetson, an odd tone to his voice, the merriness momentarily dissipated.

'Not as far as we've seen of the down, if you know what I mean. We got just to Rin's floor and then we turned back,' said Tabitha, unsure of whether to elaborate.

'I, for one, am ecstatic that we're stuck here,' said Rin.

'Aren't you forgetting something?' said Jetson.

'Oh yeh, the magical mystery doors, our doors, a quaint little set of three for each of us. They aren't the way out either, they're the doors to hell,' said Rin.

'Not exactly,' he said, smiling. 'I'll show you youngsters a trick or two, you'll see.'

'We're not in hell, are we?' said Rin, looking straight into Jetson's eyes. 'You're very cheerful if we are.'

'Exactly. I think we'd know if we were in hell – Rin, is it? I'm pretty sure it's not hell. And I'm trying to make the best of it. I can help people here.'

'Purgatory then,' said Tabitha. 'There's enough nothingness here for that to make sense.'

'If it's purgatory then we're dead,' said Rin.

'I don't think so. Look. Have you been hungry since you got here?' asked Jetson. They all looked at each other, confused, and looked back at Jetson who had the hint of a smug smile on his face. 'No?' They shook their heads, realisation dawning on them. 'Funny that, isn't it. Funny that you've not even thought about it.'

'We are dead. Aren't we?' said Rin. 'I don't remember dying, I don't remember how I got here but we're dead. That's why we don't need to eat. Dead people don't need sustenance.'

'I really don't think we're dead, Rin.'

'This isn't real then,' said Rin. 'If we're not dead then this still isn't real. Maybe it's a dream?'

'And I want to wake up,' said Diggory with slumped shoulders.

'I don't think it can be,' said Tabitha.

'No, no, it isn't a dream because you can sleep, can't you? You don't sleep in dreams, do you?' said Jetson, shrugging his broad shoulders.

'That's a point,' said Tabitha as she looked at the floor. 'I don't suppose you do. I don't.'

'Wait, that doesn't make sense, you can sleep in some dreams. This can't be a dream, though; you're not all in my head,' said Rin. 'So basically none of this is real. Which is brilliant. It's like a low-budget Matrix, only with a lot more concrete. And a lot more messed up.'

'No, don't be ridiculous,' said Jetson patiently. 'There are no evil machines keeping you prisoner, you're not wired up like a human Duracell here.'

'It is like dreaming though, even if it isn't. Dreaming is a phenomenon where as part of REM sleep you experience fictional and often bizarre events with a sense of reality. Which certainly fits what we've been experiencing.'

'Very technical, missy,' said Jetson.

'She's a doctor,' said Diggory.

'Well –' started Tabitha.

'As good as,' cut in Diggory. 'Even if you don't want to actually be one, you will be.'

'This is so much more than dreaming,' Jetson continued. 'It's so real, can't you feel it? It doesn't get any realer than this.'

'Or any scarier. How long have you been here?' Diggory said.

'Never mind me, lad, I'll help you, not to worry.' He patted Diggory on the shoulder with his huge hand. 'I'll help ye all. You won't be here as long as me, not if I can help it.'

'And how can we be sure you're not just a figment of our imaginations?' said Rin.

'Well, lassie, you can think that if you like, but you're not sure what to make of me, are you, and if you made me up then you'd have the size of me. Think about that,' he said, tapping his head.

'You can add me to the figment list too, if you like Rin,' said a strange voice.

They all wheeled round to look for its source. Standing there was a small woman, with white hair that she looked too young to possess. It stuck out at odd angles making her look as if she had been electrocuted. Jetson looked on, chuckling to himself. 'I was wondering when you were going to show up young Stacey-B; there're newcomers been left unattended to. I'm amazed I found them before you.'

'Hm, never mind about that, I'm here now. Stacey-Barbara. Good to meet you Rin.' She beamed, holding out her hand to Rin who was closest, but Rin just looked at it.

'How do you know my name?'

'I heard it just now,' she replied, looking expectantly at her own hand, and giving it a small wiggle. Rin continued to look at her blankly. 'Well,' said Stacey-Barbara. 'It's good to meet you all.' She smiled at Tabitha and Diggory.

'You too,' said Tabitha tentatively. 'I'm Tabitha.'

'Nice to meet you,' said Stacey-Barbara with renewed enthusiasm, looking wide-eyed at Diggory as she shook Tabitha's extended hand.

'Diggory,' he said flatly, keeping his hands firmly in his pockets.

'Hi, Diggory,' beamed Stacey-Barbara. 'Have you been scare-mongering them, Jetson?' she chided, hands on her hips.

'Not at all,' chuckled Jetson.

'Has he?' she asked them.

'He's been freaking us out if that's what you mean,' said Rin, looking Jetson up and down. 'Pointing out that this isn't really real life. Although that wasn't exactly a surprise.'

'Oh, he has a habit of that,' said Stacey-Barbara. 'And he is right, he usually is. But don't worry yourselves, it'll be okay,' she said, smiling.

'Usually!' exclaimed Jetson, grinning to himself. Stacey-Barbara returned a small smile.

Diggory turned to her. 'How long have you been here?'

'Not too long. And you get used to it after a while, honest,' she said. 'It's not so bad. It's all fairly inert really, as long as you stay away from the doors, and think plain thoughts.'

'Inert. That's one inaccurate way of putting it,' said Rin.

'Does everyone have a set of doors?' asked Tabitha.

'I think so, love. I don't much like them myself though. I'm a bit of a scaredy-cat really, not a fan of any of it: the dark, spiders, strange doors.'

'Scared of her own shadow, this one,' said Jetson. 'Heart of a lion though.'

'Thanks, Jetson.' Stacey-Barbara smiled.

'Wait a second,' said Rin. 'Have you been following us?'

'No.'

'You must have been,' said Rin. 'You came from down there, and we've been travelling a long way up; you must have been right behind us the whole way. Why the hell didn't you say something sooner?'

'You haven't worked that part out yet, have you?' said Stacey-Barbara.

'They've been wandering for over thirty floors,' said Jetson.

'Wow, that's a long way. I suppose you've been keeping each other company.'

'And stopping at doors,' said Jetson.

'Rather you than me,' said Stacey-Barbara.

'What are you on about, haven't worked what out yet? You must have been following us,' said Rin.

'It's easier if I show you; I'll have to show you or you might never see it yourselves at this rate. And it does make this place a lot easier, if you like the doors anyway.'

'There's still more concrete than you can shake a stick at,' said Jetson.

'Look, what are you talking about?' said Rin.

'I'll show you, don't worry Rin, but now is not the time. I have an important mission to complete first but I'll be back as old Arnie says,' she said, smiling her ridiculous grin. 'Jetson can keep you company. I won't be long, but don't go spoiling the surprises, Jetson.'

'I won't, don't worry,' he said, smiling his big, goofy grin.

And with that Stacey-Barbara left them without so much as a goodbye.

'Well, that was helpful,' said Rin.

'She'll come back,' said Jetson. 'She's been here longer than me.'

'So she knows things you don't know?' asked Rin.

'I know a lot,' said Jetson.

'Can't you just tell us then?' said Rin.

'Be more than Cheryl's worth to spoil Stacey-Barbara's fun. She loves educating the newcomers. I don't think she'd ever speak to me again. And we're both going to be here a lot longer than you lot, I'd wager, so I'd rather stay on speaking terms with her if it's all the same to you.'

'Fair enough,' said Diggory.

'She shouldn't be too long,' said Jetson.

They all settled on the landing. Rin backed against the wall, in an even worse mood now. Jetson looked expectantly at Tabitha and Diggory.

'So do you have a family, Jetson?' It was all Tabitha could think of as small talk.

'A wife,' replied Jetson.

'That's nice. Do you have any children?'

He stuttered, almost as if he might choke on thin air, and decided against answering. Instead he just shook his head. 'What about you all?'

'Rin's my sister,' said Diggory.

'Lovely that you're here together. Sharing the experience. Is there more siblings in ye family?' asked Jetson.

'No,' said Rin and Diggory in unison.

'Ah well, your parents must have been happy to have you two, looks like you've turned out well to me. They must be proud.'

The statement hung in the air. Nobody said anything. Jetson sensed the tension, and you could see the cogs turning in his head, as he tried to decipher where he had gone wrong. Tabitha watched as he looked from Diggory to Rin, obviously wondering what he should say. Diggory saved them from the awkwardness.

'Our parents are dead,' said Diggory.

'Oh,' said Jetson. 'I'm real sorry. Real sorry. How horrible. I didn't mean to speak out of turn.'

'It's okay,' said Rin. 'You didn't know.'

'Have they just died?' said Jetson, having met his fair share of the recently bereaved here.

'No, the accident was several years ago,' said Diggory.

'Don't lie Diggory,' said Rin. 'Don't lie. It wasn't an accident.'

'It's easier to lie, Rin.'

'Easier or not it isn't true,' said Rin, turning to Jetson. 'It wasn't an accident. My mother was murdered. My father stabbed her and then himself. And you don't have to be sorry. It happened, there's nothing anyone can do.'

'I –' stuttered Jetson, feeling the need to say something after putting his big foot in it.

'It's okay. Like Rin said there isn't anything we can do about it now, and you weren't to know. Maybe we should talk about something else.'

'Let's,' said Jetson, eyeing Rin apologetically. She wasn't looking at him; she was staring into the distance, scowling and sucking her hair.

The conversation continued mindlessly for some time without her. They spoke themselves into tiredness, about nothing much at all, all cautiously staying away from anything too personal. There was a reason all of them were here in Futurespan, and none of the reasons were nice. Probably best not to talk about them. So when they didn't feel like talking anymore they bedded down. Jetson settled down on his chair and the others on the floor, hopeful that Stacey-Barbara would return when they awoke to shed a bit more light on the ways of this strange place. That or, Rin thought, maybe Jetson would cave in and tell them. But when they woke Jetson would be gone.

Jetson's Encounter

Jetson blinked to life, waking from a deep but uneasy sleep, and saw to his surprise a strange glowing, ghostlike figure at the top of the stairs. He stared at it, bleary-eyed. This was new. He had been here for a long while now and this was definitely new. He opened his eyes wide and rubbed them. The figure was still there. She looked like an old woman, in what appeared to be some sort of light-blue nun's habit, and despite the eye-rubbing she was still glowing: a faint, blurry white haze surrounded her, and to Jetson it looked like a protective bubble. He pushed himself awkwardly out of the chair, not even casting a glance at the others sleeping on the floor. His eyes were fixed firmly on this new person, as he watched her disappear around the corner and rushed to follow.

He reached the next landing and she was nowhere to be seen. After briefly catching his breath he went up to the next one, also to no avail. He reached the third landing before he found her waiting patiently for him on the third step, and saw that she wasn't old at all. No, indeed, she looked a little younger than Jetson – in her mid-thirties – but she had an altogether different air about her. She seemed old. Wise somehow. She boasted an air of authority that Jetson thought he would never be capable of no matter how old he became. Perhaps it was the clothes, he thought.

She looked straight at Jetson, and made him feel like a small boy. She seemed to be looking straight through him and into his very soul, whilst she wore a strange, sympathetic smile, reminiscent of that of a doctor treating a patient who was very sick. Jetson shifted uneasily, too threatened by the woman's unsettling gaze to speak.

'Jetson,' she said serenely. 'It has been long enough now.'

'What's that, sorry?' he said, stuttering a little over the simple words.

'I'm here to help you, because unfortunately you have been unable to help yourself.'

'Who are you?'

'I'm Sister Elaina Peristo of the West Wings,' she said with a small curtsey. Jetson noticed that she put her hand to her breast where he saw the glint of a small emblem that looked a little like wings. Now he was closer he saw it was not the usual habit at all; despite the bizarre choice of colour it was not made of the ordinary harsh material but of blue silk (and it did actually look blue) with a thin, transparent layer of more silk, creating a beautiful garment that would have been more at home on a Greek goddess. On her head she wore a diaphanous veil of silk that had a faint blue tinge and Jetson saw that it cascaded almost to her hips, down past her long, dark hair. She was beautiful.

'That doesn't mean a great lot to me, Sister,' Jetson said uncertainly. 'And excuse me for saying, but you don't look like your typical nun.'

'No,' she said plainly.

'What kind of a church is West Wings?' said Jetson with a grimace.

'It's not a church, Jetson. The sisters, such as myself, bear a great weight of responsibility, and you are now part of my responsibility. You are in my Wing of Futurespan. You have been here for far too long and it is time for you to leave.'

'Well, nothing like good old-fashioned hospitality then,' he said with a small, nervous chuckle.

'You might look at it more as if you have outstayed your welcome?'

'And you have been sent to ask me politely to leave?' he said, making her smile briefly. 'I can't leave now, Sister. The newcomers need me.'

She gave him a stern look. Jetson stuttered a little but continued. 'They do, you know they need some guidance. Young Diggory is a very lost young lad and he's scared, real scared, I can see it in his eyes. I think he needs a father figure, ye know, and I never got the chance to be a father, erm, yet. I suppose, erm, anyway, I don't have children myself and he needs looking after and I feel I'm the man for the job. I feel a responsibility towards the lad and –'

'Jetson,' said Sister Elaina calmly. 'You can look for as many excuses as you like, but they won't change things for you. And you can't keep running away like this.'

'Running away?' said Jetson, his words hanging there limply, but Sister Elaina did not dignify him with a response.

She started to ascend the stairs. Jetson followed like a lost puppy, mesmerised by the flow of the long fabric as it trailed over the floor of the stairs.

'Sister, I do feel sorry for the lad though. Terrible childhood. Awful. To lose a mother so young and have her life snatched by the man who's supposed to be raising you – it's terrible. I couldn't imagine anything worse.'

'It's almost as bad as a father killing his own child,' said Sister Elaina without breaking step.

Jetson's stomach turned to ice; he stopped and felt the acid rising in his chest. He thought he was going to be sick, and took a few seconds to catch his breath. *She couldn't know. She couldn't.* He didn't even know. He pushed the thought aside; she was just making conversation. She was a nun – well, some sort of a nun. She wouldn't dig at him like that. *Would she?*

'So you see he needs some guidance,' Jetson said.

'And you're the right person to guide him?'

'Well,' he said, unsure of himself in her presence. They had rounded another landing and the Sister continued on up the next set of stairs. 'Wait, where are we going?' said Jetson.

'To help you, like I said.'

'We're not going *there*, are we?'

'Where?' she said as she kept climbing.

'To my floor.'

'That's right, Jetson,' she said slowly.

'No,' he said, stopping mid-flight. 'I can't go back there.'

'You have to, Jetson, you can't stay here. I told you,' she said with great, practiced patience.

'I don't think you understand, Sister, I can't go back there. I can't face it, not a third time.'

'You have to, it will set you free,' she said. 'You can't stay trapped here. It isn't good for you, and you're blocking up Futurespan. It's time for you to leave.'

'Reliving that nightmare for a third time will kill me, not set me free. I mean it when I say I can't do it again.'

'You can, Jetson,' she said, and she carried on walking. Her mesmerising effect meant that he followed her again, forgetting his distaste for the destination, at least for a little while.

They reached the next landing and Jetson stopped, hovering near the downward stairs. Sister Elaina turned to face him. 'You need to face it; then you can go through the other doors. They *will* set you free.'

'The first was enough for me,' said Jetson, shaking his head. 'I don't want to go back through that one, never mind any others.'

'The others are different.' She looked long at Jetson, and saw a defeated man. She saw the slump of his shoulder and the sadness in his eyes, she could see the darkness in his soul. 'Sit down. I will explain more and then perhaps you will understand better that this must be done.'

They sat opposite each other. Jetson leant against the wall, knees drawn in, looking awkwardly big in that small space without his chair. Sister Elaina sat perfectly upright in the centre of the landing, her legs tucked neatly to one side of her. 'I suppose it's better to start at the beginning. Do you know where you are?'

'Futurespan,' he said, with much less confidence in the presence of someone so obviously better informed than he. He was not used to being that person, not here anyway, and felt he had lost some of his identity. 'At least that's what Stacey-Barbara called it, and what I've been calling it.' He shrugged his shoulders.

'That's fine, Jetson, but do you know what kind of place it is?'

'It's not the real world,' said Jetson. 'I know that. But I think it's real. I think it's like being inside your own head, in a way, except you're not just in your head. And everyone's got a floor – seems to have, anyway. Mine has three doors, and so does Rin's. I'm not sure about the others; I'd wager they do too. I know lots of other floors exist.'

'Right, so what is this place really?'

'Some sort of parallel world maybe. Rin thought it was like the Matrix but I don't think it's like that. I think this is real too: real like things that are in your head are real. They're not physical but they are real. They're real to you. They're more real than the world is because you can only see the world through the filter of your mind.'

'That's not a bad way to put it, not bad at all. You don't need the whole story but think of Futurespan as another dimension, as a kind of a meeting of minds, a place where our minds overlap and intermingle. A place that not everyone gets to and indeed a place not everyone needs. You are here because you need to be, because something so significant in your life or your mind, or both, has jolted you here. Something that caused your mind to be at its breaking point, and it isn't that exactly for everyone, but for you it was. And when that point is reached you either end up here, or well, somewhere else. Somewhere from which you can never return to the physical world.'

'Why do I need to leave if I need to be here?' said Jetson. 'You said I need to be here. I don't want to be a goner instead.'

'You are here for a purpose: to go through the doors and to learn, to learn how to get back to your real physical life. You have been given a chance, Jetson. You are not here to walk up and down endless concrete corridors and stairs, staving off boredom by taking waifs and strays under your wing. This endless running away will not change the fact you are stuck here. And you will stay stuck here until you first face up to your past. And that is the first door.'

'I have, I lived through it and I relived it behind that door. Relived it and couldn't do a damn thing about it, I can't do that again. I can't watch her die over and over again. I won't do it.'

'You need to. It is the key to the rest, Jetson. You may have been through it but have you truly faced it? It is time to stop running away.'

'Why do I need to do it again? To torture me? Is that what this place is about?' said Jetson, the anger rising inside him.

'You need to learn from it, that's why. Learn that you can't change it, learn what it was meant to teach you. What you have not yet learnt. You must learn, so you don't make the same mistake again. Learn because learning from your wrongs opens the door for knowing the rights, for learning them better and stronger and deeper. Because when something hurts you badly, cuts you deeply, you remember. You remember to do the right thing next time. You get to know yourself, who you are, who you were, who you should have been but can be no longer. But you learn who you should be from now on. Who you can be if you do better. If you choose better. You can be scared all you like but it's happened; nothing is going to change that. That is why you're here. You can run forever and you still made that fatal mistake. You were still that person in that moment and that moment has gone, but recognising that gives you the freedom to be a different person from now on and that's what matters.'

Jetson had run out of excuses.

'And you missed a very important point, Jetson. You don't know that she is dead,' said Sister Elaina solemnly.

'She's alive?' said Jetson, and Elaina saw the sad hope in his eyes.

She looked straight at him. 'You need to get through the first door before you can find that out.'

'Tell me,' he said. 'Please.'

'That is for you to find out,' she said. 'I am here to guide you; I cannot do it for you. You must go up the stairs, Jetson, and through that first door. I will not drag you but it is past time and now you really must.' She curtseyed again. 'I hope you take heed of what I have said. There are not many in Futurespan who are so lucky to know these truths from me.' And with that she was gone.

Jetsonless

They woke and Jetson was nowhere to be seen. The huge wooden chair sat there unattended: Cheryl abandoned to the newcomers.

'I wonder where he's gone,' said Tabitha.

'Won't be far,' said Rin, as she sat proudly on the chair, patting it. 'It's a little high, this,' she said, swinging her legs like a little girl. 'I suppose he's a little high too.'

'He never goes anywhere without that thing though. It's like his baby, he's carried it up and down half of Futurespan, I think. It's strange he's gone without it.'

'Hmm, I bet he'll be back in a minute. No point taking it up one flight and back down again, is there?' said Rin.

'What's he gone to look at, though? Another concrete step?' said Tabitha.

'Maybe a door we don't know about.'

'You think?' said Tabitha, pausing to think. 'That would be more than a flight or two though, and we've come down quite a few flights since your floor. I still think it's strange he left his chair.'

'Maybe he thought it would be quick and he'd be back when we're still asleep, I don't know. Maybe it's a secret door we can't see or something, who knows in this bloody place, I don't know what's possible and what isn't anymore.'

'I know that feeling. Do you think there are secret doors?'

'Maybe.'

'Maybe it's his door,' said Diggory.

Rin and Tabitha both looked at him. Tabitha spoke. 'Would be strange though after all this time running around here. He's obviously been avoiding it.'

'Hmm,' said Rin. 'I don't blame him if he is. Bloody awful things, doors. Shame the way out, wherever it is, would have to be one. Unless there's just a doorframe – maybe we've been looking for the wrong thing.'

Diggory shrugged his shoulders. 'Maybe we inspired him.'

'Yeh or maybe we drove him away,' said Rin, chuckling to herself.

'Or maybe he doesn't have a door and he really is stuck,' said Tabitha.

They sat quietly musing on the possibility of Jetson's door and whether his would be any different to theirs. He himself did seem rather an altogether different entity, and somewhat of an authority on so-called Futurespan. Perhaps he did know about magical doors. Whether he did or not they wouldn't find out waiting here, that was for sure.

'Do you think we should follow him?' said Tabitha, looking at the up staircase.

'How do you know he went up?' said Rin.

'I guess I don't, but he came from up there. I suppose he could've gone down. Maybe we should go and see?'

'Maybe we should wait. He wouldn't have left his chair behind,' said Rin. 'And if he doesn't come back maybe Stacey-Barbara will.'

'Well she found us last time,' said Tabitha.

'I guess,' said Rin. 'If she really wasn't following us.'

'We can always come back here. I was looking forward to being on the road again, so to speak,' said Tabitha.

'Aren't you worried about your floor if we start going down again?' said Rin.

'I kind of wanted to go back, now I've calmed down about the door, just to see – well, I don't know, really, but it's not as if we've got a lot else to do.'

'That's true,' said Diggory, pleased that Tabitha had brought it up. He was itching to get moving. All the initial fear had faded – well, almost. He felt much better than he had, and he didn't want to sit around and do nothing. That was enough to drive a perfectly sane person mad. He knew Rin wouldn't go for it if he'd suggested it because she wouldn't want him going through another door, but since Tabitha had then maybe they could get a move on. He didn't want them to split up. Or if they did he wanted to do it with Rin's approval. She had her thinking face on, her brow furrowed like their mother's used to.

Finally she spoke. 'Okay, might as well do something,' she said. 'Not like there's a lot of places to go here anyway, I'm sure he'll follow us down if he comes back. And I'd rather go back to yours than mine. And you never know if there are magical doors, or doorways; maybe one will have appeared.' She turned to Diggory, lowering her voice. 'Don't be getting any ideas though, Dig, I'm not going back in that house again.'

He nodded, but he had no intention of leaving his other doors unexplored. They could wait, but only for now.

So they continued on down the same bland stairs. As they neared Tabitha's floor she started to get the familiar feelings of home, of a safety similar to that felt in one's own mind. It was hers in every facet, unpolluted entirely by anything else. The closer they got the more she longed to be back there again. There was a little bit of fear at the thought of the door and the horror that it held, but even that did little to dampen her eager spirit. She even thought she would go through another door. It couldn't be as bad as the first.

'Well, that seemed quicker than the last time,' said Diggory as they emerged onto Tabitha's floor.

'Downhill,' remarked Rin, still mostly in her own world.

'I'm glad we've come back,' said Tabitha.

'Aren't you scared after last time?' said Diggory.

'Maybe a little,' she said as she looked down the corridor at the doors. She knew the one in the middle would be next. 'But I feel so much better being here, I feel a lot less lost. And the doors don't scare me as much, I know more of what to expect. Even though it was awful they can't all be as bad as that one. Maybe your first door is the worst one and then, I don't know, they get better.'

'Are you going through another one?' asked Diggory.

'I think so,' said Tabitha, smiling a large, giddy grin. 'I think I am. I think that's what they must be here for. Don't you think?'

Diggory agreed silently, not wanting to anger Rin.

'Well, let me know if you find anything nice,' said Rin sullenly as she slouched in the corner near the downward stairs. 'Maybe second time's a charm.'

Tabitha ignored her pessimism, and spoke to Diggory. 'I do hope it's better than last time, I have a better feeling about it anyway. That, or I'm just excited to be here. I feel as though I'm home.'

'We'll be here waiting,' said Diggory. 'If you're sure it's a good idea.' He looked at her grinning face, realising it was pointless trying to talk her out of it. 'If it is the way out, though, make sure you come back and tell us, won't you?'

'Of course,' said Tabitha, laughing a little. 'I won't just leave you here.'

'That's good.'

'I'll probably be right back, after another venture into my future. Hopefully this is a better version.'

'I hope so too,' said Diggory.

And with a smile she walked towards her second door, as Diggory watched her a little sadly, hoping she would come back.

As the door closed after her he went to Rin, forgetting to look at the little silver numbers. 'You okay, sis?'

She shook her head. 'I'll be okay. I just want to get out now, Dig. I've had enough of this awful place.'

'I'm sure we'll find a way,' he said with a small smile, his hand rubbing her shoulder. 'Maybe Tabitha will find it.'

'I doubt it,' said Rin.

'Maybe these doors are the start. There must be a reason they're here, like Tabitha said.'

'To torture us, that's why,' said Rin, her voice empty. 'None of them say exit, do they? Maybe we are in hell.'

'I'm sure we're not.'

Rin didn't say anything else and after a while Diggory became restless, not wanting to sit too close to the negativity pouring out of Rin – that sort of thing was contagious, and someone with Diggory's predisposition had to be careful. He wandered closer to Tabitha's doors, feeling a little like an intruder, but at least the atmosphere was a bit better than Rin's. Less hostile at least, if not exactly happier. The air felt a little heavier nearer the doors and more repressed. Diggory knew it was best not to go too close to them; he didn't want to be weighed down by that feeling either. He turned to the door Tabitha had just gone through, looking at the numbers he expected to see a date ending in 0914 or later, like the last door. The future. But it wasn't. The date was close to if not the actual last date that Diggory could recall. It must have been around the time they ended up here. Strange. It read 140191190514. Tabitha was going into the past.

That wasn't good, thought Diggory, remembering his own door with a little shudder. If Rin hadn't come to get him, what would have become of him? And Rin's door to the past was like the doorway to her own personal hell. It had been torture for her. What if Tabitha's door was like that? What if it was like Diggory's and she couldn't get out?

He paused in front of the door, wondering what he should do for the best. He couldn't leave her though. He couldn't leave her to whatever fate was inside, maybe to be trapped in the past forever. He had to do something. Reaching forward he plunged himself in that heavy feeling surrounding the door. Before he changed his mind he grasped the handle and went into the fog. He heard Rin calling him as he went through, but he ignored her. Tabitha needed his help.

Amelia's Torment

.

Amelia crouched outside the door in the dark hallway. She was breathing harshly, gulping large lungfuls of air. He wasn't here but he was, he always was and he didn't like it if she cried. Besides she was a little too traumatised to cry. It welled up in her, begging for release but it wouldn't come. It hurt all the more because she had no release from it; it just bubbled and swelled in a painful torrent in her chest, hurting her heart. She knew she would buckle under it one day; there was only so much someone could carry around with them, and only for so long, and Amelia was just about at breaking point. She felt a great deal heavier than her modest seven stone. She felt as if she was carrying a volcano inside her and she wanted out of here. But it hadn't worked.

She rocked furiously now, anger building steadily, making her feel as if she was ready to erupt. She was cheated. It made her want to go and rip the stupid not-blue door off its hinges and throw it down the stairs. She wanted to go in and get a knife from the kitchen and stab his gross stomach with it, and mutilate the fat there. She wanted him to wake up to suffer it. She wanted him to know what it was to feel pain. And more, she wanted to mutilate every part of him to make sure he couldn't hurt her ever again. In all the awful years she had never felt anger like it, and she honestly thought if she didn't move she would explode.

She burst up from the floor, ready to do whatever it took now. To scream, to shout, to dance around his dead body. To smear his blood on her face. To get the knife from the kitchen and make sure he was dead. She knew in her head he must be, but the anger in her had taken over. It was consumed by a need to act, as anger often is. So she strode in through the not-blue door, slamming it into the wall as she went, and making it wobble on creaky hinges. She took the hallway in two big strides, and pushed open the door to the bedroom, and slammed into something solid that hadn't been there a minute ago. She stumbled back, almost falling to the floor before looking up and seeing with horror her father standing in front of her. She gasped, thinking she might throw up.

Not Who I Thought You Were

The fog cleared and in its place was a grand dining room, one that was all too familiar. Tabitha's heart sank; she should have realised by the numbers but she was so keen to see part of her future that didn't make her a murderer that she had stumbled head-long into an uncomfortable past. The large cherry-wood table was draped with an elegant cloth of deep red, and the silver – actual bright, sparkling silver – was set out for six. The wallpapered walls showed off an array of reds and pinks, and creams. Even the gaudy colours were beautiful after so much grey.

Tabitha looked down at herself and saw she was wearing the fitted pink cocktail dress her mother had so happily picked out for her. The pink of the fabric was startling in contrast to the grey: almost hideously bright. As she felt the fine fabric with her hands, the memories of this night came flooding back. Her ring finger on her left hand felt oddly heavy and she looked down at the sparkling diamond set in the platinum band. The one she had been carrying around for a week prior to this night, and the one she would keep carrying around for the next year or so: at least, that was the plan. Then her finger would become even heavier.

Just as Tabitha was about to turn, to go back through the door and escape before the scene engulfed her, her mother entered. Patricia Hamilton, as richly elegant as ever, with a bespoke ball-gown in cream and embellished with a gold lace-pattern, and pearls hanging around her neck. She seemed to float into the room despite the high, pointed gold heels she wore.

'Oh darling, you look fabulous, I knew you would!' she exclaimed.

And just like that Tabitha was plunged into this memory, drawn into the Tabitha of this night, the Futurespan Tabitha hovering just on the edge of her past mind, powerless to do anything except watch. She morphed almost entirely into the old version of herself, just like Diggory had morphed into his six-year-old self, albeit not as radical a transformation. Trapped, she realised with a sinking feeling that this night would play out exactly like before, and all she wanted was to run away, but it was too late. All she could do was observe.

'Are you alright darling?' said Patricia, brushing at her dress, making sure the fabric was laid perfectly.

'Yes, Mother,' said Tabitha.

'Nervous?' she said, smiling a giddy grin.

Tabitha didn't share her enthusiasm. 'Yes, a little, I guess.'

'Why not go and get Minnie to pour you a little sherry, take the edge off. Go on, run along, she's just preparing the starter. It will make you feel better. They'll be here imminently,' she said, beaming.

Tabitha did as she was told and walked along to the kitchen, carefully trying not to trip on the long trailing fabric of her gown. Sighing heavily, she twiddled the oversized gem on her ring finger, easing it up slightly and then back down, getting a little closer each time to pulling it over her knuckle. As she reached the door to the kitchen she pushed the ring firmly back down where it was expected to sit. The kitchen door was the kind that swung both ways: the type that Tabitha thought as a child was found in everyone's home, until she realised they were more commonly encountered in a commercial kitchen.

The Hamilton kitchen was the size of a commercial one and was run as if it were a business with her mother the owner-tyrant, demanding the highest standards from her small staff. The money and emptiness left by her father's untimely departure had caused her mother to embroil herself in the small details of everything. Wanting every part of her life to be just so. Including Tabitha.

As Tabitha entered she was hit instantly by the heat, and the steam in the air; she worried for her hair, or more accurately worried what her mother would have to say if she spoilt her hair. So she waited just in the doorway and called for Minnie. Instead of the ageing chef, who had always seemed like a part of the family, to Tabitha at least, she was met by Sandra, Minnie's second chef and apprentice, who would be taking over from her before long.

'Hi, Sandy,' said Tabitha.

'Hi. Minnie's busy with dinner. Can I help?' she said, not yet having learnt to mask the impatience in her voice. Tabitha was glad for Sandy that it wasn't her mother who had come for the sherry. She observed the sweat beading on Sandra's forehead and running down her red face.

'Only I have a lot to prepare too and –'

'Yes, sorry. I just wanted a sherry, please,' said Tabitha with a small, apologetic smile. She couldn't help wishing it had been Minnie who had greeted her.

'Of course,' said Sandra, rushing off to get it so she could get back to her chores. Tabitha felt a little sorry for the woman. Empathising because of the way her mother treated her, she often felt that she was more part of the staff than the family.

Minnie appeared from round the corner carrying little plates dressed with micro-leaf salad, ready to receive the queen scallops. Tabitha's mouth salivated a little; Minnie's cooking was divine, and much better than what a medical student (even a rich one) was accustomed to.

'Miss Tabitha! This hot kitchen is no place for a lady.'

'I'm not a lady, Minnie,' Tabitha smiled.

'Don't tell that to Mrs Hamilton! And you look like one to me, now out, out! Before you ruin your dress,' said Minnie, shooing her with her hands.

'I'm just waiting for a sherry. Sandra's gone to fetch it.'

'Nerves?'

'Orders,' smiled Tabitha.

'I see, well, wait for it outside,' said Minnie, looking sternly at Tabitha. 'I mean it. It's more than both our lives worth if anything goes wrong this evening, and I have enough on with the food. Now be gone with you! And good luck,' she said, whispering the last part.

'Yes, miss,' said Tabitha, pushing the door again.

'Oh, and Tabitha,' called Minnie. 'Just be yourself and you will be fine!'

If only, thought Tabitha as she waited in the corridor. *If only it was that simple.*

She waited patiently outside the kitchen door, absently fiddling with the ring again; she seemed unable to leave it alone. It seemed so big and out of place, and the platinum of the band positively glowed, especially to Tabitha's Futurespan-dimmed eyes as she watched from inside her past-self's mind. The diamond sat there boldly, glimmering a little too much for her liking. She slipped it over the first joint of the finger, and the next, and almost off. It had become a habit over the last week, since she'd received it; it just didn't feel right. Sandra appeared and she shoved the ring back on, thanking her for the sherry. She thought for a second about asking for the whole bottle but Sandra had already gone back to her preparations, and her mother would not have approved. She shook the thought from her head, glad she had at least a thimble-full; it was better than nothing after all. At least one of her mother's suggestions was welcome.

The doorbell went and her mother flounced out of the dining room.

'I'll get it, Melinda, I'll get it,' she trilled down the corridor. 'They'll soon be family after all,' she beamed, not even noticing Tabitha. It allowed her to retreat into the sitting room, putting off the inevitable meeting for a few moments longer. The sherry was gone in one swift gulp, and she concealed the dainty glass behind the world globe on the shelf of the dresser. She heard the mumblings and excited greetings from the hall, and suppressed the acid that was threatening to rise further into her throat. She smoothed the fabric of the dress down, trying in vain to make it a little less puffy. It wasn't her style at all, but her mother had insisted.

'In you come, in you come,' said her mother.

In came what she could only presume was Mrs Herbert: a short but upright lady, bringing with her an air of entitlement in conflict with her kind smile. Tabitha smiled back, looking into her small, dark eyes and realising the smile didn't quite reach them. Her black dress shimmered as she moved to hold out her hand. 'Tabitha. At last. I'm so pleased to meet you,' she said as they shook hands.

'Pleased to meet you too, Mrs Herbert.'

'Oh Elizabeth, please, easy to remember, just like Her Majesty,' she said, smiling again. 'And my husband is Frank, dear. Not frank as in blunt, Frank as in Frank,' she said, chuckling to herself.

'Yes,' said Tabitha, unsure of herself and this strange woman in front of her. This was the world she had been brought up in, what should feel like her world, but she had never felt more out of place.

'If he ever cares to join us,' said Mrs Herbert, just as a large, red-faced man with white hair emerged into the room. 'Ah here you are, Frank. This is Tabitha, and she's a beauty,' she whispered mockingly behind her hand.

'Indeed, indeed,' he said, his voice booming. 'Miss Evans,' he said, kissing her hand. 'A pleasure.'

Tabitha smiled nervously, feeling like an impostor, feeling the familiar weight of her mother's expectations on her shoulders, pushing her down.

Then in came Damian, the curve of a grin on his lips. 'Good evening, my darling,' he said. 'I hope my parents are behaving themselves.'

'Always,' said Mrs Herbert. 'He always was a cheeky child,' she said to Tabitha.

As her mother came in and saw that everyone was appropriately plied with their favourite beverage, Tabitha found herself shrinking into the background as much as possible. Damian was holding her arm, oblivious, as they talked around her. She found herself fiddling with her ring again, twisting it, wishing she could pull it over the joint, and off. Mr Herbert noticed.

'It's a proud rock, dear girl. Was my mother's. I can see you like it, good taste runs in the family,' he said, winking at his son.

'Yes, it's beautiful,' said Tabitha, retreating into herself again as the conversation turned to cut and clarity, and various other family heirlooms. She wanted to scream at them all, at the pointlessness of their sad lives, and her own.

She was grateful when Melinda came in to announce dinner, and once seated she could play with her ring as much as she liked under the table. She slid it off her finger completely, enjoying the freeness it brought, reluctantly having to replace it before raising her hands above the table to take up the solid silver cutlery. More and more these days she thanked God for small mercies such as this, small little freedoms. Without them she thought she would die.

The dinner continued, much as the conversation had in the sitting room, mostly without her. Without anyone even noticing. She sighed.

'A doctor,' said Mrs Herbert. 'Not long now, your mother says?'

'No,' said Tabitha, coming back to herself.

'We're very proud of her,' said Damian, smiling. 'You'll have your medical career, Tabitha, and I'll have my law firm. We can rule the world,' he said, laughing.

'Indeed,' boomed Mr Herbert. 'Are you looking forward to graduating, Tabitha?'

'A little nervous,' she said.

'Oh, she's always been like that,' said her mother, scolding her with her eyes. 'With no need, she's always been fabulous.'

'Good to be academic,' said Mr Herbert. 'As Damian says, it takes you far in life.'

'And a doctor and a lawyer,' smiled Mrs Herbert. 'It bodes well for the children,' she said mischievously.

Tabitha paled. 'Not yet, Mother,' said Damian. 'We need to get the wedding out of the way first, and the home of course. And Tabitha needs to be a trained GP before we think about that.'

'A GP?' said Tabitha.

'Yes, darling, we can't have you working long hours like a dog in the dirty hospitals forever, can we? No good for raising children.'

'No,' replied Tabitha, thinking that she didn't want to be stuck in an office all day listening to the everyday complaints of the hypochondriac public. She wasn't sure she had even actually envisaged her medical career, but was sure that if she had then it wouldn't have been prescription-pushing in a GP's surgery. Perhaps something calm but interesting like dermatology. Perhaps running away from it all and living in a beech hut, working as a waitress in Bali. She chuckled inside; they had it all planned out for her, but they couldn't plan her dreams. Even if they were dreams that would stay locked inside, never to be seen or acted upon, they were hers and they couldn't be taken.

'You are right, Damian. First things first. You must be looking forward to the big day?' said Mrs Herbert, looking at Tabitha as she pushed carrots absentmindedly around her plate. She looked up dutifully and smiled a small smile. 'Of course,' said Tabitha.

'It's so exciting,' said Tabitha's mother. 'I wish your father was here to see it.'

'Of course, terribly sad he's passed,' said Mrs Herbert. A small silence followed, which she broke. 'Have you looked at dresses yet?'

'Not yet, but I know a lovely boutique dress shop in Harrogate; they are divine.'

'You'll have to let me have a peek once it's decided. And we'll have to synchronise our mother of the bride outfits, it would not do to be matching.'

'Oh yes, and once the colour scheme is picked we will have to get the boys kitted out with matching silk waistcoats and cravats.'

'Yes, any talk of the colour scheme?' said Mrs Herbert.

'We were thinking red and cream,' said Tabitha's mother.

'Timeless,' said Mrs Herbert.

'And the flowers?'

'Tabitha loves lilies,' said Damian, looking proud that he had remembered a detail of his fiancée's taste.

'Lilies! Darling, they're funeral flowers,' exclaimed Mrs Herbert. 'You can't have them for the wedding.'

'It's best left to the women, son. Best left to the women,' Mr Herbert said, as he gulped the wine that was as red as his face.

Damian said no more.

'I was thinking roses,' said Tabitha's mother proudly. 'They're classic and beautiful.'

'Oh, they'd be perfect,' said Mrs Herbert. 'What of the venue?'

'Traditional country estate, after the church of course. My favourite is Oulton Hall.'

'Oh, we've been there, haven't we Frank?'

'Yes, very nice. Good choice,' he said.

'It isn't decided yet but it's a firm favourite.'

'Well, we very much approve,' said Mrs Herbert, smiling. 'And Damian was saying you're thinking of late summer next year. It will be beautiful in the grounds in August time.'

'That's just what I thought,' said Tabitha's mother.

Melinda cleared the main course away and brought out dessert. It was a chocolate mousse elegantly presented in little glass ramekins with flakes of dark chocolate on top. Damian and his father dug in, eating large spoonfuls in quick, greedy gulps. Tabitha surveyed the huge mass that was Mr Herbert, his huge belly pressing into the table, and his face reddened with much consumption of wine. She wondered if Damian would end up that way; she didn't like what she saw. Mrs Herbert was a little more reserved with her eating, but she was obviously enjoying it. Her mother was taking tiny little bits of the pudding, just coating the tip of the spoon, living her theory that ladies shouldn't be greedy. It wasn't good for the waistline. Tabitha left hers untouched.

'Don't you like it, darling?' asked Damian. Tabitha shook her head.

'It was delicious, Mrs Hamilton,' boomed Mr Herbert, taking another gulp of wine. 'It's a shame for any to go to waste.'

'If you're not having it, Tabitha, perhaps you could pass it along for Mr Herbert to enjoy?' her mother said sweetly.

'Of course,' said Tabitha, pushing it along to feed Mr Herbert's growing waistline.

'Are you feeling okay?' her mother asked across the table.

'No,' said Tabitha. 'I feel a little unwell actually. I think I need to go and lie down.' She pushed herself up from the table. 'It was lovely to meet you both, Mr and Mrs Herbert,' she said, remembering her manners. 'Goodnight, Damian. Mother, sorry I can't stay.'

'I hope you feel better, darling,' said Damian. He got up from the table, came over to her and kissed her on the cheek. 'You look pale,' he said, his eyebrows furrowing in concern.

'I'm sure I'll be fine,' said Tabitha.

'Remember she's a doctor, Damian, you should listen to her,' said Mrs Herbert.

Tabitha smiled weakly.

'Good to meet you, Tabitha,' said Mr Herbert, his mouth full of dessert.

'Feel better,' said her mother. 'Shout if you need anything. I'll get Melinda to send you some lemon tea with honey.'

'Goodnight,' said Tabitha, only letting out her long-held breath once she was outside the suffocating room.

And indeed everything played out like before. Just as Tabitha had expected it to. She retreated to her bedroom just like before, but this time instead of the door leading to her bedroom she could see through the doorframe back into Futurespan; she could see the white fog swirling, not realising it wasn't just the white fog she was seeing. Looking again at the doorframe, marvelling that she would be relieved to see the place, she ran for it gladly: the further away from the dining room and the people in it the better.

It took a few seconds for her to get back through the whiteness. Her clothes fell away, replaced with the grey garments that had never been grey before. The ring dissipated as if it had been made of fog too. She had left the night too early to replay when she had gone to bed after dinner and resolutely turned the almost into an off: off and onto the bedside table. Unsure of if it was to stay that way, but happy to play out a small portion of her dreams in reality, even if just for the night.

To her surprise, as she walked further through the fog she bumped into something within it. The fog cleared some more and she could see it was Diggory. He looked at her as if he didn't know her at all. She reached for him, but he bolted to the waiting concrete, out of her reach.

Tabitha waited, stuck in the fog for a few more seconds before she was free and through the door. Rin was at the foot of the landing 'Diggory!' she shouted down the stairs. 'What are you doing? Come back!' Then to Tabitha. 'What happened in there? I told him not to go in but he wouldn't listen.'

'It's a bit complicated,' said Tabitha. 'It isn't as bad as it'll seem, I promise. I've got to explain to him.'

Rin nodded and moved to follow Tabitha.

'No. I need to speak to him alone. Please. I'll stop him going too far and we'll come back for you.'

'You better,' said Rin, as she sat on the floor, pulling at a strand of her already moistened hair. 'And the doors are the way out,' she said sarcastically to herself.

Tabitha ran down the stairs, amazed that she didn't tumble headlong down them as she sped along to catch up to Diggory. She was one landing down before she even heard his footfall. 'Diggory, wait!' she called. 'Please, it's not what it looked like, I don't know how much you saw but would you please just wait?!' Tabitha made it to the next landing and Diggory was standing there, glaring at her. She was out of breath but the words poured out anyway; it was too important to wait. 'It wasn't my choice,' said Tabitha. 'I didn't choose him, I didn't want him. I didn't want to get married.'

'You're engaged,' said Diggory, his voice sounded empty.

'I know, I –' she started.

'You're engaged and you didn't tell me.'

'I know, I'm so sorry. I didn't know how to say.'

'All of the things I told you. About my father, about me, and the past and Rin. And you didn't think to tell me you were engaged?'

'I'm really sorry, Diggory, I know I should've told you. I see that now. I –'

'You kissed me.'

'I know.'

'You're just as cruel as the rest of them, you never really liked me. You have your posh husband-to-be waiting there for you. And don't tell me it was the future or years ago because I looked at the door.'

'Diggory, it wasn't like that. I wasn't even thinking about it. You don't know what it's like to not be in control of your life. To never be. To never even be you. And that's me, Diggory. It wasn't my choice. Not much of my whole life was ever my choice. Don't you see? I didn't, but I do now.'

'Don't know what it's like! Well, you don't know what it's like to be trapped in a prison looking out at the lunatic you've become.

To never know when you'll get out, or if. And if you do how numb you'll be from the meds they've forced down your throat. Or injected in your butt. That's not having a choice, Tabitha. Not just being a passenger in your petty little privileged life.'

'Diggory, I –'

'No, Tabitha. You had a choice. You didn't take it. You sat by and watched it slip away. You hid from your life, and you chose to.'

'It wasn't as simple as that.'

'You either take control of your own life or you don't. You had the means to.'

'It wouldn't have been that easy. I know it looks that way and I know I'm pathetic, and I know I'm weak. I know that. I might have done nothing, I might have stood back, but I didn't choose it. Not really. I didn't want it, Diggory. And I wanted to do something about it. I took the ring off, look. I put it on the bedside table. It's the last thing I remember before this place. I don't know if it's the last thing I did but –'

'You're more of a coward than me, Tabitha. You're a coward. You are weak. Why didn't you tell me?' he said with a strength even Rin didn't know he had.

'I…'

'Why didn't you tell me anything about you?'

'My life's a mess, I barely even think about it, I try not to and I wanted to escape. I was happy to be here away from it all.'

'Barely think about it?! You were sat there while they talked about your wedding –'

'And how many words did I say, Diggory?'

'That isn't the point. You sat there planning the colour of the flowers, and you didn't even mention you were with anyone to me, Tabitha, never mind engaged, never mind planning the wedding.'

'I didn't mean to deceive you, I –' She reached out her hand gingerly towards him and left it hanging limply in the air.

Diggory looked straight into her eyes. 'I thought you liked me.'

'I do.'

'Well, you should've told me. If you really liked me you would've. Your *choice* or not, you are still engaged, Tabitha. You still said you'd marry someone.'

'I know I'm engaged, Diggory, to a perfect match in my mother's eyes. He has a good job, he can provide, he has connections and all the appropriate status and I couldn't give a damn. To me he is an annoying, self-righteous pig that I don't and never could love. And it all seems so silly now that I ever went along with it. I don't even want to touch him, let alone spend the rest of my life with him.'

'Hmm,' said Diggory, crossing his arms.

'I'm engaged in his blind eyes and my mum's eyes and the rest of the world's, I suppose, but in *here*, Diggory, I'm not. I never have been.'

There was awkward silence for what felt like a very long time. Diggory spent it glaring at the floor.

'I am really sorry. I feel kind of free in here, like I can finally start to be me, and the real me wants nothing to do with that stupid man and his oversized, compensatory diamond,' she said. 'I mean it. If it was here now I'd throw it away, and if I could go back I'd end it. I promise you that, but I understand if you don't trust me now. It wasn't fair of me not to say.'

'No, it wasn't.'

'I'm truly sorry.'

'I need some time alone,' he said, curling back into himself. Tabitha was thankful, at least, that he wasn't rocking.

'I hope you understand why, at least a little bit. I'll leave you alone. But please come back, maybe after some sleep or something. I don't want to have ruined everything. I'll just be up here with Rin.' She looked back at him sadly, not wanting to leave him. 'Please come back soon, Diggory.'

He let her leave without saying a word.

Behind the Not-Blue Door

'I killed you,' she said desperately. The image of him lying on the bed, with blood oozing from him, flashed into her mind. She remembered the way she had shaken after she had fired the gun, and the feel of his warm blood on her face. It had been real, and he had definitely been dead. *Had* been. Except now he was very much alive and towering over her.

'What are you staring at?' he said dumbly.

'You were dead,' she said, still in utter shock. 'I killed you.'

'Do I look dead, sweetheart? And tried to kill me? What are you on, like you'd have the balls to. You saying you want to, eh? Well, you'll pay for that.' He pushed her towards the bedroom and her heart sank. She was sure now that she was going to throw up. But he left her there in the doorway, shouting that the washing needed doing. Amelia turned and breathed a small sigh of relief, but before it was all the way out he grabbed her shoulder. She winced, expecting him to push her to the floor, but instead he turned her around.

'I don't know what you are talking about but you better keep your mouth shut. I'm obviously alive. And thirsty. Get me a beer first,' he said.

Amelia walked numbly into the little kitchen, opening the fridge, and pulling out a cold bottle of beer for what was probably the thousandth time. She heard his lazy, stomping footsteps drag his heavy weight into the adjoining living room and sit heavily down on the grubby sofa. Amelia looked at the rise and fall of his gluttonous belly: very much alive. There was no blood, and no wounds that she could see through his filthy vest. Amelia couldn't understand it. It had been so real – had she imagined it? Had this place finally driven her mad? She wasn't sure. This felt real. The bottle felt cold against her palm, as cold as the butt of the gun had when she had shot him. This was just as real as that had been, except how could that have been real when here he was his usual disgusting, living, breathing, drinking self.

'Where's my beer, Amelia? You're slacking, come on now.'

'Sorry, Dad,' said Amelia, slipping back into her familiar character. She scurried across the room and deposited the beer into his pudgy hand, holding it by the bottle neck, careful not to make contact with him.

'I can't drink this, can I, what you want me to do? Break a tooth getting the top off it?'

'Sorry,' stuttered Amelia, berating herself for forgetting such a simple thing. Simple things were so vital to her survival in this place. Grabbing the bottle again she hurried to the kitchen and removed the offending metal, the bottle giving a satisfying hiss as the gas escaped. Again she deposited it in his hand.

'That's more like it. You shouldn't be forgetting these things, Amelia. Doesn't bode well for you. No man wants a forgetful woman. Forgetful women aren't very useful. You need to remember that.'

'I will,' said Amelia as she backed away into the kitchen, glad his attention was occupied, at least for now, with the TV and the beer.

As she went back into the kitchen she looked over at his slumped but alive form, hoping that today might be one of those days where he would drink himself into a stupor. That very thing had happened a few times, most recently on a cold winter day last December. Amelia had got back in from braving the snow and nearly slipping, laden down heavily with shopping bags. Grateful just for making it back through the then-blue door she came in to find him more than a little slumped in his usual spot. He was barely breathing, his awkward posture and extra weight lying heavily on his struggling lungs. There were beer cans strewn about the floor: his cheap stable of Special Brew when he didn't have the money for his favourite Carling Export or Budweiser. Drool was cascading down his chin and forming a pool. Disgusted, Amelia had left him there and had enjoyed a relatively peaceful night in her room, even daring to play a little music quietly. She slept well that night, lightened by the fact that maybe tomorrow his breathing would have stopped and she would wake to find him actually dead. Now she hoped it would be like that day but only this time her wish would be granted. Perhaps this way would be better than a gun – at least this way she wouldn't be a murderer. He wouldn't have turned her into a monster too.

'Don't forget about the washing, Amelia, what did I say about a forgetful woman?' he shouted above the noise of whatever mind-numbing programme he was watching on TV.

'Yes, Dad,' she said.

Going back into the bedroom, she set about collecting clothes from the floor, trying to touch as little of his underwear as possible, using only her fingertips. She cringed but at least it was a task she could set her mind to, a task that was away from him. After pilling the dirty clothes near the door she turned her attention to the bed, half-expecting to see him there cold and dead like he should be. But he wasn't. She thought that maybe she had imagined it: just another daydream. But it was different. It was so real. It happened. Except now he was alive.

Confusion reigned in Amelia; she was unable to put the pieces together. Unable to understand how she had killed him and he could be alive. She knew that both were true. Going to the bed she ripped the sheets back to the mattress which was well worn and stained, but not with blood. It hadn't happened. Or maybe it hadn't happened yet.

She took a deep breath and leant against the wall surveying the bed. It hadn't happened yet. Somehow this was before. Realising this Amelia decided she didn't want to stay here in this timeline where he was still alive. The previous one had been preferable, peaceful, despite the fact it hadn't allowed her to escape from the concrete. At least she had done it. Achieved for a moment her ultimate sorry dream of a world where her father was no more. But this time she had no gun, no way to achieve that peace again. She had to get out.

She scurried from the bedroom; poking her head out she could see the bathroom door was shut, and could hear him groaning in there, as he often did as he tried to navigate his huge weight in the narrow room. Glad he was occupied with something other than her, she bolted from the room, towards the waiting door and back into the closest thing to freedom she had ever had. Futurespan might be a strange concrete wasteland, but the only monster was tucked safely behind the not-blue door. And the door could not be opened by him.

She was thankful for how little she had seen of him, and impatient to get away from this place and think about what to do. If shooting him hadn't worked what else was there? She didn't think she could imagine a bomb. And even so she wagered it would be the same: she would go through and blow him to pieces, yet she would still be stuck. She would go and check if the little bits had somehow put themselves back together only to find him standing there, fully formed, as if nothing had ever happened.

She sank down to the concrete floor and wept, feeling more powerless than she ever had.

Diggory's Descent

Diggory descended again, glad for once to be alone, away from anyone who could hurt him. Anger fuelled him for a good few floors; he wanted to put as much distance between him and Tabitha as possible. As his thoughts turned to her, and how he had thought she was such a nice person, the anger gave way to sadness, and he slouched on the floor of the landing feeling more than a little sorry for himself. He debated going down a few more floors, back to safety. Back to innocence and blissful ignorance. Back to the only time in his life he had felt safe or secure. But Rin's words echoed in his head: *It's a trick. It was never real. It was an illusion.* And he didn't want to make Rin mad or make her cry, and he didn't like it when Rin made him feel like a silly child. He wanted her to take him seriously. She was the only person in the world that was there to look after him, and the last thing he wanted to do was to hurt her. So he scrunched his fists into little balls and pummelled them against his outer thighs, wanting to scream. He wanted to run back to the door, he wanted to feel the warm feeling of home he felt on his floor but he worried it would be too much temptation. *It's an illusion,* he thought very sadly. *It always was.*

But he didn't want to stay here alone with his sadness and he didn't want to go back and see Tabitha. So here he was. His mind wandered and he found himself wondering about his other doors. Wondering what might be behind them. He had been so preoccupied with going through the one he'd gone through, had been drawn to it so strongly he hadn't even considered the other two. He couldn't remember the numbers on them. He knew deep down that Rin was right about the first door, but the other two? Tabitha's door made him think that they would be different and a large part of him was desperate to find out if he was right. They couldn't all be the past, surely, and the numbers would tell him. If they were the future he would have to find out what secrets they held.

With that thought he got up and headed down the stairs. He promised Rin in his head that he wouldn't go back through the first door since he agreed that if she hadn't been there he might have ended up stuck playing aeroplanes forever. And as strangely safe as it was there, he knew she was right; it wasn't safe even then and living in a never-ending illusion wouldn't exactly be an improvement on his life. Things were bad, but not bad enough to want that. It wasn't bad enough to give up completely, to check out, as much as that thought had crossed his mind. The only thing that had ever stopped him was the thought of what it would do to Rin: a father who killed her mother and himself, and then an ungrateful brother who committed suicide. It wasn't what he wanted for her, even if it was often what he wanted for himself. Every time he was in his dark place, in fact, but so far he had remained with it enough for the consideration for Rin to outweigh his own dark desires. Occasionally he had slipped over the edge and Rin or some other poor soul who came across him had checked him into a strait-jacket with a one-way ticket to med-induced numbness.

Since his last spell at St. Luke's, the local mental hospital, Diggory had been a changed person. The new psychiatrist had put him on some new heavy-duty drugs that brought a whole new level of numbness, and some anxiety busters that actually worked. He hadn't felt what you would call happy, but he hadn't been to his dark place in a long time. It might not have been much of a life, but at least it wasn't a precarious one, always balancing on the edge with the threat of dark self-fulfilled annihilation. That at least brought him some comfort.

Diggory did feel like he should have done more with his life. Be doing something with it, after dropping out of school a couple of years ago, unable to cope with the pressure and face the impending exams. It was too much for the damaged Diggory to deal with. He had some sort of breakdown, cut his wrists, and Rin had found yet another member of the family lying there in a pool of their own blood. He hated himself for that. At least this time there was nobody innocent lying there with him, but he wasn't sure that

that made it any better for Rin. He was only fifteen, and the look on Rin's face when he'd come round had haunted him so deeply that he vowed never to put her through that again. His young damaged mind did think for a while that he would just jump in front of a train or off a bridge and at least Rin wouldn't be the one to find him. There would be no blood for her to traverse. But as he matured, and as the drugs started to take effect, he decided it might not involve the pain of actually seeing him there, and reliving finding their parents, but the loss of him wouldn't be any less, no matter how it had happened. So he promised himself he would try his best not to. Try his best to live, even if everything felt empty. Even if he would have given anything to make the overwhelming pain of it all to go away. He didn't want to risk being damned by the suffering he had caused his sister. His sister who'd given up the last of her teens to raise him, while she was trying her hardest to keep herself together. He would surely be damned for eternity for that.

Unless that was what was happening now? He shook his head. It wasn't bad enough for hell, not for him, and Rin hadn't done anything to deserve being in this place. She could never do anything to deserve reliving the night of the bloody shoes. Nobody deserved that. And all Rin had ever done since their parents' death was right.

Diggory felt tired with the weight of his thoughts. It was still too much for him, even all these years on. He curled up on the landing, happy he was alone; he needed some rest. Maybe he wouldn't wake up, as he had often thought; nobody could blame a man for sleeping. Nobody could be damned by their body giving up. If that happened it wasn't by your own doing. It was with this thought that he drifted to sleep.

After some time he awoke; forgetting his thoughts of slipping away into nothingness altogether, he was now more determined than ever that he should return to his floor. It was the only thing that would make him feel any better. He longed for the warm feeling of home. He wondered briefly about going back through the door, back to where everything was alright. Would it be so bad? Maybe that was why he was here: instead of becoming mad he could be Futurespan's answer to Peter Pan. But he knew deep down that flying aeroplanes forever wouldn't make him happy, as tempting as it was; Rin was right about it being an illusion. The funny thing about illusions is that once you see them for what they really are, you can never be tricked by them again. Diggory would never be able to be so truly, naively happy again. He wouldn't go through the door, but the closest he could get to that feeling was on his floor, and there were other doors to investigate.

It wasn't long before he reached his floor, and he couldn't be sure, having not counted the steps, but he thought somehow it wasn't as far as before. Undeterred and feeling as if he was home he sat for a while at the end of his corridor and basked in the warm feeling of safety. After a while he went again to his doors and stood in the centre of them all. To the right was his childhood, and his joyful naivety; he could feel the pull of it, but he wouldn't give in. He longed for its happiness again, to sink into it, and allow the demons that had since taken up permanent residence to melt away, but he knew it was all false. The illusion had been well and truly shattered.

Diggory stood there, torn about whether to try one of the other doors to try for something more palpable. He hoped they might give him some hope, that at least they might offer some glimpse into his future (if there was one). The door to his left felt strange, darker somehow, even though all three were cast in the same dim greyness. Despite the dark feeling Diggory was drawn to it: simple morbid curiosity or self-destructiveness, he wasn't sure. Unable to help himself he went to it, the number 70393130320 written simply on the door as if a door to the future was nothing more spectacular than to an office. It was six years in the future. There was perhaps a future after all. He reached out to it, awed that behind that door lay some version of his future. Perhaps not a very good one, he thought, hesitating, thinking of Tabitha. But the pull of it was strong and whatever it was he had to see it. It turned out that gazing into the future was much more enticing than his happy, illusory past.

A small part of him had expected something more spectacular to precede his future, but as he opened the door he saw the same white fog as always. He stepped into it, feeling the coldness tingling on his arms and creeping into his lungs. Breathing deep lungfuls of it he waited as it swirled and changed, getting ready to reveal this snapshot of a future.

Diggory took a breath as it started to clear, and he could make out a small room. There was a bed, a bedside cabinet and a door to an en-suite. It looked like a shabby hotel room. No, that wasn't quite right; hotels didn't look like this. Hospitals did. *Noo!* screamed Diggory in his head, his last thought being that this had not been a good idea, before he was sucked into the mind of his future self who was sitting on the bed.

He looked down at himself. He had always been skinny, but now he was skeletal. This Diggory was in control now, this future version, with the current Diggory demoted to being a mere spectator. This future Diggory was hugging himself tightly, and the spectating Diggory could feel the harsh protrusion of his ribs. *Not good,* he thought. Diggory was rocking on the bed, holding himself tightly, and emitting an odd high-pitched squeaking noise. The spectating Diggory, powerless to stop him, could only observe that this was *definitely not good*.

The entrance of a nurse confirmed Diggory's worst fear. She came up to him, shushing him and telling him it was okay. She seemed, to the spectator, to be on autopilot; perhaps she told this to many wrecked souls several times a day. The nurse eased him onto the bed, and Diggory continued his rocking supine, muttering something indiscernible under his breath.

'Roll over now,' said the nurse, her voice laced with a thick Zimbabwean accent.

Diggory continued his rocking. It seemed he hadn't even heard the nurse. She began rolling his light weight over anyway, and he did nothing to protest. Once he was prone she pulled down his shorts and boxers, exposing his white buttock before injecting him with something. She rubbed it a little, replaced his clothing and made her exit, uttering something mundane and calming on her way out. The rocking subsided slowly. And the Diggory on the bed fell into a deep, drug-induced sleep.

The spectating Diggory however, was still very much awake, and very much troubled. This was his future. A crippled shell of a man, locked away and having drugs injected into him to try and calm him into some version of normalcy. Or some quiet, easy-to-deal-with patient at least. Nothing about this was normal. And nothing about this seemed temporary either. It wasn't like the other times when he'd had a huge one-off breakdown, been admitted, drugged-up, 'treated' and shipped off under the 'care' of the community mental health team. What a joke that had been, but at least the system had shipped him out as some sort of semi-functioning human. The person asleep on the bed was not that at all. Not even close. He seemed to Diggory that he had gone over the precipice of darkness that had always lingered invitingly in his mind, and hadn't been able to crawl back out. He had gone so far into the darkness, perhaps there was no coming back. Diggory wondered how long this future-him had been here for. At a guess, Diggory thought, years: this didn't happen overnight.

He was certainly broken now. Rin's worst fear had come true. Here he was: the biggest disappointment in his family since his father. At least he hadn't murdered his wife. At least he didn't think he had. The most disturbing thing about all this for the current Diggory was the huge question mark over how he had ended up like this. He really hoped that he hadn't followed in his father's footsteps. He didn't think so: he had always been a little unstable, but his thoughts had never turned to violence or murder, at least not of anybody else. Six years surely wasn't long enough to do *that* to a man. But it was long enough to do *this* to him.

This really was *not good. Not good at all.*

He had to find out how he had ended up here. It was frustrating beyond all belief to be stuck in his future-self's sleeping head. He wasn't going to get any answers here. If only he could step outside of this Diggory and leaf through his notes or listen in on the nurses' conversation he might glean some vital clue. If delving into the past and the future was possible, then why not? But he was stuck. Stuck, and unable to even venture back to Futurespan in the hope that the third door might shed some brighter light on his future. There was no other choice but to wait it out. There was something he was meant to see here, and he didn't think it was only this. There must be more clues to come.

The current Diggory wondered how long he would sleep for,

and more to the point, how long those waiting hours would feel to him. Nothing to do but to wait, and mull over the many horrid possibilities of his ending up here. To consider the awful nature of his future, and wonder at how solid it was. Was this the way it would be? Set in stone? Surely not.

Grasping around, hating the darkness and the waiting and the unknown, Diggory realised that the answers he longed for were right here, tucked away somewhere in the darkness of his future mind. How to get at them was a difficulty, but they were here somewhere, they had to be. He could feel them whispering to him in the dark.

He hoped the answers wouldn't be what he feared. He hoped that whatever it was, that it was changeable. This empty darkness was not how he wanted to live his life.

So he called to the memories, calling them into being, calling them to show him how this had come to be. And they answered, and there was no white fog this time, but the cold whoosh and the tingling was all the same, and the darkness dissipated, revealing memories.

It all played out as if on a movie screen, giving Diggory a welcome reprieve from the darkness. He couldn't feel anything this time, and he wasn't watching through his own eyes; he was bizarrely watching himself. The scene before him was a party in a rundown house somewhere. Dance music and screaming could be heard and the flicker of amateur disco lights threw dancing colours across dirty walls. Diggory was in the living room of the house, sitting on a sagging sofa with what must have been at least his tenth can of beer in his hand. Beside him was a man smoking a bong, obviously completely stoned. The future Diggory eyed it with curiosity. The man happily handed it to him and Diggory handled it clumsily. The man encouraged him along with a couple of the other stoned people in the room. Diggory at first took a cautious drag, before taking another and then another deeper drag, before finally leaning back as stoned as the man on the sofa. He looked relaxed. He looked as if all of his troubles had slipped away. Maybe that was the idea, thought Diggory, not liking where this was going. Not liking it all.

The scene faded briefly to black and the next scene was of Diggory alone in what seemed to be his own small bedsit. He was unsure of how he actually ended up there; maybe Rin had kicked him out, or she had gone off to get on with her life. Or he had left. Who knew? It wasn't like they were going to live together forever, but it didn't look like Diggory was doing so well for himself. Diggory peered at the screen and saw that he was rolling a spliff, all of the tools neatly lined up on a tray he kept under the sofa: his Rizlas, roaches, a small pile of tobacco pulled from a discarded cigarette and his ounce of cannabis poking out of its little plastic packet. Once he was satisfied he licked the edge of the Rizla, pushing it together before putting it to his mouth and lighting it. He leaned out of the window, smoking it happily. The watching Diggory was more than a little perturbed now; trying a bong at a party was one thing but smoking it alone, in a bedsit, wasn't just curiosity, it was habit. And a bad habit, by all accounts, especially for someone with mental health problems to start with. Cannabis screws up your head.

The scene again dissipated to blackness and Diggory indeed saw that it did screw with his head. There he was in the same bedsit as the vision before, but things had deteriorated. The place was a mess. There were food cartons littered across the kitchen counters, and numerous boxes and bottles littering the floor. Diggory was sprawled out on the sofa. He looked like a tramp. The Diggory watching briefly thought at least he wasn't on the street, but looking at the state of his accommodation this wasn't really much better. He wasn't looking after himself, that much was plain to see.

The watching Diggory's eyes fell upon a familiar tray at the side of the sofa. Except this time it didn't have the comparatively innocuous tobacco, Rizlas and cannabis. This time there was a needle, a metal spoon and a lighter. He didn't know how long things had taken to get this bad. But they were bad. The facility he had seen himself in was probably for mental drug addicts. He couldn't believe he would ever be so stupid as to get into heavy drugs, but maybe he had finally found an escape that wasn't at the mercy of a rope or a train. Something perhaps that his damaged mind rationalised as better than ending his own life, or living on through his living hell of problems.

But I can't end up like that, thought Diggory desperately in his own future head. *I can't.* Deep, sickening disappointment settled on him as the scene faded thankfully to black.

The blackness was slowly penetrated by swirling tendrils of fog, and Diggory knew this nightmare version of his future was over. It probably hadn't been very long but a few seconds of seeing himself like that had been enough. He was just grateful he hadn't seen Rin's reaction in his visions. That might have broken his heart. As he was fully surrounded by the fog again he regained a sense of his physical body and could feel moisture seeping from his eyes. He was crying for the bleakness of what he had seen, and he again wondered at the surety of these visions. The past had been a concrete replica of the house, of how Diggory had been as a child. Sure, it hadn't been an exact replica of a scene, but everything else was spot on. Maybe the tray would be a bit further pushed under the sofa, maybe he would be lying on the floor, or in a different bedsit altogether in the *real* future, but none of that would matter, he would still be a drug addict. It would still lead him down the road into that dark pit in his mind that was so deep and black, no light would ever lead a way out.

He hoped it wasn't set in stone.

And with that hope he stepped back through the emerging fog, into the relative sanity of the present.

Future Dreams

Amelia had waited on her *safe* concrete landing, the one about ten floors down from the not-blue door. She went there to try and recapture some sense of peace, but the empty nothingness of it was almost as bad as being trapped in the flat. She didn't like being alone. She didn't like the strange not-blue door and the horrors she had been through behind it. She was more than a little traumatised by those. But not knowing what else to do she decided she would try the not-blue door once more.

She walked back through the door hoping something was different, that there was some clue inside as to how she could leave this place, and perhaps more importantly some clue as to how to fix her sorry life. She feared that perhaps she had already slipped into the dark depths of insanity: that would explain the gloominess of the concrete world at least. But she needed some help, a way out, anything. It was perturbing that the grey world was devoid of signs. She would have liked a 'way out' sign, or preferably a 'way out to a better life' sign; that would have been perfect.

Quite suddenly she realised that she felt different. Feeling down her body she noted that her bust was more pronounced and she had gained weight. She needed a mirror to see her face. Tumbling into the bathroom, hoping he would leave her alone long enough to see herself, Amelia made it to a mirror and the reflection staring back was not what she had imagined; she wasn't just older, she looked *old*. There were dark circles under her eyes, wrinkles forming on her forehead and her skin had lost its youthful, dewy glow: it looked grey (no surprise there). Greyness aside, she looked ill. These were the outward signs of a mind that had taken too much, of a body saying enough is enough. At a guess Amelia thought this vision of herself was a few years her senior, maybe four at the most, but it looked more like ten. *Nothing has changed*, she thought sadly. *I wouldn't look like this if it had.*

Amelia filled her hands with cold water from the gurgling tap and splashed it over her face, rubbing at her eyes hoping to wash the black marks of weariness away. Her fingers felt into the new delves on her forehead, and she wondered how haggard she would look in another ten years. Her mother had looked old and worn-out in the end. The smoking hadn't helped and had aged her more thoroughly but it was more that the life had been truly squashed out of her by him. Looking back in the mirror Amelia could see that would be her fate too; he had already squashed so much hope and life from her she wondered what she had left now. Any more and she thought maybe she would just cease to be a person one day. Perhaps that day had already come because she was still here, under his rule, her life still not her own. She was merely being lived like always, rather than living for herself and she knew this without even knowing what had become of her life, and she was at least a year past sixteen. All she knew was that being here wasn't what she wanted for herself, it wouldn't allow her to be anything that deep down she was screaming to be. But it wasn't that easy to escape, she knew that too. And here she impossibly was, years down the line, knowing that nothing of any importance had changed.

'Amelia,' came the shout from the living room. The shout she wished her gun had silenced forever.

Amelia hurriedly dried her face and went into the living room. The man in there was largely unchanged, just wider now in proportion with hopefully an equally enlarged liver. It saddened Amelia to see that he was undoubtedly grey, not even a hint of yellow. Although there were no colours here still, so he could be yellow really. She hoped so.

'Yes, Dad?' she replied, standing in the doorway, debating leaving already.

'Give us twenty, will ya,' he said, not even turning to look at her.

'Sorry?' said Amelia, confused.

'I know your little secret. I know you've been working extra at the Dog and Horse and I know Dick will have paid you yesterday so cough up, you can't live under my roof for free you know. You're a woman now, aren't you?'

Amelia, unsure of herself, whispered something to appease him and drifted back into the corridor into her room opposite the bathroom, leaving the door open so she could hear if he moved: she didn't want to be surprised by him. She had an escape now back into the world of concrete and she intended to use it.

Looking around her room she could see it hadn't altered much, the older version of herself no doubt saving every penny to get out of this dump. Although perhaps not saving much if he was always asking for it like this. Casting her eyes around, surveying the cheap, battered furniture, with the white veneer peeling to reveal nothing remotely similar to real wood beneath. Everything about this place told Amelia she wasn't good enough: everything from the crappy furniture to the childish pink bed-sheets. Looking around her now she wondered where her mother had ended up, if she was living in a tower block with peeling furniture or had made a life for herself somewhere and had silk dresses and oak cabinets. Amelia sometimes liked to think of her mother like that, living a nice life after all of this. But another part of her thought that if that was the case there was no excuse for not coming back for her daughter, so she could live a nice life too, instead of leaving her here to rot. Her mother had never even sent her a card, or even better any money, and he was too lazy to pick up the post so she knew if there ever had been anything he hadn't taken it. In these thoughts, and her anger about all of her wasted years, and the state of her face, she realised she did blame her mother. She was weak. She was meant to look after her but instead she had run, which Amelia had always understood. What she couldn't understand was why she had never come back for her, and it turned out she did blame her for that.

Shouting from the living room (something about keeping him waiting) roused Amelia from her thoughts. The money. The money she, in some future continuation of hell, had earned, and now he wanted to take it. Not wanting him to chase her out again, she decided to give him the money and hope it would appease him long enough for her to quietly exit this future hell and go back to the concrete solitude. Worse, in some ways, but better that she was away from him and much better that she had not yet aged so ungracefully. Looking about her she realised she had no idea where the money was. Where would an older Amelia hide it? She had never had any money to hide before. Considering the various hiding places – under the bed, in the bedside drawer, in the wardrobe – her eyes settled on a bag hung on the handle of the door. Rooting inside the cheap plastic she found a brown envelope with her name scrawled across it. Inside she found two twenties and a ten. Even though she knew this wasn't strictly real, her heart still leapt with the realisation he wouldn't be getting it all. As she went to put the remainder of the money back where she had found it she stalled thinking again. She pulled the other twenty out and hastily stuffed it in the inside of her pillow, putting it on the underside so the shape wouldn't be seen through the cheap fabric.

'Took your time,' he said as she approached. 'Weren't counting it, were you?'

'No, Dad, here,' she said, holding out the twenty.

He grasped it and her hand, holding it firmly, squeezing it a little too hard. She tried to pull away but he held her firm. 'You won't be planning to be up to no good with what's left of that money now, will you? Not planning on doing anything silly now?'

'No,' Amelia whispered.

'You sure about that?'

'That's most of it, I don't have much left, I'm not going to do anything silly.'

'Promise?' he growled.

'I promise.'

He released her hand. 'Good, now go and use what's left to get a Chinese. Want the works: beef curry, spring rolls, chow mein, fried rice and those crackers. Need a nice treat now you're a working woman, don't you think? Make up for the hours I gotta do without you around.'

Amelia was shocked; even though she should've known this was what would happen, she was still shocked after all these years. His cruelness was more than her delicate heart could bear. 'I've only got a tenner left, Dad.'

'Well, I'm sure you'll sort it out. You were resourceful enough to get that job weren't you.'

'Yes,' she said quietly. 'I'll go now.' Stopping at the bedroom she fetched her envelope, leaving the twenty under the pillow, hopeful that if this future did happen that the future Amelia would find it there and it would give a little glimmer of hope that she was just a little bit closer to real escape. Clutching the envelope she opened the blue door, taking one last look at the shabby flat, hoping she wouldn't be doomed to spend another three years or more here, before she walked solemnly into the fog.

Jetson's Struggle

Jetson lay on the landing, eyes shut, head swimming with the conversation with the nun. *You don't know that she is dead.* He hardly dared to think about those words and what they meant. If he thought about them he would have to face up to what he had been doing here, and how long he had been here for.

He was glad he had been pretty much right about Futurespan but it didn't make any of it any easier. Every fibre of his being wanted to run back down the stairs and pretend that nothing had happened. To guide the newcomers as usual and not say a word to them or even to Stacey-Barbara. To pretend that the nun had never existed and to spend what would feel like weeks or months with the newcomers, to help them, to go through their fear with them. *Hypocrite,* came a voice loud inside his head. And he knew it was right. Telling Diggory there was no need to be scared when he was the biggest chicken in Futurespan: that made him a hypocrite alright.

He dragged himself up off the ground. *You don't know she's dead,* echoed the serene voice of Sister Elaina. That had given him hope, as much as he hated it. He wasn't sure if it was enough hope to relive what he had thought was her death, or if not hers then – no. He couldn't bear to think about that. He would just go back down the stairs and –

HYPOCRITE! came the voice again, screaming for attention.

He had to face this. The nun was right that it had been much too long, and he couldn't stay here forever. *You don't know she's dead.* Maybe he could face it with hope. Hope that it wasn't as he thought. Then he would unlock the other doors and finally get some answers. Finally face the uncertainties he had been avoiding.

He stepped onto his landing with mixed feelings as always. The sense of the familiar, and the somewhat friendly was strong here. He supposed it was because it was his. But he felt sick, not just to his stomach, but to his bones. Sick with guilt and regret. He did not want to do this. But he had to know.

He stood outside the offending door, feeling the emotions pulsing from it. His emotions from that day spilled out and gripped him. Hot anger, followed by waves of sick, grim disbelief and regret. Backing away from it his mind turned to the other doors; he needed a minute. He stood outside the one to the left. There didn't seem to be any feeling from this door; it felt as if it was dead. Jetson shuddered at the thought. The numbers read 111063030614. This one was in the future. He turned to the other. That was, too. He sighed, and reached for the cold handle. He grasped it and he tried to turn it: no luck. He went for the other one and it was the same – there was only one option left, as deep down he knew there would be.

Jetson stood at some distance from the door, sizing it up, knowing he had to go closer. He had to go through it again. He had to go back through the door, back down the rabbit hole, back into hell. He couldn't keep running around this place like a demented hobo. At least he had had a home, and now it was time to revisit it. Back to that day. Back to start the journey to see what happened next. It was time. It was. The nun was right.

He stepped forward, shaking inside. Anger washed over him and regret settled low in his gut. He breathed through it and grasped the deathly cold handle. Puffing his breath out forcefully he pushed it down, pausing for a second before going through the door. The fog swirled around him, penetrating his skin, making him feel as if the cold, grim sickness was infiltrating his body and gripping every cell. He felt terrible, and was desperate to turn back to the plain safety of the concrete.

You don't know she's dead. He clung to that.

The fog cleared and Jetson was sitting again at his kitchen table, on that fateful Saturday in April. His Futurespan-self receded into the background of his mind, as it had done on his first time through the door, and he relinquished any control of himself, destined only to watch as the events played out just as they had done. He would behave just as he had, powerless to do anything more than relive, without change, the worst moment of his entire life.

Jetson put his hands down and felt the familiar oak beneath his fingers; he liked the roughness and the notches. It had been passed down from his grandfather and despite his wife's protests he refused to get rid of it, as it reminded him too fondly of the happy moments of his childhood. He looked at her now as she stood staring out of the window at their small garden, her head cocked slightly to the side as always when she was thinking, allowing her straight brown hair to just touch her right shoulder. She looked innocent: like butter wouldn't melt, he thought. But Jetson knew that was a façade. He felt the anger building up inside him, coming deep and strong and fast. Threatening to burst out of him in a fury and engulf all his reasonable senses. He could hear his blood pounding in his ears and he wanted to throw his beloved old table across the room. How could she! He felt a growling anger growing inside him; he glared at her. She smiled at him, the upturn of her lips faltering as she saw his expression.

'Whose is it, Sonia?' he growled.

'What are you talking about? What's the matter?' she said, those big eyes of hers full of concern, and her free hand resting on her protruding stomach.

Jetson's eyes rested there, thinking of the baby and of whose baby it was. It fuelled his rage. 'You,' he spat. 'You're the matter.'

'Jetson, I –' she stammered. 'What's wrong?'

'Whose is it, Sonia? Tell me.' He glared at her, swallowed by anger.

'Jetson, I don't know what you're talking about, you're scaring me.' She put the cup carefully down on the counter and took a small step back.

'That,' he said again, pointing at her swollen belly. 'Whose is that?'

'Our baby? Is that what you're talking about?'

'Is it ours though? That's the question,' he said with his eyes wide and his voice wild.

'Of course it is. Where's all this come from?'

'I'm not blind and I'm not stupid, either. That's where it's coming from, Sonia.'

'What do you mean? Speaking to me like this isn't good for the baby,' she said.

'All concerned about the baby, I see,' said Jetson. 'His baby.'

'It's your baby, Jetson. Our baby. Of course I'm concerned about it. I have no idea what you're saying here. You sound like a madman.'

'I have been mad,' said Jetson, clenching his fist in a ball. 'But I'm not now.'

'It's our baby, of course it is because we're married for god's sake – what do you think of me?' she said, hurt showing clearly in her voice now.

'It's never happened before, Sonia. Five years since we wed and no baby. Not until now. And I've been mulling that over. And it's funny that there's a baby now, don't ye think? Now you've been spending so much time with him.'

'Who?'

'Mike,' said Jetson. 'Who else, Sonia?'

'Mike? I've been helping him.'

'I bet you have.'

'Jetson,' said Sonia, appalled, her hand protectively on her stomach and tears in her eyes. 'I can't speak to you like this. I think you need to think about what you're saying. I'm going in the bath.'

As she left the kitchen Jetson sat there seething, shaking with rage. But he wasn't finished. He stormed up the stairs and into the bathroom where Sonia was folding her towel over the end of the bath. The water was running, sending plumes of hot steam up into the air.

'You didn't answer me,' said Jetson. 'Don't you think it's funny that we've never conceived a baby before, not in all these years?'

'No, it happens all the time. Now's our time, it wasn't before. The body has its own mysteries. And that's all the mystery there is to it. I'm pleased we have a baby on the way. We've waited long enough.

I thought you were pleased too. '

'You were spending more time with him six months ago than me, Sonia. We hardly had chance to get pregnant. What are the chances really after five years?'

'Jetson, you're being ridiculous. You need to calm down. I need to have a bath and relax. Stress is bad for the baby, the baby we've waited so long for. So just go away and think about what you're saying, will you.'

'I know what I'm saying. You're just trying to hide it because I've guessed the truth.'

'I'm not. Leave me alone now.'

'No. I've had doubts for months – ticking over in my mind, driving me mad.'

'Not now Jetson. Not when you're like this,' she said, turning her back on him to pour bubble bath into the flow of water. Jetson watched as the many little bubbles formed, and then he leaned over and turned off the bath.

Sonia looked at him, with big, sad eyes and tears streaming down her face. 'I need to have a bath.'

'Well, I need to talk to you.'

'Jetson, I don't know what has gotten into you. I don't want to talk to you until you've calmed down.'

'I only ever wanted a baby, Sonia,' he said sadly. 'It broke my heart that we couldn't and then I was so happy. But I've been such an idiot all this time and I want answers.'

'About what? It's our baby, of course it is. What else can I say?'

'About the fact that suddenly there's a baby when you've were spending all your time with him.'

'Mike was struggling. He was lonely. I thought you understood.'

'And you kept him company. Nice, Sonia. Real nice.'

'Jetson, you're impossible,' she said, pushing past him out onto the landing. Jetson followed her, shouting her name. She turned with one foot over the edge of the top step.

'Why, Sonia, why do that to us? Did I disappoint you so badly as a man that you thought you'd look elsewhere and bring a cuckoo to our nest?'

'He lost his wife, Jetson!' she screamed.

It all happened quickly then: she turned, losing her footing slightly. Jetson went to grab her, not to stop her from falling as he didn't realise she was, but to stop her from leaving. As she leant back and away from him she lost her footing completely, and fell backwards down the stairs, tumbling as she went.

She smacked against the floor of the hallway with a sickening crunch. Jetson stood at the top of the stairs looking down at her.

The Futurespan-self in his mind was seeing it for the third time and seeing himself the same as he always was, stunned and still before rushing down the stairs, desperate that he couldn't rouse her, horrified at the awkward angles of her body. He'd hurried to the phone and grabbed it, his large fingers jabbing the nine three times, his panicked voice saying his wife had fallen down the stairs, saying it was an accident when he knew it was his fault. He looked down at the broken body of his wife, worried his rage had ripped what would be a permanent, irreversible rift between them. The wait for the ambulance had felt like a lifetime as he had crouched next to her, stroking her arm, listening to the simultaneously comforting and haunting sounds of her breathing. He thought that he would prefer it if she was screaming; at least then he would've known the blood pouring from her head wasn't the last of her faculties running out onto the floor.

The paramedics came and sprang into action, injecting her with drugs unknown to Jetson, bandaging her head, strapping up her ankle. They attached oxygen and monitors as Jetson stammered that she was six months pregnant, and that she had slipped. They bundled her away from him, as he didn't feel able to move and they'd established he wasn't hurt; they implored him to ring someone, and said they had to hurry. Jetson didn't remember anything after that. Just her limp and broken body being wheeled away from him out of the door.

None of that happened this time. This time Jetson stood there motionless as he looked down at the still body of his wife and the blood slowly seeping into the carpet. He watched this as the white fog swirled around him. He looked away, distraught that his wife was now lying down there instead of safely in the bath as she would have been if he hadn't turned into such a monster. He'd lost control of himself and look where that had got him. His wife unconscious on the floor. So he walked away from the scene, knowing it didn't matter how quickly he called for an ambulance; all this had already played out. He was disgusted with himself, relieved to see the door to Futurespan where the bathroom door used to be, the white fog permeating from it.

Jetson came out of the door gasping, feeling as if he was going to choke. Tears streamed down his face and great sobs shook him uncontrollably, making it even harder to breathe. He didn't even notice that Elaina had reappeared and was standing there, just as serene, until she spoke to him. 'It's okay now, Jetson. You can breathe. It's done now. It's all in the past.'

Jetson carried on sobbing and shaking, still trying to breathe.

'It's done, Jetson, and you can't change it. You can only move forward into the future.'

'I can't,' Jetson sobbed.

'You can. You must. You must go through your other two doors now. I would recommend the one on your left first. You need to do it now before this sadness consumes you again.'

'It never stopped.'

'But it numbed, and it got a little easier to bear. You must do it now before Futurespan consumes all that is left of you. Do it now for yourself. Do it now for Sonia.'

'What if I killed her, what if I killed the baby?' cried Jetson.

'Then it is done. But you don't know. She might not be dead, the baby might not be dead and here you are rotting and running away. If you don't go through those doors you will spend an eternity here never knowing what happened to Sonia and the baby. Is that what you want?'

'No,' sobbed Jetson. 'No.'

'Then go through the door, Jetson. That one,' she said, pointing at the door she had mentioned earlier. 'Go now.'

Jetson looked at her, long and hard, knowing that she was right. He had felt the weight of the darkness of this place, the weight of his guilt and sadness heavy on him lately. It had been growing heavier, no matter how far from his floor he roamed; no matter how far he tried to run it was with him always. Some actions are too big to ever be hidden, or to hide away from and Jetson had finally realised this.

He took the distance to the door in three huge strides, and flung it open, rushing into the familiar white fog. Hoping he had something left to rush in for.

Diggory after his Door

Diggory had slammed the door shut. He'd been wrong to think the other doors would be better. It was worse. Far worse. He should have listened to Rin and stayed away from the awful things. Maybe she was right and they were gateways to hell. Whatever they were they tortured whoever went through them.

Diggory was torn: both traumatised and comforted. Tempestuous emotion clung heavily to his chest. The scene behind the door was awful, haunting, his worst fear realised. And he would be powerless to even end it all. Yet he was comforted he was on his floor; despite the horror, he still felt safe here. It still felt like his.

Maybe he should be glad he had seen it. Maybe they were a warning, like Rin had said. Tabitha went through her first door so she would never become a doctor who killed people, and Diggory would never become a locked-in lunatic, trapped in a drug-induced coma for forever. He hoped that was it. He didn't want what was behind that door to become his grim reality. It would destroy Rin, even if he wouldn't be with it enough to comprehend the awfulness of his life.

Maybe Rin was right about it all being an illusion. The first door certainly was. Maybe the future was too. And they weren't the way out. But there must be a point to it all, otherwise why would the doors be here? That at least filled him with some hope that he had been shown his future for a reason. Maybe it was to warn him, and if the future behind that door wasn't inevitable then maybe he would get a chance to change it. That would mean there was a point to the horrors behind the doors. But it didn't fit for Rin's door – there was no changing that. Perhaps they just didn't understand the point yet. The point seemed to be to hurt people, and if that was their purpose then they worked splendidly.

Diggory curled himself up, exhausted by it all.

Jetson's Door

The fog cleared around Jetson and he found himself outside the door of a hospital side-room, his head level with the little window, allowing him to see through. He peered in but could only see the foot of the bed. The open Futurespan door stood directly behind him, white fog swirling angrily. The sounds of a hospital ward echoed around him, but he couldn't see anything except the doors he was wedged between. He'd had enough of doors to last him a lifetime and here he was stuck between two of them. He knew that turning back wasn't an option – the nun was right. So it had to be the other door.

Looking at the bumps showing through the hospital blanket, he felt ill. The sense of foreboding was palpable in the air, and he felt as if he was standing at the top of the staircase again. He didn't need to see the rest of the body to know whose feet they were. The fleeting bolt of anticipation, of near-excitement at seeing Sonia again after so long alone was gone as soon as it had come. It was replaced by trepidation. He didn't know what would come next. All he knew was that she was here by his doing.

You don't know she's dead.

He swallowed. His gaze was fixed on her feet, tiny peaks under the blanket, still and unmoving. He hoped she was sleeping; surely she must still be breathing otherwise he'd have been brought to the morgue instead of here. Had to be: Jetson was sure the nun wouldn't have said that, and then let him open the door to see her dead. Even if it wasn't a definite future, she wouldn't do that, he was certain of it. Well, pretty sure of it: she wasn't your typical nun after all.

He supposed it was time to face whatever it was.

He opened the door slowly and the rest of the body came into view. The still form of Sonia was lying there and Jetson recoiled from the sight. She was connected to a number of tubes of which Jetson didn't know the purpose. He found himself unable to move any further into the room and stood there simply taking in the terrible scene, quite unable to go any closer. One hand rested on the door handle as he watched the rise and fall of her chest powered by the machine: what must be the breathing tube snaked into her mouth, held in place by tape. The sound of the puffing bellows of the machine pushing the air into her lungs was grotesque; worse even than the sound of her body smacking against the floor. He edged slightly closer and saw that it was as he feared: her stomach was flat, deflated and empty. He didn't know what had happened to the baby.

He barely dared get closer, and looked away, desperately hoping that when he looked back she would be well, and he wouldn't be responsible for this horror. But the scene was of course unchanged.

After a few more moments of sadly watching he went slowly to her side and held her hand. It wasn't as warm as he remembered it being, but he sat there next to the bed, holding it tightly, hoping the temperature wasn't a bad sign. Sonia's face was barely recognisable: pale and obscured beneath the array of unnatural tubes coming out, she looked like something from a movie, not his wife. His hand reached out as he gently felt for her stomach beneath the blankets, just to be sure, and found it was as flat and empty as it looked. His heart sunk to depths it hadn't before. The baby must dead, and it was all down to him.

Jetson tried speaking to his wife but he found his throat was utterly choked; he couldn't believe he'd done this. Couldn't believe how stupid he'd been. He clasped her hand tightly, willing her to wake up. 'Sonia, I'm so sorry,' he said finally. 'I'm so so sorry. Please wake up. Please forgive me, I never meant to hurt you. Please.' The last word hanging there felt misplaced and empty. Powerless. It echoed their last awful conversation *Please, Jetson*. To think of it made Jetson feel sick. If only he'd listened to her before she'd ended up tumbling down the stairs, before she had ended up in a hospital bed and it was somehow too late.

The door clicked open and in walked a doctor in dark blue

scrubs with a black stethoscope hanging proudly round his neck. 'Ah, Mr Guthrie, I'm glad you're here, but I'm afraid the news isn't good. We've had the test results back. Mr Guthrie?'

Jetson had been staring at his wife, still not fully able to comprehend what he was seeing. What he had done. He looked up at the doctor. 'Will she be okay?' he asked.

'I'm very sorry, Mr Guthrie, but things aren't looking good.'

'Can't you fix it, Doctor? Will she wake up?'

'We've been over this, do you remember?' said the doctor with practiced patience. 'I know it's very difficult for you to absorb but the chances of Sonia waking up are very slim. She's very weak, she has been in a coma for over a month now, with the added complication of her haemorrhage leading to a complex surgery and loss of your baby. Her body has been through an awful lot.' He sighed, a frown on his face accentuating lines that were now a permanent feature, probably from years of standing in similar rooms delivering similar news.

The baby was dead. He had lost everything. He had killed his baby, and possibly his wife as well. He was the very worst kind of human – he hurt those he should have loved. This time irreversibly. And all down to his stupid irascible nature.

'We have the results of the EEG scan, the test for brainwaves,' the doctor continued. 'There isn't much activity, I'm afraid. We would have expected much more recovery by now and we aren't seeing it. I doubt that this will improve; it is highly unlikely that this activity will ever increase to normal levels. The damage in her brain is extensive.'

Jetson was stricken: this is what he had feared all along. What he had been running from all this time and now she lay cold and nearly dead in front of him. Every time he looked at her he could see her falling down the stairs and could hear the sickening crack over and over again. He saw the blood seeping from her damaged head – what was her mind running away into the carpet.

'I thought she was going to be okay,' said Jetson.

'Her condition has always been very serious, Mr Guthrie. I know it is so very difficult to comprehend but she has not regained any kind of consciousness or independent function. When we tried to take her off the ventilator last week it was not successful: she cannot breathe for herself. It has been over six weeks now and without the equipment she wouldn't even be able to breathe. I'm going to consult the head neurosurgeon at the RVI to check there isn't something we're missing, but things are not looking promising. I really do stress that you need to prepare yourself.'

'I thought she was going to be okay, Doctor. It's all my fault. There's nothing to be done?'

'I very much doubt it. The body has undergone too much trauma. The amount of bleeding in the brain, despite the operation, causes significant damage and even if we could get her to breathe for herself, or if it were possible to wake her up, we would probably find that she would not be the person she once was.'

'Would it affect her personality?'

'More than that. She might not be able to do things for herself, probably wouldn't be able to do anything. And the chances of her waking up at all are minimal at best.'

'She'd be a vegetable,' said Jetson, stricken. 'There'd be no chance she'd wake up as Sonia?'

'There is very little chance she will even wake up at all, let alone waking up unaffected. The chance is so small, I wouldn't like to say, but cases of someone waking up from something like this at all is one in millions. Waking up without a scratch, so to speak, would be a miracle. I'm so very sorry.'

'So you're not expecting this special consultant to help then. Just a matter of course?'

The doctor nodded. 'I've looked at the research. We like to get second opinions sometimes too. I wish I were wrong, Mr Guthrie. I wish I could help your wife, but her injuries, I fear, are too much.'

'Thank you, Doctor. Thank you for telling me the truth.' Jetson looked at the young face of the doctor, and could see the weight of these no-chance lives on his shoulders. All he saw was sadness and resilience, no judgement, and Jetson could never thank him enough for that. 'I never meant any of this. I never meant to hurt her. I never thought a stupid argument could end up here.'

'I know, Mr Guthrie.' *Nobody ever does,* thought the doctor.

'I didn't think it would come to this,' said Jetson sadly. 'What happens now?'

'Now, Mr Guthrie?'

'Now if there's nothing to be done.'

'Well, I will talk to the neurosurgeon, but I… Perhaps the best thing is to have some time to start to say goodbye.'

Jetson nodded, and the doctor excused himself. He sat holding her hand as the in-out of the ventilator continued. Tracing the lines of the tubes protruding out of her mouth, into the compressing chamber and the wires that came out the back out of it, chasing into the wall to the plug. The everyday pug in the everyday socket, the switch firmly held in the on position. He was transfixed by it, haunted by the fact he knew he would have to turn it off. Pull the plug on her life –and it was all his fault.

She might not be dead, thought Jetson with sadness: maybe nuns do lie.

His wife was dead behind this door. As good as. And he'd have to be the one to make the final decision. His decisions had already landed them here. Poor Jetson didn't want to make any more, but he supposed there weren't really any to make. Not here. He'd made his jealous decision and now was the time to find out where it really had landed them.

He very much hoped it would not be back in this room, that this was not fixed. He hoped he would be seeing his baby born, not his wife and baby both dead. He squeezed Sonia's still hand, looked once more upon her face deformed by tubes and unconsciousness, and prayed he would only see this now in nightmares. After kissing her hand he stood, and went to the door back to Futurespan, the same white fog waiting to welcome him into its angered embrace.

She might not be dead. He didn't look back.

Amelia's Realisation

Amelia emerged from the fog into the concrete wasteland again. She clutched the envelope like a talisman, to remind her that her plan was flawed, that there had to be another way. Oh, how she wished he had stayed dead. It had taken so much to pull the trigger; it had devastated poor Amelia to find him alive again. To find herself in a future that she couldn't believe she had ever imagined would be any different. Planning to escape at sixteen, she scoffed at herself: not likely. Not possible.

She clutched the envelope, sadness settling in her chest; she felt utterly hopeless, tortured, helpless and unsure. She stepped over the threshold and back into the concrete, but as she did so the envelope she clutched dissolved into nothing. She grasped at the air but it was gone.

Her reminder was gone, but the truth remained in her heart. She'd have to find another way. There had to be one. Maybe there was another door somewhere. Maybe a door to somewhere better. It was worth a look at least. She didn't want to go back through that one again, and she was sick of hiding all alone.

So she starting walking up the steps and away; there was nothing to be done here.

Jetson

Jetson emerged from the white fog into the greyness again. The nun was back, standing there inhumanly still and perfectly poised. Her expression was exactly neutral: no hint of anything. There was something a little unnatural about that. Jetson couldn't shake the feeling that she was from another world. He was in another world of sorts, after all: a world that she knew better than him. He wondered if she lived here, haunting the halls. But he wasn't sure that would be possible. In fact, he wondered what kind of nun she was at all giving people false hope like that.

'Is it real? Is that what's happened?' asked Jetson. 'Because she isn't okay, and neither is the baby,' he said angrily. 'And you made it sound like she would be okay.'

'I said she might not be dead, Jetson. What did you see? Is she dead?'

'As good as. And the baby is gone,' he said, his voice gruff.

'The baby has died. Not gone. Died.'

'So it's all true,' said Jetson sadly.

'I didn't say that. In that version of the future the baby has died. But that version may not be the version that is aligned with your reality.' She surveyed Jetson's sad face, and clarified this. 'That is to say, it might not have, as you say, "really happened".'

'It might not have?'

'It is just one version, Jetson. And here lies the other,' she said, indicating the opposite door.

'I don't want to see any more,' said Jetson.

'It can't be any worse than the last door, can it?' she said plainly. Jetson shook his head, feeling like a child. 'Well, then, you'd better go and see what it is. We've been through this, Jetson; you have been here long enough and I can't have you here any longer.'

And Jetson knew she was right. He had to face reality. There couldn't be a worse reality than what he had just seen: not unless it was a funeral this time. He didn't think it would be, though. This door had a better feel to it. A feel that made him nervous: nervous in a not wanting to get his hopes up kind of way. This door might not be real either, and he had a feeling that he hoped it would be.

'Come on, Jetson,' she said, her hand on his shoulder guiding him towards the door. He didn't hesitate this time. He had to see what it was.

As the fog was clearing Jetson found himself again seeing a hospital bed. The door back to Futurespan was standing open at the end of the bed, so that anyone on it might be able to look through into the concrete jungle. Except the woman on the bed had other things on her mind, and even if she hadn't Jetson was pretty sure he was the only person in the room who could see the impossible door. He turned his attention in full to the woman on the bed: his wife. As her face came into focus he could see she was glowing with rosy cheeks and dewy skin, sweat running down her face and hair stuck to her forehead. Despite that, to Jetson she looked like the most beautiful woman in the world. And she was alive! He wanted to run to her and drown her in kisses and never let her go; he could barely believe that she was real. His heart felt as if it was bouncing in his chest; he had never felt so elated in all his life. As stepped towards her he collided with a woman in a navy nurse's uniform, who seemed to have materialised from the Futurespan door.

'Careful, Mr Guthrie,' she said. 'You don't want to be knocking the midwife out before we're done here, do you?' There was a smile in her voice.

'N-no,' he stuttered and felt like an idiot. He looked at Sonia again; she was panting now. He had been so awed she was alive he hadn't realised she was giving birth. He thought he might collapse. The fog cleared fully, and Jetson managed to stay upright, watching the midwife as she checked the monitors near his wife's head.

'Baby's doing well, Mrs Guthrie. Just need to examine you again now, see how we're getting along, okay?'

Jetson stood there agog at the whole scene; it was like watching a dream. It wasn't real. But neither was the black-grey hell or sitting by the ICU bed. It wasn't all possible. But then neither was reliving her falling again and again and again. Except that was real. That had happened. It was Jetson's fault. Who knew how real the rest was, but he hoped beyond all else that this was the real version. That this was what would happen. Not her lying limp in an intensive care bed with an empty stomach; please, Lord, anything but that.

'Mr Guthrie, are you okay?' asked the midwife, frowning in concern. 'You look a little pale.'

'I'm okay,' said Jetson, mentally shaking himself. He looked back at his wife, struggling through the pain, and he could see the beads of sweat on her face, and could smell her musty scent in the air. This was as real as it got. 'I'm fine. Just look after my wife, don't be worrying about me.'

She smiled. 'Well, that's what I'm here for. But I don't want you collapsing on me. Go and have a seat there and make use of those hands.'

Jetson did as he was told and balanced on a small plastic chair at the head of the bed. He grasped his wife's hand, and she smiled a very small smile. 'I am glad you came,' she said.

'Of course,' said Jetson, rubbing her palm, enjoying the heat and the hot, steady pulse of life. He grinned.

'Of course?' she said through ragged breaths, wincing as the midwife carried out the promised examination. 'You still don't believe me.'

'None of that matters now,' said Jetson.

'It doesn't matter? No! We've only had months of awkward silences, Jetson. Months of you pretending to be happy about a baby deep down you don't even think is yours.' She whispered the latter part angrily, almost hissing. 'And me pretending it's okay I fell down the stairs. It's okay because it was an accident. It's okay because I was fine and *our* baby was fine. Well it's not okay, Jetson, because it happened because you didn't trust me and you didn't believe me.'

'I'm sorry, Sonia, I'm so –'

The door clicked as the midwife slipped out and Sonia cut

Jetson off. She shouted more loudly now there wasn't a third party to hear. 'I'm not finished. Months, Jetson. Months of trying to forget you don't trust me, of pushing down how much that hurts. And we're literally about to have a baby. And I could not think of a worse situation. Or a worse time. And I'm so scared.'

'Look, Sonia, I'm here now. I'm here and I'm not going anywhere and I am really sorry. So sorry you wouldn't believe. And it will be better, you might not believe me but it will be, I promise. But we can't sort it out now.'

'I don't believe you, Jetson. You were like a madman, and I know you didn't mean for me to fall but I've never seen you like that. It terrified me. And even after, I was so scared something would happen again. It can't have been any good for the baby. What if the baby isn't okay?'

'The baby will be fine, Sonia, I'm sure it will. It has good genes – with you as a mother how could it not be beautiful.'

'And you as a father,' she said, panting still. 'I hope it isn't as pig-headed.'

'Me too,' said Jetson. 'I'm sorry, Sonia.'

'Well, I'm scared,' she said.

'I'm right here,' said Jetson. 'I'm not going anywhere. I promise.'

The midwife had come back in and was busying herself at the end of the bed, acting as if she hadn't heard a thing. 'Right, Mrs Guthrie, it's time now. You're fully dilated and ready to push, so let's get that baby out into the world.'

Sonia didn't respond; her sad eyes bored into Jetson. 'I'm here,' he said, squeezing her hand. 'We can do this.'

Her gaze softened a little and some determination returned to her eyes. Jetson couldn't have left her if he tried. He never wanted to leave her now; he was scared if he took his hand away she might melt into nothing. He was here for her; of course he was. But as for the baby? That was still a question mark in his mind. He had walked the many steps trying to escape from his suspicious mind and his guilty conscience, but had found little solace in trying to outrun either. The torturous, intruding images still thrived there. And he still didn't know for sure.

He realised now he had a choice: to trust the woman he had vowed to love and cherish, or to let doubt and fear tear his marriage apart. If he went as far as proving the baby was his, there would be no marriage left for it to be raised in. There almost wasn't now. He rubbed the small gold band on his wife's finger and let the memory of how much he had loved her that day fill him up. That man would never have doubted her.

A part of him of him thought that once he saw the baby he would know for sure. He was certain he would know in his heart. But as the midwife shouted for Sonia to push Jetson realised he wasn't going to get that chance. Not today, anyway. White fog rolled in around him, gathering around his ankles. He tightened his grip on Sonia's hand only to find he was clasping nothing. He reached around desperately in the nothingness trying to find Sonia again. He had a choice, and as that thought dawned on him, rolling white fog closed in around him completely. He couldn't see anything. 'Sonia!' he called out to nothing. The warm hand had melted away, just as he had feared, and he was alone in the fog. Jetson wept. He had broken his promise, and Sonia was gone.

Diggory's Encounter

Diggory awoke to whimpering echoing from below his landing. For a moment he thought he was back in the psychiatric ward listening to another patient from down the hall, and was glad, despite the greyness, that he wasn't. Just as he thought he might have been imagining it altogether, it started again, proving that here, at least, he wasn't mad. This time it was more of a cry than a whimper. Diggory pushed himself up, knowing it wasn't Tabitha or Rin, and was pleased for the moment it wasn't. As he stepped off the landing he felt the momentary tug of regret at leaving the fuzzy warmness of his floor, but curiosity drove him on and he didn't pause, knowing he could come back. The whimpering voice didn't sound like the kind of person to stop him.

He rushed down the stairs, taking the steps quickly. The whimpering continued; the noises sounded like hollow, desperate cries. Diggory could feel their pain as if it was radiating up the stairs next to the sound waves, and it hurried him on. He hoped it wasn't some new twisted trick of this place. Hoped instead that it was someone he could help, something he could actually do. Something in the here and now, if that was even possible in this place. He felt as if time was stuck here, but it felt more like the present than anything else, more like the present than the life before now had. He felt more in control of this, now the fear had subsided a little anyway. And now there was someone who needed his help. He turned the corner, hugging the wall of it with his hand to let him swing round quicker. He took the rest of the stairs in large, quick strides. The crying was louder now, a desperate gasping and gulping, nearly a choking between the strangled sobs.

He came to the bottom of the stairs and on the landing he found the source of the noise in an awkward heap in the corner. It was in the form of a thin, gangly girl. Her light coloured hair was straggly and hung over her face, swollen from crying.

The girl gasped as she saw Diggory. She stood up and slowly backed against the wall, her sprawling legs moving awkwardly. Diggory thought she looked a lot like a trapped animal and he was worried that she thought he would hurt her. She stood shaking against the wall. 'Who are you?' she said.

Diggory gave a small smile. 'I'm Diggory. What's your name?'

Amelia just stared at him with wide, scared eyes.

'It's okay. I won't hurt you. I heard you crying, are you okay?'

She looked at him suspiciously, and wiped her eyes. 'I'm sick of being here.'

'Well, that makes two of us,' said Diggory, sitting down at the other end of the landing, not wanting to frighten her any further. 'I take it you haven't found a way out?'

'No. What are you doing here?'

'The truth is I'm not sure. I don't want to be here. I don't know about you but this place scares me.'

'I thought I was the only one here,' said Amelia. 'I don't know how long I've been here but it feels like forever, and I thought it was bad before but this is so much worse. I'm so alone and I've no idea what to do.'

'Me neither. Is that why you're crying?' he asked gently.

'That, and I lost my envelope,' she said sadly.

'Envelope?' asked Diggory.

'It's a long story but I thought it would help remind me. But it disintegrated as I came back through the door.'

'You found your doors?' he said.

'I've found a door,' said Amelia. 'I think it's the only door, but if it's the way out I don't understand because I've tried everything.' She looked terrified and her hands shook. 'And I mean everything, everything I can think off and I'm still stuck.'

'You've only got one door?'

'It's the only door. There's just stairs and landings, and my grey front door.'

'It isn't the only door,' said Diggory.

Amelia's pupils visibly dilated. 'What do you mean?'

'I'll show you,' said Diggory, and Amelia followed him up the stairs, feeling for the first time here a little less alone.

'Have you found a way out?' she whispered.

Diggory slowed his steps a little. 'No,' he admitted, his voice low, his eyes on the floor. 'But I didn't say I had. I just wanted to show you there are other doors here, that's all.'

'Okay. Well, it would be different. If they're anything like mine I guess I won't want to go through them though.'

'No,' said Diggory. 'Even when they're not yours they can be painful ' He paused. 'I just figured that if there are other people's doors. Maybe there are others. Maybe they're out…'

'Maybe there's a door to heaven somewhere,' said Amelia.

'You think we're dead?' said Diggory, not sure he wanted to hear her answer.

'I don't know,' she said. 'But I almost hope so. And then we can go on to something else, something better.'

'I've felt like that before,' said Diggory. 'But I think I'm usually running away from myself.'

'Hm,' said Amelia. 'I don't think it is like that with me. I'd like to have a chance to be me though. To go on and be free to be me, that'd be great.'

'Yes, it would be,' said Diggory.

'You want to get out?'

'More than anything. Like you wouldn't believe. At least I'm not curled up on the floor now.'

'Sorry?'

'Never mind. I've gotten a bit more used to it, and the company helped. But at least I'm not terrified now.'

'I am.' There was a pause. 'Did you say company?'

'Yeah. Haven't you seen anyone else at all?'

'No, I've been alone. Always alone,' she sighed.

'I'm sorry,' said Diggory. 'It's not nice being lonely.'

'No,' said Amelia. 'Who else is there?'

'My sister Rin, and a girl we met called Tabitha. Oh, and Jetson. A huge guy with the even bigger chair, you must've seen him? No? He's been wandering this place for ages. Up and down. It's a wonder *he* isn't mad. Mind you, he did seem rather attached to that chair – calls it Cheryl or something.'

'Oh,' said Amelia, wondering if she should have been scared of him: he was a man, after all. But he seemed so much like a little boy that she felt safe with him. In fact, she hadn't felt scared even for a second, and she found herself looking at him in wonder. She really didn't think that Diggory would ever want to hurt her. He was kind and good – of that she was utterly sure. She was walking close enough to feel the brush of heat radiating from Diggory and she smiled that for once she wasn't alone, or alone with someone who wanted to hurt her. She felt safe next to this kind stranger – safer than she ever had in her own home.

'Rin's a bit harsh sometimes but she is good at looking after people. Always has been with me. We can look after you for a while and if Jetson ever comes back he can help too. He knows more than we do. I think you'll like Rin,' continued Diggory.

'I wish I'd had a sister.' She paused. 'Actually no, I don't. The company would be nice but it's better like this.' *Better that it was only me,* she thought.

'Sometimes I wish I was an only child when Rin's in one of her moods but I don't know where I'd be without her, so I'm glad really.'

'That's nice,' said Amelia.

They walked up the few steps to his floor. Amelia looked on in total surprise, her eyes flitting between the doors.

'They're my doors,' said Diggory.

'Yours?'

'Isn't your door yours?'

She thought about it. 'Yes. It's my front door, except it isn't blue anymore.'

'Strange that you've only got one,' said Diggory. 'We've all got three.'

'Really?' said Amelia. 'Mine's just the same front door as ever; I thought I was still in the tower block when I first got here.'

'Yes,' said Diggory, chuckling a little. 'This place is a bit like a tower block, isn't it.'

'I guess,' said Amelia, giving a small smile. 'I thought I was going mad when I first went through and everything was grey. I was going to go to Jimmy's – the hospital across the road – until I realised I couldn't get out.' She paused. 'Have you really all got three doors?'

'Yes, we haven't been through them all though, but they're there.'

'And they're all like this?'

'Yes,' said Diggory.

'I wonder if I have any more,' said Amelia.

'I don't know but I think we should carry on, as much as I'd like to stay. It feels safe here for me. But I think we should go and see if Jetson can help you, if he's come back. He said he can help people.'

'Okay,' said Amelia, still transfixed by the doors, but she followed Diggory. 'My name's Amelia.'

'Good to meet you,' said Diggory. 'Come on.'

They walked up several staircases in comfortable silence, Diggory's worry about seeing Tabitha outweighed by his desire to help Amelia. Amelia was happy that she was no longer alone, and was still trying to process that there were other doors and other people here: all here, the whole time, while she had been all alone.

'Nearly there,' said Diggory, as they entered Tabitha's floor.

'More doors,' said Amelia, looking at them in wonder.

'Yeh,' said Diggory, pushing on quickly, not wanting to dwell on what he had seen behind one of them. 'They won't be far now, come on.'

After a little while he rounded the corner of the landing to see them both there. Rin was sitting, legs swinging like a child's, on Jetson's chair. Tabitha sat cross-legged on the floor. He couldn't hear what they were saying from where he was. Rin noticed him first and her raised eyebrows caused Tabitha to turn and scramble up to greet him.

'Diggory, I'm so glad you've come back. Are you okay?' she said, her eyes big and watery, filled with hope. 'I'm still sorry,' she said, pausing a few feet from him, holding her hands limply in front of her, wanting to reach for him.

He looked down at her, his gaze steady. He said nothing.

'How much further –' Amelia halted just behind Diggory, having seen Tabitha and Rin. She was frozen like a cornered animal, unsure of whether to trust or run.

'It's okay,' said Diggory going to her. 'This is Tabitha, and back there is my sister Rin.'

Rin came to join them. 'And this is?'

'Give me a second, Rin, this is Amelia. I found her a few floors down; she's been here longer than us.'

'Not another Jetson, are you?' asked Rin.

'Does she look anything like Jetson?' said Diggory.

'Pleased to meet you, Amelia,' said Tabitha.

'Me too,' said Rin.

'How long have you been here?' asked Tabitha.

'I'm not sure,' Amelia replied. 'Feels like a very long time.'

'Well, at least you're not carrying a chair around,' said Rin, and they chuckled.

'I'm surprised Jetson isn't back yet,' said Diggory. 'I wonder where he's gone…'

Jetson

Jetson stepped back out of the fog onto the concrete, rubbing his eyes. The nun stood there, at the opposite door, unsurprised. She said nothing to him, just looked at him so deeply that he felt again she was assessing his soul. He thought that she might be able to; she was no ordinary nun, after all. He looked back then, unsure of what to do, but glad all he could see was fog. This was the first time he was sure in his heart he had had enough of this. He had a choice ahead – at least he hoped he did – and not the kind of empty choice he had just faced. Finally, though, he was ready to face it: as ready as he would ever be. He looked at the nun, and wondered if she could hear his thoughts.

The nun nodded her chin the tiniest amount and raised her left hand towards the top of the doorframe. In a brisk movement she swept her hand down, and the door was gone in a small flurry of dust. Jetson gaped at the empty wall. She then performed the same movements on the door near him– the door of hope, Jetson thought – and his chest tightened as it vanished into dust. Then she moved to the third door; this time she did it slowly, and he saw that the doorframe remained but the door was gone, leaving plain concrete behind.

Now she stood a few feet back from the door-less frame and held out both hands. She stood still as if summoning strength: maybe from God, Jetson mused. Then all of a sudden light erupted from her hands with such force that it pulled her towards the wall. Jetson stared wide-eyed at the bright white light blasting from her palms. He was agog, no longer the un-shockable veteran of Futurespan. The light coated the empty space inside the frame and started to take physical form. As the nun moved her hand down slowly the light was directed to form a solid door: a door that was pulsing with the light, glowing brighter and brighter as the nun strained with the effort. Jetson watched as the last of the light trickled out of her fingers, leaving the glowing door complete. It was a brilliant contrast to the dull of everything here: a bright shining light in the greyness. It was blissfully devoid of numbers. Jetson was truly awestruck for the first time in his life.

The nun looked at Jetson with reverence now, and nodded again. Her hand was still extended towards the door. 'It's time, Jetson,' she said. Then she gestured for him to come forward. Jetson obeyed, pausing just before the door, looking at the nun. 'It is time.' She smiled at him now with a kindness in her eyes.

He put his foot forward slowly, edging towards the door, holding his breath, unable to believe this moment had finally come. As he neared the door he felt a tiny pang of regret for what he was leaving behind. Futurespan had been his comfort, his safety, his sanctuary, and he felt a little sad for not saying goodbye to Stacey-Barbara, but he knew she had to find her own way. He thought briefly of Rin, Diggory and Tabitha and hoped they would have it easier than him. He hoped they would look after Cheryl too; she had been more like a friend to him here than anything. A childlike part of him longed to take Cheryl with him but the thought fell away as his foot left the ground. He laughed at himself. Friends with a chair! Time for the real world. The nun was right. And with that thought he was ready; whatever the outcome, he knew he couldn't go back in time. The only place left was to go forward, to find out his future. To return to the real world once more, make his decisions, and live. Properly live again. Properly live for the first time.

Whatever the future held.

He strode the last few steps, turned quickly to the nun and said, 'Thank you,' as he briefly touched her wrist. He felt tingling, as if some invisible coldness was pulsing through her. Whatever it was, it didn't matter to Jetson now. Everything about her exuded power, and he was pleased to have known her, pleased that she had helped him be free, but he knew she was so far removed from him and his world, it was best not to worry about her any further, and to accept the brief time he had known her. He would never forget her, or this place, but now it was time. He was finally leaving Futurespan behind.

He grasped the door handle. It felt much like the nun, except colder, and more intense, almost alive. He turned it and pulled it open. No white fog this time, just a blinding bright white light. He walked straight into it, into the future, into life…

The Different Door

'So this is the chair, the one the man you were on about has a name for?' asked Amelia.

'Jetson's chair,' said Rin. 'It is.'

'He calls it Cheryl,' said Tabitha, her eyes flicking over Amelia before settling on Diggory.

'Cheryl?' said Amelia.

'I know,' said Rin. 'Seemed okay, apart from that. Well, as okay as anyone who's been stuck in this godforsaken place can be. Though we're not sure where he's gone.'

'I thought he'd have been back by now,' said Diggory.

'Us too,' said Tabitha. 'We came back here to wait for him.'

'Have you been to look for him?' asked Diggory, looking up the stairs.

'No,' said Tabitha. 'He seemed pretty keen that we didn't go up there, and we did think he'd have been back by now.' She paused. Rubbing her hands together, she looked up at him a little sheepishly. 'And we were worried about you.'

'Yeh,' said Diggory. 'Well, never mind about that. I think we should go and find him. He's the only one who's going to know how to get out of here. And I really want to get out. Amelia does too.'

'Yeh, I agree he's our best chance,' said Tabitha. She moved a little closer, speaking only to Diggory. 'We'll go and look for him in a minute. But I wondered, could I have a word with you, Diggory? Please?'

'Okay,' he said, a little reluctantly, and then they headed down the stairs, Diggory first with Tabitha following a good distance behind.

Meanwhile Rin surveyed the young girl in front of her. She was a mess.

'You okay?' said Rin. Amelia nodded from her curled-up position on the floor. Rin looked dubious. 'We can help, we'll find Jetson. He said he'd help us.'

Amelia gave a small smile. 'I can't believe you've all been here.'

'When you've been on your own?'

Amelia nodded.

'Well, you're not on your own now, are you,' said Rin. 'At least we can stick together in this awful place.'

'I agree. Awful isn't bad enough,' said Amelia.

'I was going to say bloody awful, but I thought in the presence of a young woman it wasn't the most appropriate language to use,' said Rin, making Amelia laugh a little. 'Looks like you've had it worse than us anyway?'

'It's been bad. I thought the before was worse but this…'

'Did you have to relive something horrible?' said Rin as she sat down next to Amelia.

'My life.'

'What, all of it?'

'Just like before, day after day, always the same story behind that door. Always was.'

'Did you try the other doors?'

'I didn't have any other doors,' said Amelia. 'I didn't know there were any until I met Diggory. And from what he said about other people's doors, then I don't think I'll be trying those either. The one door was bad enough.'

'Wait, didn't you have three doors?'

'No, just one.'

'All of us have three doors. We each have a floor and at the end of the corridor there were always three doors.'

'Mine wasn't like that. Just my front door, that's all. Unfortunately,' she sighed. 'Were yours all like Diggory's?'

'Yes, except they all had different numbers on. The little silver ones, we worked out they were our birthdays and the date of what was behind the door. It was Diggory first: his past, we followed him in, he turned all little again and I had to drag him out. Not good. Then Tabitha's. Three doors again. She went through one: the future, and it wasn't great. And Diggory followed her through the last one: the past. I don't know what happened there but they had a falling out. Can't have been good. None of them have been.'

'What about yours?'

'I have three as well. We thought everyone had three. Guess we were wrong. So your door didn't have any numbers or anything on it?'

'Just the number four. Hanging the same wonky way it always has. Except the door used to be blue.'

'So did these jeans,' said Rin. They both giggled. 'Good job I was never really a colour person.'

Amelia looked at Rin, a bright curiosity in her eyes. 'What about your doors?'

'What about them?'

'You said about Tabitha's and Diggory's but you just said you had three doors? Did you not go through yours?'

Rin paused, looking down at her hands. 'I did. I wish I hadn't though.'

'Not good?'

'No,' said Rin, shaking her head. 'None of them are.'

'This place isn't.'

'Seems that way. Shame none of us know the way out.'

'Let's hope this Jetson person does.'

'I agree,' said Rin smiling.

'Though,' said Amelia, pausing. 'It's better now at least. Having company is better than my old life; at least I'm not alone here.'

'We won't leave you, and despite how bad the before was, we can't stay in this place forever. It's creepy apart from anything else.'

'Yeh, it is I guess,' she said with a small smile.

'We'll work it out.' Rin grasped her hand. 'I promise. We can't live here forever,' she said, hoping very much that that was true.

In the meantime Diggory and Tabitha were standing on the next landing down, a few feet of awkward silence between them. 'So?' said Diggory.

'I'm sorry, Diggory. You're right. You're right that I had a choice. It was up to me, it was my choice and I didn't take it. But I realise that now. And I realise I should have told you.'

'Good.'

'I never meant to hurt you.'

'I know.'

'I like you. And I know what you saw there, and how weak I've been is going to affect your perception of me. But I hope it hasn't ruined any chance. I hope that maybe we can start again?'

'Let's just find Jetson, Tabitha, and we'll see,' he said, turning away after his eyes had lingered a second too long on her lips. She knew she might have a chance, and she wouldn't blow it next time.

'Okay, Diggory. I know I don't deserve it.'

He didn't answer her; he just kept walking as she followed him up the stairs in a silence that was at least a little less awkward.

The group reformed, and with their new addition in tow they headed up the stairs together. They left Cheryl behind, sure in the knowledge she would still be there when they got back, and none of them as strong or motivated as Jetson to haul her up the many stairs. Even one flight would have been an effort, and who knew how many they would have to traverse. Jetson had been gone a long time, at least it seemed that way, and could be quite a lot higher up by now. None of them minded too much; they were all glad to be together and to not be facing their own demons, much happier in the distracting adventure to find another lost wanderer.

Rin worried about how she would feel going to her floor again. She didn't want to go near the door ever again, but the chance of getting out of this place all together outweighed that thought. If it meant getting out she could go to her floor. She would just go to it and walk straight past it, just keep going up.

It didn't take as long as they thought. A mere four flights up and the mood changed. It was as if the air was heavier, and they all felt a sense of dread. 'Maybe we should go back,' said Diggory. 'It doesn't feel safe here.'

'I know but we've got to find Jetson. He needs to help us,' said Rin.

'I think it's Jetson's dread we're feeling,' said Tabitha.

'Me too,' said Amelia, motioning to Diggory. 'It's okay to be scared but nothing here will hurt us. Whatever it is, it's hurting Jetson. Not us.'

'Okay,' said Diggory. 'But I don't like it.'

'None of us like it, Dig. That's why we need to get out of here.'

They carried on in silence for another few uneventful flights. The feeling didn't dissipate but it didn't strengthen either. It was bearable even for Diggory. On the next landing they came across a small but familiar change of scene. Tabitha spotted it first. 'Numbers,' she said and ran up the last couple of stairs. The others joined her on the landing and indeed there were numbers. Numbers and an arrow, just like the ones they'd seen before all of their floors. They read: 11106314.

'Well, we're on the right track. Guess you were right about it being his floor, little bro.'

'It had to be important or he would've come back. I hope he's okay,' said Diggory.

'Me too,' said the girls in unison, and they giggled.

'Strange though,' said Diggory. 'It wasn't here before, was it? We should have reached Rin's floor first.'

'Everything here is strange, Dig. Maybe the floors move – wouldn't that be wonderful? Then we'll never find the exit, if there even is one,' Rin said, relieved she didn't have to go near the door again.

Nobody responded to Rin. They carried on up, and sure enough, on the next flight of stairs, instead of opening out into the usual small landing, it opened out into a long corridor, just like all the others.

'Jetson's floor,' said Diggory. 'Feels worse here, but better too.'

'Yeh,' said Rin.

'What's that?' said Amelia, looking down the corridor, her sharp eyes spotting an anomaly the others had missed. Following her gaze they looked down to the end of the corridor and saw what had got her attention: something was glowing.

'What is that?' said Rin.

'One way to find out,' said Tabitha, shrugging her shoulders, and with that they all eagerly went down the corridor.

It seemed that the corridor went on for a long time, but as they got closer the glowing intensified, and they could see more.

'Is that a door?' said Rin.

'Yeh,' said Amelia. 'I think so.'

'Is that a glowing door?' said Tabitha.

'Wow, a glowing door, now, that would be new,' said Rin.

As they neared they could see that Tabitha and Amelia were right. There was a glowing door here. It was bright white, with pulsing light emanating from it. Diggory reached his hand towards it and he felt heat coming from it as well. He and the others all stood there, awestruck by the beauty and mystery of the door.

'Wow, it feels so nice,' said Amelia. 'I wish my door was like this.'

'You don't think it's the way out, do you?' said Rin.

'It's Jetson's,' said Diggory.

'Do you think we could go through it?' said Rin, eyeing up the door.

'I don't think so,' said Tabitha.

Rin went closer, reaching her hand towards the handle.

'You shouldn't touch it, Rin.'

But it was too late. Rin touched the glowing silver handle and immediately withdrew. 'Ow,' she said. 'It burnt me.'

'I said you shouldn't have.'

'Well, it's a bit late for that now,' said Rin.

'Is it okay?' asked Tabitha, peering at Rin's hand. 'It looks okay.'

'I didn't think you could hurt in this place. At least there isn't a mark,' said Rin. 'Well, I guess it isn't the way out for us.'

They went back to staring again at the door, all of them awed by it. They stared so long that it hurt their unaccustomed eyes, but they all found it impossible to look away. That is, until a voice came from behind them and startled them all out of their shocked state. Poor Amelia spun around and backed away so fast she accidentally bumped into the door and was pushed away from it, as if by a force field; she ended up on the floor. Rin helped her up, both of them glad it hadn't burnt her.

Stacey-Barbara was the owner of the voice. She spoke again now. 'I didn't mean to scare you. I'm ever so sorry.'

'We didn't expect to see anyone else here. How did you get here so fast?' asked Tabitha.

'What did you say?' said Rin, staring at Stacey-Barbara. She was the only one who had half-heard what Stacey-Barbara had said at first.

'I said I'm glad Jetson has finally found his way home,' she said, smiling. 'It's a happy day in Futurespan. If only we could have a party.'

'Is that what the glowing door means?' asked Rin.

'Yes. It means success. An exit. A one-way ticket out of Futurespan for good.' She smiled, genuinely happy for her old friend.

'An exit?' said Rin. 'The way out.'

'Jetson's way out.'

'How did he do it?' asked Diggory.

'That's the mystery,' said Stacey-Barbara. 'If I knew that then I wouldn't be standing here would I.'

They all looked back at the door; it had a mesmerising quality.

'So Jetson's gone?' asked Amelia.

'Certainly is, my love,' smiled Stacey-Barbara. 'I'm so pleased for him.'

'He was supposed to help us,' said Diggory.

'You'll be just fine with me,' she said, smiling.

'You didn't answer my question,' said Rin. 'How did you get here so fast?'

'Come on, I'll show you, I said I would. But let's get off Jetson's floor first. I feel like I'm standing on his grave.'

Not entirely sure what she meant, and more than a little reluctant to leave the presence of the warm, glowing door, they followed her three floors down.

The Sliding Doors

'Not all doors are made equal,' said Stacey-Barbara matter-of-factly, once they were all assembled on the landing.

Rin was reminded of her insufferable primary school teacher Mrs Summers and it made her feel as if she was seven again. 'Don't you mean not all *people* are made equal?' she said, her petulant child coming out.

'And it's true,' said Diggory, looking at Tabitha.

'Now, now,' chided Stacey-Barbara in true Mrs Summers' style. 'Not all doors are the same here; some are special.'

'I wouldn't describe any of the doors we've seen as special,' said Rin. 'A trio of hells for each of us. And there aren't any other doors, except Amelia's, and that glowing one up there that burns you when you touch it.'

Stacey-Barbara raised an eyebrow.

'Wait, don't tell me – they're invisible?'

'Not completely right there, Rin, but not completely wrong. Besides you don't have to go through all three doors. In fact you might not even have three,' said Stacey-Barbara.

'But we've seen them,' said Diggory. 'I do. Rin does, and Tabitha.'

'Yes. Yes. Futurespan is a kind of projection, you know; controlled by your mind. To some extent at least. You have been affected by the projections of the others around you. Some people only have one door. Some people's third door is the way out, or their second. Sometimes even the first. You saw three doors, but you, Diggory have been through?'

'One,' said Diggory, unwilling to admit to the others he'd been through his second door. 'But I can't only have that one, I was a child.'

'No, probably you have at least two. It might only be two. And you, Rin? You've been through one? Your second might be the way out for you. Saying this, you might have created doors together, your collective consciousness saying there are three doors each. Knowing it into being. That's why you can't see the other doors. I like to call them the sliding doors. Come on, I'll show you.'

'How come there isn't any colour here but there is behind the doors?'

'I'm afraid I don't know everything, Diggory.'

'Mine doesn't have colour,' said Amelia. 'It's always the same, still black-and-white, and grey, just like this place. And why is it always the same? Why is he always there? I'm always trapped there with him.' Her voice was breaking. Rin put a protective arm around her. They all looked at Stacey-Barbara who looked uncharacteristically unsure of herself. She looked as if she was debating whether to tell them something. Amelia's eyes pleaded with her and finally she spoke.

'There is a rumour,' she said slowly. 'A rumour about doors that are black-and-white behind. They call them true Futurespan doors, and I think yours may be one. Where you can see not just one scene play out as it has done or will do, but you can see many versions of a future. You can play them all out, and you're fully aware and in control of yourself: no being whisked as a bystander back into the past.'

Amelia nodded. 'How do I get it to stop?'

'Only you can know that. There is an answer somewhere behind that door. It's something you can control.'

'I don't control anything in that flat.'

'You can control yourself. Your mind is your own child.'

Amelia didn't say any more. Neither did Stacey-Barbara, having divulged the extent of what she knew about true Futurespan doors.

Rin was the first to speak. 'So what were you saying about invisible doors?'

'Follow me,' said Stacey-Barbara. 'And you'll see they're not invisible at all, they're sliding.'

They went up the stairs, to a floor they knew wasn't there before, and at the end of the corridor on this new mysterious floor there were indeed doors of which they had never seen the like before. They were silver and glistening, and as Stacey-Barbara approached, they were indeed sliding.

'A lift?' said Rin. 'There's a bloody lift?'

'You'll see,' said Stacey-Barbara.

They all crowded through the sliding doors and into the silver box. Instead of the usual side panel, there were dozens of little rectangular buttons, each with tiny silver numbers on. They extended around the entire walls of the lift, so every surface was coated with them except for the floor and the ceiling, and presumably the back of the sliding doors.

'It is a lift,' marvelled Tabitha.

'How many are there?' asked Diggory, craning his neck to look around.

'Countless. You could walk this place literally forever,' said Stacey-Barbara. 'In fact I intend to. But that's another story. Anyway the light grey ones are your floors, and mine,' she said, pointing to one very low down. 'Someone else gets in and their button will be grey too. You can walk to other people's floors without them; you can cheat your way to them if you like but you wouldn't want to. And you won't feel very welcome if you do. It's not right to go traipsing through somewhere that doesn't belong to you. But anyway it makes it easier for you to get where you should be going. When you're ready to go there.'

Stacey-Barbara came out to make room. She smiled at them all slightly squashed in the small space, keeping away from the walls.

'Don't worry,' she chuckled. 'The other buttons won't work easily. Anyway I'd better leave you to it; you don't need me.' And she turned to go.

'Wait!' said Rin. 'How do we find this again?'

'Easy, now you know it exists. You just have to know it in here,' she said, tapping her head. 'And so it will be.' She gestured towards the lift. 'I have opened your minds.' She smiled. 'Who needs to get out when you can have so much fun.'

'We do,' said Rin and Diggory in unison.

'Yes. Yes. That is the way for you, and I'm pleased for you all, I'm sure you will succeed. But it isn't the way for me. I am a Futurespan wanderer, and with Jetson gone I suppose I am *the* Futurespan wanderer. And long may it ever be,' she said, beaming.

'Well, good luck to you, Stacey-Barbara. I hope you'll be happy here,' said Tabitha.

'Thanks for helping us,' said Diggory.

Rin and Amelia said their thanks too. Stacey-Barbara waved, and smiled. 'Now be gone with you before I squeeze in there too! Goodbye!' And with that the doors started to close as they watched the disappearing shadow of Stacey-Barbara through the closing slit in the lift.

They looked at each other, and then at the panels that were theirs, each working out which numbers were their own, and realising the height of them corresponded to the order in which they found their floors. Diggory – Tabitha – Rin.

'So where first?' said Rin.

'Amelia's,' replied Diggory. 'She's been here the longest.'

'I'm not sure I'm ready,' she said in a small voice.

'There'll never be a good time to face it. And the sooner you do the sooner it can stop altogether,' said Diggory. 'I want to see your door glowing just like Jetson's. If he found a way then you can too.'

'O-okay,' she said, finding a strength in his eyes.

'Okay?' said Rin.

'It's that one,' she said, pointing to the number that was in the column to the left of the others, a little further down than Rin's. Rin pushed it and the lift burst into life. It was like taking off in a plane, and all of them instinctively squatted against the force.

'At least it's quicker than walking up the steps!' shouted Rin.

'And less soul-destroying,' said Tabitha.

'Definitely!' said Diggory.

They clung on, waiting for it to stop, hoping Stacey-Barbara was right about the other numbers not working, as they pressed against the button-filled walls, or who knew where they would end up. It took a good few minutes, but it was certainly quicker than walking would have been. The lift came to a dead stop, with a final whoosh for good measure, and the sliding doors opened.

'This it?' said Rin.

'I think so,' said Amelia, peering slowly out of the doors.

'It's okay,' said Diggory. 'We can just go and have a look, and you can go through when you're ready to. We'll be right here.'

'Aren't you coming out?' she said.

'Yes, we are,' said Rin, grasping her small hand. 'We'll be right outside.'

'That's what I meant, right here on your floor. Come on, let's check this thing has worked,' said Diggory, exiting the lift.

'I think it has,' said Amelia.

'It feels right?' said Tabitha.

She nodded. 'Feels wrong.'

'Just keep thinking about Jetson's glowing door, and about how the before wasn't as bad. You said it was bad but not as bad as this, so let's get you away from this. You can do it,' said Diggory.

'Yeh, come on,' said Rin.

'But it's better now; here's better than before with you all here,' said Amelia, pulling back towards the lift. 'I don't want to go back in there again, please. It's so much better here now I'm not alone.'

Rin turned to her, holding her little hand in both of her bigger ones. 'We can't stay here forever, Amelia. We can't and neither can you. We're right behind you. Remember Stacey-Barbara said you're in control. They're just projections of futures. They aren't real.'

'Not yet,' Amelia whispered.

'Maybe not ever,' said Rin.

Amelia looked up at her with watery eyes. She nodded barely perceptibly, but she started walking. Rin squeezed her hand and smiled. They all walked together down the corridor, towards the not-blue door. Amelia held Diggory's hand now too, like a child in between her parents.

'I don't know if I can do it,' she whispered as it came into view.

'You can,' said Diggory. 'Just take control. You can do anything you set your mind to, Amelia. It's all in your mind.'

'I know you're right,' she said, with a deep breath. 'But I get so scared.'

'You can do it. Go on, the longer you wait the scarier it will get. We'll be right here.'

'Okay,' she said very quietly.

'What scares you?' said Rin, holding both her hands now. Amelia looked at Rin and then at Tabitha and Diggory.

'Me and Tabitha are going to wait near the lift, erm, make sure it doesn't disappear. You can shout us if you need us.' Diggory squeezed Amelia's shoulder. 'You'll do fine.'

Tabitha and Diggory left, and Rin and Amelia sat a little way from the door, Amelia eyeing it warily.

'What is it that's so bad?' said Rin. 'Can you tell me?'

There was a long pause. 'He hurt me,' said Amelia. 'Every day, one way or another, he hurt me.'

'I'm sorry,' said Rin, rubbing her hand.

'Me too,' said Amelia. 'All I used to wish is that he would die. That all the booze and awful fast food I had to get for him would be too much for the fat lump and he'd die. I'd dream about waking up one morning and finding him slumped on the sofa.'

'That's terrible, Amelia,' said Rin, feeling a kinship with this damaged child.

'You must think I am. Wanting my dad dead when most people want their parents to live.'

'My parents didn't hurt me. At least not when they were alive. But I understand. I wished my already dead dad dead, after what he did to Mum. I wished him dead and her alive. But all that wishing never changed anything.'

'I shot him,' said Amelia.

'You shot him?' said Rin. 'Is that how you ended up here?'

'Oh no, I shot him here.'

'Oh,' said Rin. 'How?'

'I found a gun on the stairs. I must have *imagined it into being,*' said Amelia in a Stacey-Barbara voice. Rin giggled. 'But it didn't work.'

'It didn't?'

'I'm still here. No bright glowing doors for me. When I went back in to check he was dead, he was up and walking around as if nothing had happened. I couldn't believe it.'

'Maybe you don't need a gun,' said Rin. 'Maybe it's like Stacey-Barbara said and you have everything you need already.' She tapped Amelia's head, and Amelia giggled.

'I wouldn't mind another gun, though. I could probably get one if I thought really hard but I know it's pointless now, so maybe not. It took a lot to pull the trigger and then to find him alive again. I couldn't go through all that again.'

'I think you need to go back in. It's your only door. There'll be a way.'

'I know. I wish there was another one with a big "way out" sign on it.'

'Me too,' said Rin. 'But we all have our own doors and we all need to leave. Soon, hopefully, and I'm not going to leave you here. You are not going to be the next Stacey-Barbara, do you hear me?'

'Yes,' said Amelia, looking up at Rin. 'You'll make a good mum.'

'Maybe one day.'

'Thanks, Rin,' said Amelia. 'If it works then I hope I can see you in the outside.'

'Me too. Maybe after all this we'll be connected.'

'I hope so. Life's no fun all alone like mine,' said Amelia.

'No, well, hopefully the reason we're here is to fix whatever's wrong,' said Rin.

'Do you really think so?'

'I do, otherwise there wouldn't be any point. We've all been confronted with our problems, with what was wrong or awful in our lives. There must be a reason for that. Even if some of it can't be changed, that's the problem with the past, but you have the power to change your future.'

'But I can't fix it.'

'Maybe Futurespan can and maybe the annoying Stacey-Barbara has a good point. Maybe you're stronger than you think. Maybe you can control it in your mind. Maybe that's the key to getting out.'

'I'll give it a try,' said Amelia with a small smile.

'You'll do it,' said Rin. And with that they had a final embrace and Rin watched as Amelia approached the not-blue door for what would hopefully be the last time.

Facing the Not-Blue Door

Amelia approached the door with the same grim sickness as before, only this time it didn't reach her head. She was sick to her stomach with fear and dread, and her legs felt so heavy she couldn't force them to go faster. But her head felt clear and bright, and most importantly hers.

Meeting Rin and talking with her and the others had strengthened her. These strangers had shown her more care in however long it had been than her sorry excuse for a father had ever shown in her whole life. And Stacey-Barbara was right; it was her mind, and for the first time she felt she was its master. If she'd been strong enough to imagine a gun into being, and strong enough to pull the trigger, she was strong enough to defeat the monster with her bare hands – or her bare mind. And even the wanderer who'd been crazy enough to name his chair Cheryl had managed it. If he could do it then surely she could find a way. Strengthened by the memory of the bright door, and feeling as if she was still bathed in its warmth, she walked through the door feeling for the first time like the master of her own destiny…

The flat was still entirely grey. A true Futurespan door to the end. Everything was the same, but she was completely different: brave, strong, powerful and with a fire that she had never had before. She felt as if she were seeing things clearly for the first time. Striding confidently into the living room she held him in sharp focus, seeing him for what he truly was. And for once instead of fear there was anger: anger and disgust at this sorry excuse for a man.

'Get me a beer, Amelia,' he said gruffly.

'I won't,' she said.

He pivoted slowly, reminding Amelia of big ships that couldn't manoeuvre quickly due to their size. He glared at her, angry at being defied. 'You won't?' he spat.

'I won't.' Amelia stared straight back at him with none of the usual terrified aversion of her eyes. This time she wasn't going to let him get an inch.

He pushed himself up from the sofa, seeming to swell up, reminiscent of a bull walrus making its clumsy advance on land. As he came towards her Amelia stood up straighter and held her head higher.

'What did you say?' he growled, looking down, close enough for her to smell his stale breath.

'No,' she said, looking him straight in the eye.

He stopped short, and stared at her, confused. 'You what?' There was venom in his voice, and he looked at her as if she was worse than dirt on his shoe.

'I said no, I won't get your beer. I won't wash your clothes. I won't do what you say. I won't do anything.'

'Oh, I think you will,' he said, anger in his voice.

'No I won't.' She held his gaze firmly, even though she was craning her neck to do so.

'You need putting in your place again, girl? I knew you were stupid, but I didn't think you were that stupid.'

'I'm not. I'm not stupid and you're not going to hurt me any more.'

'And you think you can stop me? You silly girl,' he sniggered.

'You can't hurt me any more. I won't let you.'

'You're not in charge here, little miss. I thought you knew that. Looks like you need reminding' He took a step to close the small space between them further. Amelia stood tall as he brought up his huge hand; stepping forward he smacked her full force, the whole of his palm colliding hard with the side of her face. The force of it sent her staggering backwards, almost causing her to fall. Still she stood steady, resisting the urge to put her hand to her throbbing face.

'You want some more?' he said, bringing his hand up again. This time pain rocked through her, and she felt something snap; she heard it ringing loud in her ears. It was coupled with wet, sticky blood pouring from her nose and the taste of metal flooding her mouth. She pushed herself back up from the floor and wiped some of the torrent from her face. She stared at him, looking right into his black eyes, seeing what emptiness and evil looked like, and facing it head on for the first time in her life.

The monster glowered at her, but he was confused. Angrier than she had ever seen him, and yet she wasn't scared anymore. 'You can do what you like but you won't hurt me. Not in here.'

'Look at your face, you stupid girl. You're mine and I can do whatever I want to you. I thought you'd learnt that,' he growled.

He advanced and pushed her to the floor. Amelia didn't have a chance to get back up before he kicked her in the stomach. It took the wind out of her. She gasped. But inside she was still smiling. He kicked her hard, three times, once on her thigh and two connecting heavily with the softness of her abdomen. The pain coursed through her and she could barely breathe; it was so powerful it threatened to make the world black instead of grey. But she willed herself to stay conscious. She had to finish this; if she stopped now she might never get up the courage again. With difficulty and much pain she got to a shaky standing position. As she surveyed him glaring at her, heaving to try and catch his breath, she saw with wonder that the image of him was a little bit fainter. And despite being bruised and broken she felt stronger than she had in years. She felt indestructible.

'You can't win any more,' she said. 'I'm more than this.'

He grabbed her, shaking her small body. 'More than this,' he growled. 'More than this? You're nothing. Everything you are is here, you're nothing without me. Nothing, do you hear?' The shaking intensified.

'You can't hurt me,' said Amelia, her voice trembling with the vibrations of him shaking her. 'I am more than this. I'm worth more than you. You can't hurt me any more.'

All of a sudden the brightness in her mind seemed to overwhelm her. She collapsed in his arms and he chuckled, letting her drop and prodding her with his foot. Saying something that was indiscernible now, and whatever it was it no longer mattered. She had never felt so powerful. The light welled up in her mind, filling it completely and making her head feel as if it might burst. The light that she felt so strongly now in her mind burst out of her; exploding from her head were beams of blinding bright white light. One of the beams hit her father square in the chest and his body splintered into fragments of light.

Just like that he was gone: no gun required.

He was gone and so was the room, and so was everything except the feeling in Amelia's head. Everything felt warm and happy, and hopeful. The light kept pouring from her, until she knew her whole imaginary flat was gone; it had dissolved it all. Even Futurespan, at least for her, was melting with the power of it. She felt drained by it, and she lay on the floor, convulsing a little and slipping into a strange sleep as the last of it blasted from her. All there was now was peaceful whiteness.

Finally, she was free.

After Amelia

The three of them waited for a very long time. So long that Tabitha imagined afternoon had slipped into evening. She felt sleepy and before long all three of them were on the floor, backs against the wall, looking bleary-eyed at the door opposite, waiting to see if Amelia would return.

Tabitha drifted off into an uneasy sleep. All she dreamt about was concrete steps: unlimited staircases of them. Not what she had ever thought of as hell before, but the blinding monotony of it was soul-destroying. She dreamt of that and the doors; she dreamt of the 140191020914 door briefly. Even in her dream she was saddened by it, appalled at herself for being so useless, so spineless. She should never have been a doctor. She should never have even started It, let alone let it get so far. To actually think of herself working as a doctor in a hospital was laughable. Looking at it now she couldn't believe she hadn't done something about it sooner. It had never been what she wanted to do, not ever, but Patricia Hamilton wanted a doctor in the family, and she was a woman who was more than accustomed to getting what she wanted. She had guided Tabitha with the firm hand of interference for years, grooming her for doctor-ship. Everything from *triple science will be best at GCSE*, to *all the best students choose the sciences for A-level*, to *you're a bright girl, you should be no exception. The Hamiltons were always bright, Tabitha.* She could hear it all now as clear as day. It had never been her life.

Diggory meanwhile stirred as bright light streamed through his eyelids. For a moment he thought it must all have been a bizarre dream; there was no Tabitha, no Amelia, no Futurespan. He was in his bedroom, the sun beaming through the thin, useless curtains as usual. He shuffled and felt warmth next to him, felt the hard concrete beneath his bum: Futurespan was real. He wasn't sure if he was relieved or saddened by it, but he blinked his eyes open and saw the source of the light. It was Amelia's door.

'Wow,' said Diggory. The door was glowing a bright fantastic blue. He pushed himself up, and went towards it, feeling warmer the closer he got to it. 'Tabitha, Rin, wake up! Look at this.'

'Oh wow, it's just like Jetson's,' said Tabitha. 'Only blue.'

'Did she do it?' said Rin groggily, her eyes squinting.

'Yeh, look.'

'Whoa, it's warm,' said Rin, holding her hand a few inches from the door, 'and happy. I hope she's happier now.'

'She did it!' Diggory reached to Tabitha and hugged her tightly, then pulled back, shocked at himself. He looked right in her eyes. 'She did it.'

'She did,' said Tabitha smiling before he let her go.

'Well, there's hope for us,' said Rin. 'At least we know it's possible to get out of here now, without staying as long as Jetson.'

'Yes, we still don't know how though,' said Diggory. 'But I'm glad Amelia did it.'

Tabitha looked in wonder at the door. 'I think it must be different for everyone.'

'In what way?' said Rin.

'Well, what's behind the doors is very different for everyone, isn't it, but it all seems to be some sort of problem or significant point in our lives – past or future. So the way past them must be different. I think we have to work out why we're here,' Tabitha said.

'And behind the doors is the key?'

'Only key there is,' smiled Diggory.

'I guess I knew deep down,' said Rin.

'Poor Amelia. Her life back in the real world sounded worse than this.' Diggory looked sadly at the door, wondering.

'Hopefully it will be better now,' said Tabitha, rubbing Diggory's arm.

'I hope so.'

'At least it will be a real life; I just hope it improves. I hope that's the reason she was here,' said Rin.

'Maybe that's why we're here, so that all our lives can be better afterwards,' said Tabitha.

'Yeh, maybe,' agreed Rin.

'Or to stop us making mistakes in the future. Just think, now I know what happens when I'm a doctor, I can just not become a doctor. I've realised I don't even want to be one. And once I get back to my real life I can put an end to the ludicrous madness of my life and actually turn it into *my* life.'

'It's a nice theory, Tabitha, but there's nothing me and Diggory can do about our past.'

Tabitha shrugged her shoulders a little, knowing there wasn't much she could say to that. Diggory was rubbing his hands together, uncomfortable again now he was without Amelia. He had liked having someone to look after, someone who needed help more than he did, and now he felt like the baby again. Weak and powerless and scared, and he hated it.

'You okay?' said Rin. He looked up to see both her and Tabitha's looks of concern. At least somebody cared, and despite her economy with the truth, Tabitha did too. For once someone other than his blood. Diggory's heart swelled a little and he felt a tiny bit braver. He nodded to them, summoning the courage to speak. 'Can…' was all he managed at first. He paused to take a deep breath. Tabitha was about to speak, but Rin held her hand out to stop her. Diggory inhaled and tried again. 'Can I go next?'

'You sure?' said Rin.

Diggory nodded. 'As long as you'll be okay?'

'I'll be fine, Dig, always have been. I will be now.'

'Okay, because if I leave it any longer, or end up alone, I don't think I'll be able to, and I want out.'

'Okay,' said Rin. 'Let's go. Let's do it. Since there's no other way out.' She held out her hand and Diggory took it, and Tabitha took his other, and they walked back to the lift together, echoing their journey here, except Diggory was the child now. Inside there were only three buttons to choose from.

Diggory's Floor

They stepped out of the lift and to Diggory it was like coming home. He felt safer here than he ever had since he'd been that little boy with the aeroplanes. As they came out of the lift he smiled, and released all the air in his lungs in one big, happy sigh.

'Not scared now, huh?' said Rin.

'Not of this floor. I don't know about the doors though.'

They walked down to them, and to their surprise found there was only one.

'Maybe they disappear when you've been through them or something…' said Tabitha.

Diggory eyed up the doors. 'It's gone. The future one has disappeared.' He stared at the blank space where the door had been, wondering if that meant his awful future wouldn't be realised – or maybe it meant something different altogether. 'Maybe I don't have a future any more. You don't think I'm going to walk through the other door and die, do you?'

'I'm sure you won't, Diggory. What would be the point in all this then?' said Tabitha.

'Maybe Jetson and Amelia have gone to Heaven,' said Diggory. 'Would make sense with the bright glowing doors.'

'It's probably just like Stacey-Barbara said and now we're more aware of things here we can see them properly. Maybe you never had three doors. You just thought it because –'

'But my floor was first,' said Diggory. Nobody said anything else. 'I think I want to just wait here for a little while before I go through. I think I'd feel better if the other doors were still here; it'd feel like there were more options, more time.'

'Maybe you don't need more time now. Maybe you're ready?' said Tabitha.

'The past door is gone too,' he said.

'Just because it's disappeared doesn't mean it isn't going to happen, or hasn't happened,' said Rin. 'You must still have a future, Diggory, because you have a past.'

'Mm,' he said, not wanting her to know the horrors he had seen in the future. He hoped desperately that it was different. He went to the solitary door: there was no date, just 70393, numbers confirming it was his with no indication that it led to the past, future or otherwise. 'It isn't what I was expecting,' he said glumly. 'I think I just need some time.'

So they all sat on the floor again, drifting in and out of uneasy dreams. Diggory was torn, a familiar confusion of emotions tearing around inside him. He felt happy and warm that he was here; he felt himself, whole. But this was surrounded by a darkness, a threat of what waited behind that strange, lonely door, and he was terrified of it. It was the same darkness that had been inside him for as long as he could remember. The darkness he rarely lived a day without. Even in those odd moments of respite he felt exposed in his happiness, and knew the darkness was waiting at the edge of everything he did – ready to claim him. It was more familiar than the light, and a large part of him was often relieved to creep back into its dark embrace.

Looking at the door he felt as if he was standing on the precipice of something, maybe a cliff, and he didn't know what would happen when he stepped off (or 'in', as the case might be). Maybe he would plummet to his death. Maybe he'd find he was wearing a parachute and would glide safely into the soft water. The dark side of him, the scared side, the one that said bad things happen, was saying *you'll only be disappointed*. That bad things happen always, and it was best to not even try for the light… The side that usually won the battles and had won the war was the side that did not want to go anywhere near the door. And now it was screaming at him: even that side of him didn't want to die. Not usually, anyway. He couldn't get the idea of ending up in a straitjacket out of his head. He didn't want to go back to a mental home again, and a part of him was very scared that if he didn't sort his head out he would end up in one forever, just as he was behind that terrible door. A part of him knew he was already in a straitjacket in his head. The real Diggory was trapped.

Bad things do happen, he said to himself. *They do. They have. They probably will again*. He looked at Tabitha and the smallest of voices in his head whispered *but good things happen too.*

Tabitha saw him looking and smiled. 'You worried about the disappeared doors?'

'Something like that,' sighed Diggory. He looked over at Rin, who was either asleep or pretending to be. 'I don't think you realise how messed up I am.'

'We're all messed up, Diggory,' she said as she took his hand lightly in hers.

'Me more than most.'

'Well, look at the mess I've made of my life, and I didn't go through anything like you have. I don't even have an excuse. What happened was bound to leave you a little messed up; you were so young,' said Tabitha.

'Hm,' said Diggory, staring at the door. 'I'm terrified that if I go through the door that that will be it. That will have been my life. And I spent most of it terrified of my own shadow. Paralysed. Alone. Sad. Pathetic. Not realising that I still had a life to live and that worrying bad things would happen didn't make it any less likely they would.'

'No,' said Tabitha, soothing, stroking his hand.

'I don't want to go through that door and be dead. I don't want to have failed and let everyone down. Mum would be so disappointed.'

'It's not your fault. She would understand that it's not your fault.'

'Maybe. She'd still want me to live. Really live.'

'Of course.'

'And Rin. I've let her down too. She gave up everything. All her life for me. To look after me and make sure I was okay, and how do I reward her? Me being a mental, pathetic mess and hiding in the dark.' He looked at Tabitha, and saw true care for him in her eyes. 'And if that door is the cliff edge, the end, then I don't get all of this – what was the point? Why was the first door my childhood? The last time I felt safe, secure, happy. Maybe it was to torture me, to remind me of what I can never have back.'

'Do you think that door was trying to tell you something else?'

'No, only that. Just to torture me, reminding me of the last time I felt anywhere near normal, the time before hell started. Before I was broken.' He laughed. 'Maybe that's it. The door was the last time I was okay. I never recovered from what happened with my parents. I could never move on from it. That's why it was behind the door. I've been like this ever since.'

He was looking at the floor, his eyes wide, a little excitement rising in his voice. He didn't see what Tabitha saw: the door at the end of the corridor, the door he was so worried about, was starting to glow very faintly, just at the bottom, as if a light was on the room beyond.

'It was showing me that everything comes from there,' said Diggory. 'In a lot of ways I'm still that little boy. Wanting safety and security. Wanting to be assured everything is okay, wanting attention, wanting to be held tight. That little boy is inside me, and he's in too much control. I've grown up, and I need to grow up in here too.' He tapped his head, still not noticing the now half-glowing door. 'And it's down to me, Tabitha. I can choose to stay in the darkness. Make excuses that it wasn't my fault, I didn't create it. But I'm creating my life now and I need to choose the light.'

Tabitha nodded at him, smiling.

'However hard it is, I need to choose not to let the darkness in. Every day. I need to fight it.'

'Look,' said Tabitha.

'What?' he said, seeing her grinning. 'What is it?'

'Look at the door Diggory.'

He turned and looked wide-eyed at the bright glowing door. 'Oh my god.'

'You did it.'

'I must have… as long as it isn't the door to heaven. Because I definitely want to live. At least it doesn't look like the door to hell.' He hoped it wasn't the door to the future he'd seen – he'd do everything he could to make sure it wasn't.

'You'll be just fine, Diggory, you're free now' said Tabitha with a slightly sad smile.

Rin stirred. 'Light,' she said, holding her arms in front of her eyes. 'Wow, another –' She stopped and groped around, letting her breath out as her eyes fell on Diggory, standing now, transfixed by the door. 'Diggory. What did you do? How did you do it?'

'I –' He found himself unable to speak.

'He realised he already knew the way,' smiled Tabitha.

Rin raised her eyebrows. 'But he isn't wearing red slippers. However will he get home?'

'Slippers?' said Diggory dreamily.

'Our own little Dorothy!' laughed Tabitha.

Rin giggled and clicked her heels together.

'Dorothy?' said Diggory. 'It's my door.'

'Never mind,' said Rin. 'Well done.' She hugged him to her tightly.

'Thank you,' he said.

Rin smiled as she and Diggory broke apart. He fell into Tabitha's waiting arms and they hugged each other close. 'I'm scared,' he whispered.

'I know,' said Tabitha. 'But you'll be fine. I'm so pleased I met you, and I hope to meet you again. Out there. I hope we remember.'

He nodded. 'I will. And good luck.' He turned to Rin. 'I'll see you on the other side, sis; be strong. The past is over, it's all about the future now…'

She smiled and the two girls came together to watch as Diggory approached the glowing door and grasped the handle. The light that streamed out blinded them, and they turned away, covering their eyes. When they looked back he was gone, and the still glowing door stood closed. A glistening reminder of hope in the greyness.

After Diggory

'Wow,' said Rin.

'Yeh.'

'He's really done it. I didn't know if he would. He's come a long way from the rocking boy on the floor I wanted to take to hospital.'

'Yeh. He's conquered his fear. I'm so pleased for him,' said Tabitha.

Rin nodded, still staring at the door. 'I wonder what it will be like in the after – you know, back in real life. Will we remember any of this? Or will it be like nothing ever happened?'

'Surely there would be absolutely no point in any of this if we couldn't remember it? Then things would play out exactly as they would have done before.'

'I guess. I just wonder if it won't be like a dream, and as soon as you wake up it starts fading, until just like that you're brushing your teeth and you can't remember anything of it.'

'This isn't like a dream, though,' said Tabitha.

'You said it was before, right when we first met Jetson.'

'It isn't exactly like a dream. And I think we all know Jetson was right and somehow it is real. It isn't normal life, it isn't what you'd say is "real life", is it – and we know that, so I don't think we'd forget it, not like a dream. Dreams happen in your subconscious. We can choose here, we can think, we can decide so this must be our conscious. And you don't just forget what's happened to you.'

'Not usually, but this isn't usual, is it. The glowing doors might not even go back to real life and even if they do then maybe walking into that light causes some sort of amnesia or something. I don't know.'

'Are you worried we'll forget?'

'Like you said it's pretty pointless to go through all this just to forget on the other side of those doors. There wouldn't be a point then. For the first time in a long time I'm not worried about Diggory. Wherever that door takes him I'm not worried about him because I heard what he said. The penny's dropped and I know he'll be okay now. He's ready to make something of his life and that's somewhere I didn't know if he'd ever get to. I always worried. Always. And now he's ready. If we get back and that's all undone, that and me having to relive finding my mother cold. If that's all for nothing then –'

'It's okay, Rin.'

'You don't know that.'

'I feel it. There is a point, there is. I feel it in my bones. Come on, let's get back in the lift and see if you really have three doors or not.' Tabitha held out her hand and Rin grasped it, not letting go. They reached out together and pushed the button 180984: Rin's floor.

They exited the lift onto Rin's landing. Rin laughed. 'It is like coming home. And I guess home wasn't great, so it's accurate.' She shrugged. 'A part of me just wants to stay here. I don't really want to face whatever it is.'

'You can do this, Rin.'

'I hope so. I wonder if it will be the future. A part of me can't see much of a future, I've been so focused on getting through the present and forgetting the past. It would be strange to see what it holds.' She looked down the corridor and saw there were still three doors, but none were glowing. 'I suppose I better go and find out. It can't be any worse than the past.'

'No, and if it's the future remember it hasn't happened yet. Remember what you said to me. You'll have a chance to change whatever it is. If it is the future then I think you're seeing it so you will change it. However bad it is then remember that.'

'I will,' said Rin, taking a deep breath.

'Good luck.'

'You too.'

'I guess this is goodbye then.'

'No offence but I hope so. I hope the other door disappears. And we might not meet again, so thanks. Whatever upset Diggory you helped him more than you know, and it's been good to have the company.'

'Thanks, but I have a funny feeling we will meet again,' said Tabitha smiling.

'Let's hope that there's colour next time, and I don't mean behind one of these damn doors.' They laughed.

'Here's to colour.'

'Yes. If only we had a drink to toast it with.'

'Next time,' said Tabitha.

'Next time.' With a touch of her hand on Tabitha's Rin walked towards her second door, hoping it would be her last. Tabitha sat and waited, alone.

Rin's Other Door

Rin stood in front of the door. Tabitha waited on the landing, close enough to be able to watch out for glowing doors, but not near enough for Rin to even feel her presence. Like so much in her life she knew that this, too, she had to do on her own. So she stood there outside this second door, alone, waiting for something to happen; thankfully nothing did. No blood came spilling out of this door. No darkness this time. No pulsing. No horrible feelings. In fact there was just nothing. The door felt barren. She moved a little closer, and still there was only emptiness and coldness. It felt dead. The feeling of nothingness gave way to sickness and fear in Rin. *Doorways to hell.* She reached out and touched it. Nothing except the echoes of herself in her head: *doorway to hell*.

No! she screamed in her head, and backed away from the door.

It can't be, said Rin to herself, unable to shake the third visit of A Christmas Carol from her mind, feeling just like Mr Scrooge at the gateway of the cemetery, only her gateway was the door. The dead, empty door. *Please no,* she whispered to herself. *Please don't let me be dead. Don't let me be dead.* Reaching out to the door, she hoped she would feel something, anything as long as it wasn't heat from *the doorway to hell.* She shook her head hard. *No, no, no. Don't let me be dead.* She chanted the words over and over in her head like a mantra. *Don't let me be dead, don't let me be dead.* She paused, squeezing her eyes shut, wishing away the dead, empty feeling, wishing life into the door. But it didn't come. Nothing changed. She opened her eyes and reached slowly towards the handle, half-expecting to feel something as she neared it, but as she grasped it all she felt was coldness. It chilled her to her bones. She took a shaking breath and turned the handle, wanting to be able to let go of the freezing thing.

The door swung open. As she walked into the white fog it was like walking into a walk-in fridge. The fog swirled around her, the coldness of it clinging to her skin and penetrating deep inside her. She thought it might freeze her heart. As she stood in the fog she wondered if she was going to come out the other side somewhere cold. Perhaps she'd moved to Iceland in this future, and would now know to avoid the cold. Or maybe she'd taken a job at a factory or a restaurant and was getting something from the fridge. Maybe she'd taken a job at a morgue. *No,* she said to herself, trying to stop the train of thought, but it carried on. *Maybe you're in the morgue,* said the evil voice inside her head. *No!* screamed the scared Rin. *No. Please don't let me be dead. I don't want to be dead.*

It was then that the fog started to clear, and with it the coldness dissipated a little too. Rin was thankful for that. Coldness was linked in her head irrevocably to deadness. Her body was shaking as she strained her eyes to see through the whiteness, to see if there was anything that looked like a morgue. She desperately hoped not. As the fog began to clear, to her relief she could make out a window looking out onto open sky. And as it cleared a worn brown sofa came into view, and then the whole of a dreary living room: it was a sorry sight. But it wasn't a morgue.

Rin found herself in a postage stamp of a hallway, a few feet from the living-room doorway. The kitchen was obviously hidden around the corner in the living room: the bin giving it away. It was a cramped, claustrophobic place, and Rin wondered who lived here in this sad tower block.

The fog was almost clear now and she looked down at her skin to see it morphing and changing before her eyes, the smoothness of youth giving way to the wrinkles and prominent veins of old age. She felt herself shrink and hunch a little, and reached her gnarled hands up to her face to feel the lines there. She must be old. She felt old, but not only that: she felt as empty and cold as the door had. Her clothes had changed into sagging rags, and the transformation was complete.

Well, she wasn't dead. She couldn't help thinking she might as well be. This woman she had become, obviously the future version of herself, was barely a woman at all. Barely a person. She felt utterly devoid of life, hopeless to the point of carelessness. She walked slowly around the sorry apartment, seeing no sign of another. Back in the hallway she found the door to the cramped bathroom: only one toothbrush. There was a small handheld mirror above the sink; Rin grasped it tentatively, not sure she wanted to see herself, and held it at arms-length.

She took a deep breath before taking a long look at her future reality. The face that stared back was old. No. Haggard. With deep ingrained lines on her forehead, and down the sides of her mouth – frown lines. She was pale, her hair was a mess, and the clothes looked like something a homeless person in a hostel might wear. She didn't even want to think how she had gone from now to this. The woman in the mirror had not looked after herself at all.

I might as well be dead, Rin thought to herself sadly, *but I don't want to be.*

She looked around the flat; there were no photos anywhere. She had never been much of a photo person but she had expected that to change. Maybe to have had a family of her own, one that was at least the non-murderous side of normal, but there was no evidence of that here. No baby pictures, no carefully kept keepsakes – and no wedding ring.

In the kitchen there was a calendar neatly stuck to the fridge, plainly devoid of notes. The only entry for the whole month (Rin noted it said 'November 2046') was to remember to pay the phone bill at the end of the month. As if someone with a life like this could forget! *What else was she doing?!* thought Rin angrily. Keeping the house tidy for one, she saw, surveying the kitchen. It was truly spotless. Everything had its place. There were no dirty dishes in the sink, and not even a used cup in sight. The counter-tops sparkled, with no crumbs besmirching their surface. You could have quite happily eaten off the floor.

Clearly she lived here alone, in this carefully kept prison. With nothing else in her life.

Rin had seen enough. She ran out the door.

Rin's Future

Tabitha waited, wondering what was behind Rin's door, hoping it wasn't something else awful. Rin had been through enough. Tabitha pondered on how long it might take for the door to start glowing, but found she wished it would take a while; she was pleased, for the moment, to avoid facing her own fate.

The sound of the door bursting open shook her from her reprieve. She looked up to see Rin running down the corridor towards her. Tabitha stood up, puzzled at what could possibly compare to Rin, at the age of seventeen, finding her mother and father dead. Rin ran right at her, almost into her, stopping just short. She grasped Tabitha's hands, tears pouring down her face.

'What happened?' said Tabitha. 'What is it?'

Rin just stared at her; she looked sad to her soul. Tabitha pulled one of her hands from Rin's tight hold and rubbed her shoulder with it.

'It's okay now, Rin, it didn't happen, you're okay.'

'But it's going to –' said Rin. Half of what she said was lost in sobs as she threw herself at Tabitha, crying hard. Tabitha put her arms around her, but the experience was so alien with the usually unaffectionate Rin that it felt like hugging a crocodile. All the same it was good that Rin was finally letting some of her demons out. If anyone needed a hug it was Rin and Tabitha was happy to oblige.

'I'm sorry,' wailed Rin, in a muffled voice as her head was nestled into Tabitha's chest.

'It's okay, Rin, I'm here. You're safe now.' Tabitha rubbed her back, wondering what could have reduced Rin to such a state.

'I need to get away from it,' she said as she made for the stairs.

'Okay,' said Tabitha. 'It's okay.'

They went down to the next landing, Tabitha following Rin. When she reached her the sobs had subsided a little.

'It was horrible, Tabitha,' said Rin. 'I don't want to end up like that. I think I need help.'

'I can help you. What can I do?' Tabitha hoped Rin didn't want her to come through her door; as curious as she was, she didn't want to have to deal with whatever horror was inside. She had enough with her own doors: she needed all her strength to face them.

'I don't know how to do it, Tabitha. I don't and it will always be like that, I won't be able to change it. I always thought it would be Diggory whose future I had to worry about and I was too bloody blind to see it was my own. Stupid girl.'

'Hey, Rin, look we've all realised things here. We got the chance before it was too late. That's good, right?'

'Not if there's nothing you can do about it.'

'You don't know that, Rin. What would be the point of you being here, of you seeing it, if you couldn't change it?'

'Some kind of sick joke. Maybe I was right all along.'

'You know that isn't true.'

'It was so real,' said Rin, tears still streaming down her face.

'I know,' said Tabitha as she held her hands tightly. 'I know that. Mine was real too, it was awful. But I've got to remember it isn't, and you do too. It hasn't happened. Maybe we'll believe that more when we're back in the real world. We can change the course, Rin – we can.' Rin sat down looking defeated. Tabitha sat next to her. 'Tell me what happened.'

Rin took a deep breath. 'It's what's going to become of me. I'm going to end up old and alone. Not married, no family. Just me.'

'That's what you saw?'

'Yeh. That's my future. Bitter and alone, and obsessively clean – since I'll have no people or life to get in the way of the cleaning schedule.'

'You must have people in your life. What about Diggory?'

'I don't know about him. Probably too busy having a life to bother with me. It didn't look like I had anyone anymore. I think I actually succeeded in driving everyone away and shutting everyone out. But I didn't like it. Not at all. It was such a sad life – no pictures, nobody there, nowhere to go. I don't want that to happen to me. It was all so empty.'

'Maybe you just need to let people in,' said Tabitha hesitantly, feeling as if Rin might snap at her and put up the spiked, barbed-wire fences at any moment.

'It isn't that easy.'

'I know it isn't but I think that's what you're meant to see from this. That if you do shut everyone out then you will end up alone.'

'I know that.'

They sat in silence for a few minutes, Tabitha feeling a bit awkward but deciding to persist regardless. Rin needed to hear this. It needed to sink in. 'I'm just trying to help you, Rin. You don't have to shut me out. I'm not hurting you.'

'I know,' said Rin. 'It's hard to trust people. I wasn't the most trusting anyway, I've always been what you might call cynical but that never used to be all I was. But now –'

'I know it can't have been easy,' said Tabitha.

'No,' said Rin. 'It wasn't at all. When your…' She stumbled over the word, and finally spat it out. 'Father. A man you trusted, a man who was this huge part of your family – not without his problems granted, but we all trusted him… He did make us happy. We all made each other happy. And one day you come home to find him dead in the garage.' Her voice was choked now. She took a breath and carried on. 'That would have been bad enough. It would have been horrendous. It would have ripped us all apart. But Mum would have been there and we could have put ourselves back together, but he killed her. He took her from us. And if he could do that to his own wife, his own family? It showed me, proved to me, what people are capable of.'

'I'm so sorry. I can't even imagine what you went through, what you still go through now. But people are capable of good things too.'

'I know. But he was, and look at what else he was capable of. I had no idea,' said Rin. 'None at all. He was troubled sometimes, and sad, but I never thought he would hurt anyone else. And it just plays over and over in my mind, what she must have gone through. She can't have known either. Our mother was one of those rare, kind, true-hearted people – she would've got him help. She would've helped him. If she had any idea she would've made sure me and Diggory weren't there with him. She can't have known anything – then one day the husband that she loved so dearly murders her with their young child sleeping upstairs, and leaves her and then himself in a pool of blood for their oldest child to find. I just thank god it was me instead of Diggory – god knows what it would've done to him. He's been broken enough without seeing that. That image is burnt in my mind forever.'

Tabitha reached out for Rin's hand, and Rin let her take it.

'I can never get it out of my head. It haunts me every day. It's even haunting me here.'

'That's why it's your first door. It's where it all started, why you ended up here, why you're stuck. Just like mine. I'm here because I've been doing what everyone else – namely my mother – thinks I should do. I've wasted five years to become a doctor and what a disaster that would have been.'

Rin stared at the concrete, turning over what Tabitha had said in her mind.

'Like Diggory's,' said Tabitha. 'His first door was a scene from his happy childhood. He's stuck and broken because he can't get over the fact that it's gone. That even the memory of it is besmirched by what your father did. But Diggory has found a way past it, or at least made a start – that's how he's gone. Your door, having to relive that awful night was showing you –'

'I can't get past it. I can't just forget it.'

'It can never be forgotten or fixed, but maybe you can find a way past it. A way to lessen its hold on you and let you be freer to live.'

'Mum would have wanted that, and on top of it all I feel like I'm letting her down. She had such an open heart, and mine is barricaded. And that future there, my future, would break her heart.'

'You can do something about it now. You can make her proud. I bet you already have, raising Diggory all alone. She would understand how difficult it has been for you.'

'It would have broken her heart,' said Rin. 'I'm glad she died without knowing what a monster he was. I'm glad she died and didn't see it coming. Maybe she would have been proud at how grown up I was, how I didn't abandon Diggory. But it wasn't what she wanted for us. She would've seen the path I was on, the path that would lead to the sorry broken life behind that door.'

'Now you see it too; you've seen it before it's too late.'

'She always thought I was too hard, "old before my time", she would say. But I had to be, didn't I, after what happened. It wasn't a choice anymore.'

'Yeh, you did a great job, Rin.'

'I did the best I could.'

'Exactly,' said Tabitha. 'It's just like my door, just like what you said to me. You can change it. You can see that if you continue you'll end up sad and alone. You've seen that you have to let people in, even if it's difficult, or you'll end up all alone.'

'Yeh, it is difficult,' said Rin. 'It was easier just to shut everyone out.' She took a breath. 'If you can't even trust your father, who you thought was a good man, then who can you trust? I lived with him for seventeen years and if I hadn't seen it myself I wouldn't have believed he could murder my mother. Didn't think he had it in him. Turns out he did.'

'You've had it really hard. It would have broken most people, but you've been so strong.'

'Too strong.'

'Yeh maybe a little,' said Tabitha.

'Maybe I can turn my determination into the determination not to become a bitter old woman.'

'Sounds like a plan,' said Tabitha.

'Diggory can help me for a change. I think he'd like that after all the years of me telling him what to do. And if I meet you in the real world then you can be my first friend. Got to start somewhere right?' Rin gave a small laugh.

'I'd be honoured,' said Tabitha.

'It's a start – just about the only one I can make in here. Aren't exactly a lot of people around are there. I hope it's enough for me to leave.'

'Me too,' said Tabitha. 'Maybe you should go and see.'

'Maybe *we* should go and see,' said Rin, a little begrudgingly. 'I can't do everything by myself, can I, unless I do want to end up as that woman.'

'No,' said Tabitha. 'And if we do meet on the outside, we could help each other: I could do with being stronger and more independent, and you could do with letting more people in.'

'Yeh, I think we could both get something out of it,' said Rin with a smile. 'If I do go now, aren't you scared about your doors, about how you'll get out?'

'A little.' Tabitha paused. 'Well, a lot. But I need to do things on my own, I think that's the reason I'm here. I think I had to be last. Not that I want to be.'

'You'll be fine, you'll work it out. You were going to be a doctor, after all: not exactly short on the intelligence front.'

Tabitha laughed. 'Yeh, just a bit short on the decision front.'

'You'll manage,' said Rin, smiling. 'Come on, if Amelia and Dig and hopefully I can manage, then you can.'

'Yeh.'

'Hopefully I've done it now, let's go and see.'

So they walked up the flight of stairs in silence, having said everything that should be said. Both of them felt a difference in the air. Both of them were thinking this was it. It was out for Rin, and in Futurespan alone for Tabitha, just as she had started. They climbed slowly, each with their own trepidations. Rin was realising that she was more scared there would be a glowing door than not. It would mean she would have to face up to things. To face up to her life. To make changes. All the things she had been avoiding since they died. She had just been trying to stay afloat for Diggory, taking each day as it came. But that wouldn't be an option anymore.

As they saw the horizon line of Rin's landing they both focused on it, Rin straining her eyes for the first sign of anything glowing. Her stomach dropped as her head bobbed above the floor level and she couldn't see any glowing door. She really did want to leave, but she was frightened, as most people are when it comes to taking control of their lives, and facing up to the problems usually avoided. Deep down she didn't want to stay here in this place. She did want to leave, and start living again, however difficult it might be. Though with no glowing door that wasn't possible, and she had no idea what else she could do.

Tabitha joined her on the landing, as she stared sadly at the distant doors. 'I haven't done it.'

Tabitha surveyed the doors; she couldn't see any of them glowing either. 'Well, let's go and look properly.'

'No, it's pointless,' said Rin, turning her back on the doors.

'Come on, you can't see everything from back here,' said Tabitha. 'It can't hurt.'

'It already does. It hasn't worked.'

'Just trust me, let's go and see. Sometimes it's worth listening to someone else you know. Let's just try.'

'Okay,' said Rin reluctantly.

They walked slowly and silently towards the doors. The middle one did look a little different from the others. Rin didn't say anything but her steps quickened. Tabitha let her go first. As they approached they could see that the middle door was glowing very faintly. It wasn't like Jetson's door or Amelia's, but it was how Diggory's had started out. Maybe there was more of a family resemblance than Rin liked to admit. She ran to it and put her hands on it.

'It's warm,' she said, leaning on it.

Tabitha nodded.

'How do I make it glow like Diggory's?' said Rin, almost to herself. She stood thinking quietly for a few moments. 'How did Diggory do it?'

'He realised the significance of his doors,' said Tabitha, shrugging.

'I thought I had.' Rin sounded a little stumped. 'The first door,' she said, looking at it warily, still worried that blood might seep from it again. She clutched this third door, hoping it would give her some peace. Third time lucky. If only she could make it glow.

'The first door?' prompted Tabitha.

'The first door was there to remind me of how that night changed my life completely, not only because of what happened but of how I reacted to it. How I changed, and closed off and hid myself away from the world. How I stopped living for me at all,' said Rin, speaking to Tabitha, directing her attention away from the door.

Tabitha, echoing her experience with Diggory, saw the door glowing more. She said nothing to Rin, this is what she needed to do.

Rin continued. 'It meant I didn't trust anyone. I forgot all the open-hearted ways my mother had taught me. I didn't want to let anyone in, and I didn't.' The door was brighter still, and Rin turned to it, remarking that it felt hotter. 'It looks brighter, Tabitha. Look. Is it brighter?'

'Looks brighter to me,' said Tabitha.

Rin grinned. 'Maybe I can do it, maybe I can get out. The second door showed me what I don't want out of life. Showed me where the path I'm on will take me. It scared me.'

The door was glowing even more brightly now, but not yet brightly enough. Rin looked at it and then back at Tabitha. 'What else did Diggory do?'

'I don't know, he just realised what the doors were telling him and what he wanted out of his life.'

'Well, I want...'

'What do you want, Rin?'

'I don't want what's behind there,' she said, indicating the other door. 'I don't want to be a bitter old woman. I don't want to be old and alone.'

'So you want a family around you?'

'Yeh, I want Diggory there, and hopefully his wife and children.

And I'm not sure what else.'

'Do you want a family of your own?'

'I suppose deep down I do, but I'm frightened it will end up like mine. I'd be scared that the man wouldn't be who I thought he was.' Rin paused. 'I suppose what I really want out of life is to live it. To do what I want. To be my own person, and to stop carrying around this bitterness like a weight around my neck. That's what I'd like.'

And with that the door was at its full strength, glowing strongly amid all the dim greyness. Tears were rolling down Rin's face, and her hands were reaching out to the door, basking in the warmth flowing from it. First, she turned to Tabitha and grasped her, hugging her tightly. 'Thank you,' she said. 'Thank you. I hope I see you out there.'

'Me too,' smiled Tabitha, admiring the glowing door and realising the other two had fell away into nothing.

'Bye, Tabitha. Thank you. Remember you'll be okay.'

And with that Rin opened her door, beaming, and Tabitha watched as blindingly bright white light shot out of the door. Rin shielded her eyes a little, giggled to herself with happiness at her achievement and walked through the light, leaving Futurespan behind.

After Rin

So Tabitha found herself alone on the concrete staircase, just as she had started. But she had come a long way since then, and not just in steps.

She had more of a sense of her future now, of what her future should be – *and will be,* she thought. It wasn't her mother's future any more – it was hers. Even if the only things she knew were that it would not include a marriage to a 'suitable' man whom she didn't love, and that she wouldn't be Dr Hamilton: at least not practising. Whatever her future held it was not ending up being a bewildered junior doctor without a clue. In fact if she was honest with herself more than a small part of her hoped that it might include a marriage to a less-than-suitable, slightly unstable manic depressive. At least that's how her mother would see him, but to Tabitha Dig was so much more than that, and he wouldn't care if she wasn't a doctor. And they had shared all this together. They had helped each other see what they should do with their lives, and Tabitha thought there could never be a more important experience. If he could forgive her.

Her only real fear now was not seeing Diggory and Rin again. She even hoped she would see Jetson again, too, or that at least she would find out that his life was okay now. And she hoped things would be better for Amelia as well. She truly hoped all of their lives would be good now. Futurespan was a chance, an out, an opportunity, and Tabitha intended to grasp it with both hands.

She thought all this as she walked down the never-ending stairs, purposefully avoiding the sliding doors – at least for now. She needed to clear her head before it came to facing her doors. There was symmetry about it too. She had started off aimlessly walking these many steps, and now she was doing the same, only with more purpose. Once she had thought about it all a contentedness settled on her: true and heavy, and very welcome. The future was still unknown but she knew for the first time she would pave its way and alter its course. She would do it whilst being unavoidably herself in every facet possible, in every strength and weakness and character flaw; she would finally allow the real Tabitha Hamilton to be released into the world. She had been locked up for far too long, and it wasn't doing the world any good, least of all Tabitha.

As the feeling of contentment settled in her chest she reached the next landing and there were the glistening doors of the lift. There was no need for her to walk any more. She felt she had reached all of her conclusions, and she had finally reached the end of her road in Futurespan. It was time to go back, and to finally stop hiding.

Tabitha got into the lift and took a deep breath before reaching out and pressing the one remaining glowing button. She was going home. She stood in the button-filled lift, feeling the whoosh of the passing floors, hoping that she would be greeted with an already glowing door. She wasn't entirely convinced that that would be the case but she remained hopeful. Slightly haunted by the thought of Stacey-Barbara and Jetson, despite the success of the latter, she didn't want to be here as long as either of them. Especially not alone. Futurespan wasn't exactly a dark place: more of a dim place, as it looks to the eye. It reminded Tabitha of that odd time just before dark when the light takes on a surreal quality. Since arriving here she had had that uneasy feeling you get after waking from a strange and unsettling dream. The dream persists and so does the uneasy feeling weighing down your stomach even though your brain knows you can't actually come to any harm. That was how Futurespan felt to her, and she would be happy to leave that feeling behind.

So it was with this feeling that Tabitha exited through the sliding doors for what she hoped would be the last time. She was surprised to see, however, that she had arrived at least a floor away from hers – for some reason the lift had stopped short. She put one foot back into the lift to check the solitary glowing number. It read 140191. It was indeed supposed to be her floor. Shaking her head she left the lift again – at least she wasn't miles away now, she could feel she was close. But she couldn't help feeling a little hurt – by a lift! All the others had been brought directly to their floors yet she had to walk down more concrete stairs, after she had decided she was done with that. *Maybe they were ready,* came a little voice from inside her head. *Maybe I'm not,* Tabitha consciously added to the first errant thought, agreeing with what it implied. *Maybe I'm not as ready as I thought.*

So she slowly walked down this slightly longer 'lift landing', as she thought of it, her thoughts turning to all that had happened since she arrived in Futurespan. She thought fondly of Diggory and how he had gone from a whimpering boy to an empowered man ready to face the world. Tabitha was proud of Rin for recognising that not all people would hurt her, and even though there were ones that would, a life without them would be pointless. Curiously she thought of the mysterious Jetson, and how he had finally managed to leave this place by who knew what means – they'd never even found out why he was here. Must have been something very difficult to face for him to avoid it for so long, to prefer to stay here lugging Cheryl around. So she was glad for Jetson, and glad for them all – this place, she thought, was a crossroads, not a place for staying long-term. Maybe even Stacey-Barbara would realise that at some point.

The only one she wasn't entirely pleased for was poor little Amelia – little even though she was taller than Tabitha, for she was little in every other sense of the word. Tabitha worried that where Amelia was going back to, from what she and Rin had said, was much worse than Futurespan. Poor Amelia didn't even have friends. It saddened Tabitha deeply to think that herself, Rin and Diggory were the closest friends Amelia had had. And aside from teaching her some personal strength and giving a much-needed boost to her shattered confidence Tabitha didn't really see how Futurespan had helped her. Maybe it had let her see that she was worth much more than her situation, which was perhaps the most important lesson anyone can learn – the true value of self-worth. But Tabitha couldn't help thinking that what Amelia really needed was practical help, and in terms of that Futurespan hadn't provided her any that she could see. And what could Amelia do? She was only a child. Even if a real-life gun materialised, and Tabitha wasn't sure if Futurespan reached that far, it wouldn't do much to help Amelia's desperate situation. The last thing she needed was to be a murderer or to have to stand trial, even if she got off on self-defence. One monster would be gone from her life, but what about those in her head? Diggory could have told her those were not so easy. Or maybe Futurespan helped to fix those kinds of monsters? Tabitha wasn't sure; she just hoped that Amelia would be okay. That maybe they could find her on the outside and help her. That would be a worthwhile start to her new life. The one thing she liked about the idea of being a doctor was helping people; perhaps she could find a safer way to do that.

She had a feeling that leaving Futurespan was only the very first step, and that there would be many more difficult, real steps to come.

Tabitha came back to herself and realised that she had gone on autopilot and walked herself to the middle of the staircase, so far that she could see the start of her floor. Her future. She stopped there feeling as if she was on the precipice of the rest of her life – as if all of it balanced on a knife-edge. As if whatever decision she made now would irrevocably pave the way for everything to follow and there would be no second chance. She wondered if everyone felt this way before they left, but she thought perhaps not. She felt this way because she had to decide. Taking charge of her life needed to start today. She strode up the last of the steps, emerging triumphant onto the landing ready to do it. Except the view was not what she was expecting. Instead of one gloriously glowing door ready for her to stride through, to Tabitha's horror there were two.

The third door that was there before had vanished – or perhaps it had never existed at all? She had a feeling that these two doors weren't even the same as the ones she had already been through. For a start, there were no long numbers, just 140191. And aside from that they were both faintly glowing, as Diggory's door had to start with. It wasn't the full, brightness of success; it was the dim glow of a choice that had to be made.

Tabitha didn't like this. She didn't like this at all. She'd come so far, realised so much, she couldn't help feeling a bit bitter that by the time the others got to this point they were pretty much ready. They didn't have two doors to choose from, and at least they weren't alone like she was. But she could see the irony.

Come on, she said to herself. *You can do this. You can.* But she didn't budge from the spot where she stood. Holding her breath she tried again to urge herself into action, knowing it was what she needed to do. What she wanted to do. But maybe she wasn't brave enough. *You can't stay here forever.* With that thought stuck in her head she put her left foot tentatively forwards, forcing herself to keep putting one foot in front of the other, slowly shuffling towards her fate. Still a little unwilling to decide, unwilling to risk falling off the wrong side of the knife.

She shook her head; this couldn't continue. It was her life that was happening in front of her, that was being lived on her behalf for the satisfaction of those around her, namely her mother. And she needed to take control and decide what she wanted to do with it.

As Tabitha stood there, in the dead centre of the corridor between the two doors, not giving priority to either, she could see clearly that she was on a knife-edge. Whatever she chose now would decide everything. If being stuck in this place didn't give her the kick to change her life, if seeing the things that she had seen here, seeing her future play out for her – the one she didn't want – didn't make her do something about her life then she had no right to her life anyway. Might as well not have one at all. She didn't want that but she was worried she wasn't brave enough to take control. It would be easier just to give up and concede. Tabitha had spent too much of her life doing that. It had become more than a habit. It had become all that was truly left of herself, and she wasn't sure where the rest of her had gone.

She would have to find out. That, or hide from herself and the fact that it was her life forever; and deep down in her gut she knew if she wanted to actually live then that was the only option. As scary and risky as it was, as abhorrent as it was to the Tabitha who just wanted to stay hidden away in herself, it had to be done. If she chose the easy door, back to the before, then she might as well stay in Futurespan with Stacey-Barbara and find a dark corridor somewhere to curl up and die. And a part of Tabitha wanted that.

But that scared the part of her that wanted to live. That part was pulling at her and screaming, wanting to drag her (she realised) to the left-handed door, which was glowing a little more brightly. The door to the future worth living. The door to the unknown.

She took a deep breath. She had to do this. She had to. *Have to, have to, have to…* Tabitha said it to herself trying to convince the rather larger part of herself that that was true. It was a nice thought to take over her life and change everything but it wasn't very practical. Her mother would probably kick her out if she heard Tabitha didn't want to be a doctor, and then Tabitha would have no home and no money, and would have totally wasted at least five years of her life. Oh, and she would have to leave the fiancé she didn't even want; well, at least that part wouldn't be so bad. But all of the other worries and the thoughts of her mother's response to the latter crowded her mind. They swam up, causing crippling anxiety to ripple through her body, paralysing her, as it had for most of her life.

What if, what if, what if?

How can I? Can I? Could I?

I can't. I'm scared.

I need to do what they say.

I can't choose.

I'm not good enough.

Maybe this is for the best.

But there were no real voices here, as indeed there were no real people to produce them. All of the real people had left (Stacey-Barbara excluded). The voices were from the ghosts in her head, crowding there, smothering her with their oppressive words and their instructions for her life. There was nobody real here to push her into a decision, to coerce her and control her. But she was still letting it happen – the voices in her head were screaming at her, pulling her towards the right-hand door. It was too much for her weakened and downtrodden mind to bear. Her heart was suffocated and she felt as if she couldn't breathe.

Her heart needed her to be true, and to stop listening to the ghosts. Her heart wanted to be listened to, but she had been ignoring it for so long now, she had forgotten how to listen, and all she could feel was pain in her chest and screaming voices hurting her head. She collapsed on the floor, on the invisible central line, sitting on the fence of her life, unable to move as she descended into a shaking, sobbing ball.

Goodbye Futurespan

Tabitha shook herself. The two doors were still there, and she had to decide. She had to make a choice. She wiped her eyes and forced herself to move. Approaching the door to the left, she reached out and felt that it was warm, just like Rin had said. It not only felt warm, but it felt utterly different from anything she had ever felt and she knew that this was the door to a life where everything would be changed.

She turned then to the second door, knowing what she would find there. For all its destructive, marginalising power it felt safer. Easier. That was the reason she had been going along with it her whole life, wasn't it. It was easier to. Simpler.

Now she had a choice.

It was cruel but she had to decide.

She thought again of all of the people she had met here, and how they had all found a way out. Although there was nothing to say if what was behind those doors was good. They *felt* good. Tabitha wanted that. And standing in the middle of her doors she wasn't sure if either of them felt good. But she had to decide.

She had to go home. There would be a lot of work to do when she got there. Starting with giving back that overpriced rock that was waiting on her bedside table. The arrogant excuse for a man could perhaps give it to her mother – since she thought he was such a good match! Her mother wouldn't be pleased, though, about Tabitha calling everything off, but Tabitha found, happily, that she did not care. It was her life. An unsure one, maybe, but it would be hers, and it wouldn't conform to the neat little blueprints her mother had drawn up. Not anymore.

A feeling of nervous excitement welled up inside her; for the very first time in her life she realised she could choose. And she didn't want to choose her mother's way anymore. She longed to go towards the left-hand door, but the old tug of familiarity and ease pulled at her. Did she dare carve out a way for herself?

Looking straight ahead she saw the corridor now looked so much longer than it had been. At the end of it she thought she could make out a figure in a blue dress, watching her. Her right arm was slightly outstretched, as if she were a strange Futurespan air hostess pointing out the exits. Tabitha looked away, sure her mind was playing tricks on her; she had been here too long. When she looked back she saw that the figure was gone; perhaps it had never been there at all. Tabitha looked at each door in turn, her eyes settling longer on the one to her left – the one the figure had been pointing at. *No,* thought Tabitha, *the one I imagined the figure was pointing at. Because that's what I really want.*

Tabitha walked towards the left door, towards terrible fear and great hope for a future that was truly her own.

Epilogue

Monday 21ˢᵗ of July 2014 - 2 months after Tabitha's exit from Futurespan.

'Dr Tabitha Hamilton,' said the Dean.

Tabitha stepped up on stage, careful not to trip over her graduate's gown. Tilting her head up to see past her cap she saw her mother weeping openly. She shook the Dean's hand, smiled for the photograph and exited stage left, with her hard-won degree in her hand.

Once the ceremony was over she went out in procession with the other graduates, and met her mother outside. All of the graduates busied themselves congratulating each other on their degrees, and shaking hands with lecturers and university officials. Tabitha's mother was talking with her programme lead, Dr Hawthorne, about how well Tabitha had done. Tabitha cringed: another of her mother's many ploys to get her to put her medical training into practice.

'Well, well, *Doctor* Hamilton,' said a familiar voice. It couldn't be! Tabitha whirled around, and impossibly, it was. Standing in front of her was Diggory with Rin next to him, both of them in the flesh in the real world. They were real. These last two months she had lived in a dream, trying to make sense of Futurespan and wondering if she would ever see any of them again. She had even wondered if any of them really existed outside of her own head. She had no way to find them, no surnames, no town; they hadn't talked about any of it.

'You're real,' said Tabitha, her voice breaking a little. She reached out and awkwardly embraced them both. They grinned. 'How did you find me?' said Tabitha, just able to get the words out.

'I heard your surname when I followed you through your past door,' said Diggory. 'Turns out there aren't too many Tabitha Hamiltons graduating from medicine. None, in fact. And we thought we might all live close in the real world and Leeds Uni is the closest to us so I started there. And there you were.'

'And here you are,' smiled Rin.

'How did you know I'd be here? We all know I'd make a terrible doctor.'

'We didn't know for sure,' said Rin. 'But we thought after nearly five years' work, doctor or no you'd be here to pick up your qualification.'

'Exactly right,' smiled Tabitha, still in shock. 'I'm not going to be an actual doctor. In fact I don't know what I'm going to be. But at least I didn't do all that work for nothing. Plus my mother can say she has a doctor in the family, which appeased her a little, even if I've never been practising.' She looked at them both. Now in full Technicolor she saw that Diggory's eyes were blue. 'I still can't believe you found me.'

'Us neither,' they said in unison, and laughed.

'But I'm very glad you did.'

'Me too,' said Rin. 'You're going to be my first proper friend. Remember?'

'I remember,' smiled Tabitha.

Tabitha's mother came over. 'Tabitha darling,' she said, before looking down her nose at the casual dress of Rin and Diggory, in their jeans and t-shirts. 'And who may you two be?'

'Mother, this is Rin and Diggory. They're my friends.'

'I've never heard of them,' said Mrs Hamilton.

'Well, they are my good friends.'

Mrs Hamilton didn't seem convinced. 'Tabitha dear, we have a lunch reservation with Mr Johnson and his son Toby.'

'Mother, I've told you I don't want to meet his son,' said Tabitha under her breath.

'He graduated from medicine last year. I thought he could tell you all about what you're missing by not using that medical degree.'

She looked pointedly at the scroll Tabitha was still grasping.

'Mother, I've told you I'm not going to be a doctor,' Tabitha said. Rin and Diggory stood there awkwardly.

'It is what you've trained for,' said her mother.

'What you wanted me to train for. I'm not having this conversation again. I don't want to be a doctor and it's my life. And I'm not coming to lunch. Give Mr Johnson and Toby my apologies. I won't sit there for hours while you make me feel bad about what I've chosen for myself. I'm going to celebrate my achievement with my friends. Come on,' she said to Rin and Diggory.

They walked away from her mother, who stood in a stunned silence. For all of Tabitha's out-of-character behaviour over the last couple of months, she still thought that she would come round, and had put her radical change of course down to nerves. Standing there and watching her daughter walk away with apparent friends she realised Tabitha really had changed. She didn't bother calling after her.

'What should we do then, Doctor?' said Rin.

Tabitha laughed. 'Get a coffee, there's a good place around the corner.'

They made their way along in happy silence, past the many graduates and parents crowding the streets of the campus.

'I still can't believe you found me,' said Tabitha. 'I think I'm in shock.'

'I can't believe how easy it was,' said Rin.

'We did have to wait a bit, though, to see if we were right,' said Diggory.

'I was starting to think that maybe I'd imagined you. I think it was my way of coming to terms with never seeing you again.'

'At least we had each other,' said Rin.

'Yes,' said Tabitha. 'I wish I'd had someone I could have asked. I thought I was mad to start with.' They approached the coffee shop. 'Have you found anyone else?' asked Tabitha.

'Let's sit down and we'll explain,' said Rin.

They got seats in a booth around the corner, out of earshot.

'Have you found Amelia?' asked Tabitha.

'We looked for her first,' said Diggory.

'Immediately,' said Rin. 'We wanted to help her so badly.'

'Is she okay?'

'She's better,' said Rin. 'Her father's dead.'

'Really?' said Tabitha. 'How?'

'That's the funny thing,' said Rin. 'When Amelia left Futurespan she found herself walking out of the bright light, and standing in front of the not-blue door, except that it was blue again. She was *home*. When she went inside her father was dead. Bullet wounds to his chest and head.'

'You're kidding?' said Tabitha.

'I'm not. They never found a gun, or a shooter; the police have given up hope. Amelia thinks that somehow she actually murdered him, and we tried to convince her otherwise but what can we say?'

'It matches what happened in Futurespan perfectly, she told us,' said Diggory. 'It freaked us out. Never mind Amelia.'

'But she's coming to terms with it now; she's coping a lot better.'

Tabitha stared into the coffee shop, turning the scene blurry as she went into herself. The enormity of it, especially after spending so long wondering if it had all been some terribly vivid dream, was too much for her to take in.

'So what's happened to her?'

'Foster home,' said Rin.

'Oh,' said Tabitha. 'That's awful. Doesn't she have any relatives?'

'They're looking for her mother, but Amelia has mixed feelings about it. Her mother did leave her with that monster after all. And it isn't all bad. She's much happier in the foster home than she was before. She says it isn't too bad, and she's made some friends. And she isn't scared all the time.'

'The carers like her because she's good with the chores,' said Diggory. 'And she was over the moon to see us. You'll have to come; we're going on Saturday.'

'I'd love to,' smiled Tabitha. 'How did you find her?'

Diggory and Rin exchanged a look.

'With some difficulty,' said Rin. 'All we had to go on was that she lived in a tower block near Jimmy's, with a blue door.'

'With the number 4 on it,' said Diggory, still the numbers man.

'There are several tower blocks near the hospital,' said Rin. 'We were sure we'd get arrested for trespassing but we managed it. We snuck into five of them before we finally found the one, and if we'd been much later we'd have missed her.'

'She was packing up her clothes with a social worker when we got there; it was pure luck we didn't miss her.'

'I'm so glad,' smiled Tabitha. 'Even if you had never found me, to leave that poor helpless girl alone would have been terrible.'

'I agree,' said Diggory, looking at his watch. 'I'll be back in a minute.'

Tabitha and Rin just smiled at each other. 'Thank you,' said Rin.

'No problem,' said Tabitha. 'It all really happened, didn't it?'

'It did,' said Rin.

'Do you think Amelia really killed her father?'

'Think about it, Tabitha, what other explanation is there? Someone breaking in while Amelia was busy being tortured in Futurespan and shooting her father just the way she thought she was imagining shooting him? Not very likely is it?'

'No,' said Tabitha.

'Not that I would ever say that to Amelia. Last thing she needs is to keep thinking she's a murderer. But I suppose she'll realise in time that it was somehow for real.'

'Poor Amelia.'

'Hm. At least she's free, and he had it coming.'

'Futurespan made her a murderer though.'

'It set her free. Maybe it was the only way.'

Tabitha was glad she hadn't had a true Futurespan door. What a thing Amelia would have to come to terms with. At least her father couldn't hurt her any more though; that was a blessing.

Diggory came back holding several newspapers.

'What's with the papers?' asked Tabitha.

'We think Jetson's probably local too,' said Diggory. 'But with hardly anything to go on, we just keep searching the papers, hoping for something. There's no Jetsons anywhere. Here.' He handed her a couple. Rin was already riffling through hers.

'Start at the back,' said Diggory. 'We check all the announcements, even the obituaries. Then we scan the stories to see if we can see any Jetsons.'

'It's been a long couple of months,' said Rin.

'I bet,' said Tabitha. She started looking through her own paper. 'Surely there must be a better way?'

'With no surname everything's a dead end,' said Diggory. 'There's too many Jetsons online.'

'Hey, look at this,' said Rin.

It was an announcement that read: 'Mr and Mrs Jetson Guthrie are proud to announce the birth of their baby girl Elaina Stacey Guthrie. Born on the 11th of July 2014, weighing 8lb 10.'

'Do you think it's him?' she said.

Diggory and Tabitha shrugged.

None of them knew. None of them had known why Jetson had been in Futurespan, but they all hoped whether or not it was their Jetson that wherever their Jetson was he would be happy in his new life.

They hoped that they all would be.

'Well here's to colour,' said Tabitha clinking her cup against Rin's and then Diggory's.

'Here-here!' said Rin, taking a gulp of coffee, to toast it.

'I'm so glad we found you,' said Diggory quietly.

'Me too,' smiled Tabitha.

'And me,' said Rin, grasping both of their hands, and smiling the broadest of smiles.

They held each other's hands, together now, and all hopeful of a bright future in the real world.

About Georgia Duffy

I have always loved stories and I am a complete book addict. I have written for as long as I can remember, but only recently have I found the courage and determination it takes to actually make it to the end of a novel: Futurespan is my first! I am originally from the North East, where my supportive family (Mum, Nan and Granddad) still live. I went to the University of Leeds and gained my Radiography degree in 2011, and have since been working as a Radiographer (x-raying people) in North Yorkshire, where I met my lovely boyfriend Karl. I am an ENFP (Myers-Briggs personality type) for those who might be interested. I care passionately, and often way too much, about anything that is truly important (or captures my interest). I adore fantasy as I love to immerse myself in and dream up interesting, complex worlds that capture the imagination. And I have forever been fascinated with the human condition, and the idea of fate. It is amazing how one seemingly small decision can change the path we're on completely and irrevocably. Stories just seem to find their way into my head. Writing is my biggest love, and being published my hugest dream come true. I have forever been inspired by amazing authors such as Stephen King, Margaret Atwood, Phillip Pullman and Hugh Howey to name just a few. If I could achieve even a fraction of what they have I would be a very happy writer!